A
Harlequin
Romance

OTHER
Harlequin Romances
by MARGARET MALCOLM

Many of these titles are available at your local bookseller,
or through the Harlequin Reader Service.

For a free catalogue listing all available Harlequin Romances,
send your name and address to:

HARLEQUIN READER SERVICE,
M.P.O. Box 707, Niagara Falls, N.Y. 14302
Canadian address: Stratford, Ontario, Canada.

or use order coupon at back of book.

NOT LESS THAN ALL

by

MARGARET MALCOLM

HARLEQUIN BOOKS   TORONTO
WINNIPEG

Original hard cover edition published in 1972
by Mills & Boon Limited, 17-19 Foley Street,
London   W1A 1DR, England

© Margaret Malcolm 1972

Harlequin edition published June, 1972

SBN 373-01607-7

Printed in Canada

1607

CHAPTER ONE

HE couldn't believe his luck.

For weeks—it seemed more like months—he'd been looking for some quiet place where he could work undisturbed. He didn't care what sort of place—it could be a cottage or a bungalow or even a caravan. But it must be somewhere quiet. That was essential. But apparently impossible. Cottages which were once isolated were now either on a new arterial road or on the perimeter of an airport. Bungalows, he discovered, rarely came singly. More usually they were part of a development and were crowded against each other like hens in a battery. As for caravans—he shuddered at the memory of the camping sites he had visited. Hundreds of caravans stacked in neat rows and thousands of shouting, squalling children, to say nothing of transistor radios bawling without cessation.

And then, quite by chance, he saw the advertisement, not in an estate agency, but on a hand-printed card in the small crowded window of a general store where he had stopped to buy something for a picnic lunch.

The first time, he read it automatically as one does any single notice in a shop window. Then, as the penny dropped, he read it again incredulously, but with sudden surging hope.

"TO RENT for three months or longer by arrangement. Canal butty (i.e., living quarters, no machinery) permanently moored half a mile west of Yeoman's Lock.

ACCOMMODATION: well equipped galley, living room, sleeping accommodation for two in comfortable cabin. Extra bunk can be made in living room. Modern sanitation, Calor gas stove and refrigerator.

NOT SUITABLE FOR CHILDREN. No dogs, radio, television or musical instruments permitted.

A perfect haven for those who value isolation and peace.

Rent per month—"

But he didn't stop to read the last line. He must have it! Absolutely must, whatever the rent. It was surely the perfect answer!

He went into the shop, only to have to wait while the pleasantly plump woman in charge attended to two earlier customers, and exchanged all the local gossip.

At last it was his turn.

"That—that advertisement in your window." He was almost stammering in his eagerness. "Is it—is it still available?"

"Oh yes, sir," The woman looked at him curiously. "Would you be interested?"

"Very much indeed! It sounds just what I've been looking for. I'll take it!"

"What, without seeing it?" She gave him a doubtful look. Just what sort of a man was this, as young as he was—and good-looking—who wanted to hide himself away—and why? Didn't seem natural like—The doubt was so evident that there had to be an explanation.

"Yes, without seeing it. I'll take a chance. You see, I'm a writer, and I've been hunting for somewhere quiet where I can work undisturbed. This sounds ideal."

"Oh—a writer!" The woman's face cleared. "That's funny, now! It belongs to a writing gentleman, but he's gone abroad looking for some sort of colour for his next book."

"Local colour, I expect. Well, how about it?"

"Well, if you'll write down your name and address—and Mr. Thomas did say I was to ask for the first month's rent down—"

"Fair enough! Give me a piece of paper—"

But instead she produced a small black notebook which had evidently been prepared for just such an occasion as this, for, as she opened it at the first page, he saw that it was headed:

"Long-boat, *Seven Stars*."

"Now, sir, if you'll write your name and address, then

I'll put down each time you pay me. Would you like a pen, sir?"

But he had already taken his own pen from his pocket and wrote :

"John Lindsay,
31A Faber Street,
Bloomsbury, London, W.C.1."

Then, as she studied it carefully, he took out his wallet and counted out the necessary notes and added a few coins from his pocket.

With the payment entered in the little black book, he was the official tenant of the *Seven Stars*. He drew a breath of relief. But he wasn't allowed to seek his sanctuary yet. Boring though admittedly useful information was given with the key.

"It's Calor gas, sir, for both cooking and the fridge. If you go into the ironmonger's shop opposite, you can make arrangements for delivery of fresh supplies with Mr. Mangell. There's two containers on board, so what you do is let Mr. Mangell know as soon as you've emptied one. Then you never get caught without. He looks after the dynamo that does the electric light as well if it goes wrong. Then there's food, sir. If you care to give me an order, my son will bring it all down to you when he gets home from school."

"Thanks, Mrs.—?"

"Watchett, sir. My husband works up at the farm yonder—" with a jerk of the head.

"I see. Well, thank you very much, Mrs. Watchett, but I'll take supplies for a few days with me. After that—" He left the remark in the air, but in fact he'd made up his mind that he always would fetch and carry his own supplies. He didn't want a gangling schoolboy disturbing his peace !

It was only just as he was leaving that he remembered one important question.

"How near to the canal can I park my car?"

"Oh, quite near, sir. You go down the lane opposite and when you've passed a stile, you come to a field gate with an old barn just inside. You can park your car in the

7

barn—but you have to pay Mr. Jobling, the farmer who owns it, for that. He only charges a pound a month. Then there's a small gate in the hedge and when you're through that, you're on the canal bank. Shall I tell Mr. Jobling you want to make use of the barn?"

"Yes, please. And now, food—"

A quarter of an hour he set off burdened with two heavily laden carrier bags. Mrs. Watchett watched him from the shop window as he got into his car and turned down the lane.

"Quite a nice gentleman, though a bit abrupt, p'raps. Looked as if he might have a bit of a temper, too, with that square chin and the frown creases between his dark eyebrows."

"I wonder what Miss Alice will make of him?" she pondered as she went back behind the counter. Then, with the vestige of a chuckle : "And I wonder what he'll make of Miss Alice?"

Incredibly, the advertisement had not exaggerated the amenities of the *Seven Stars*.

The galley *was* well equipped. It was also very conveniently arranged and spotlessly clean. The cabin *was* extremely comfortable, but it was, in fact, the sitting room which gave him the greatest satisfaction. To begin with, it was larger than he had anticipated. He thought that a second sleeping cabin had been sacrificed to achieve this. The fittings were plain and sensible, the two armchairs well sprung and upholstered. But best of all from John's point of view was the solid kitchen table set under a window which looked on to the off-side bank of the canal. The middle third of the table top was covered by a stout piece of felt marked with four small round indentations. With relief he recognised them as the unmistakable impressions left by a typewriter. So, notwithstanding the restrictions about noise, the sound of a typewriter was permissible. He thanked his stars that the boat's owner was also a writer, particularly as he had left behind him a small but useful selection of reference books—the Bible, two volumes of Milton and a complete Shakespeare, a good dictionary and an equally good

Thesaurus. John blessed the absent Mr. Thomas with considerable fervour. Anyone who couldn't write here simply hadn't anything to say!

Having inspected his quarters, he went out on deck and momentarily frowned. As far as it went the advertisement had told the exact truth—but not all of it. No reference had been made to the fact that the *Seven Stars* was not the only long-boat moored here. There were two others; the *Pride of London*, adjacent to the *Seven Stars* though with about a boat's length of water between them and beyond her, the *Rosebud*.

John's scowl deepened. Gone was his dream of absolute solitude. In fact, one or two people might be worse than a crowd if they happened to be of the gregarious type.

Still, presumably they, too, would be restricted about noise and might appreciate peace and quiet as much as he did. Moreover, on neither boat was there any sign of life. Perhaps, after all—

He turned his attention to his surroundings, and with these at least he could find no fault.

The canal, he knew, had not been used commercially for years, and there were evident signs not so much of neglect as of indulgence. On either side was a towpath backed by a hedge which had been allowed to take up far more space than would have been convenient in years past. In the main, it was of hawthorn. Falling petals drifted lazily like perfumed confetti on the slight, mild breeze. Then there were dog-roses, pale pink and white, whose delicate beauty surely warranted some more euphonious name.

At the base of the hedge spires of meadowsweet reared their creamy-white umbrellas and vied with purple loosestrife to delight the eye. Masses of forget-me-nots, the bluest John had ever seen, fringed the towpath, trailing down to the water and even drowning some of their blossoms in it.

And as the perfect complement to all this beauty, somewhere high up in the cloudless sky, a lark was throbbing out its heart—

John stood motionless, drinking it in, conscious of a

sense of peace and well-being within himself that he had not known he was capable of feeling.

"Good afternoon!"

Startled, he spun round so sharply that he almost stumbled.

A woman was standing on the near side bank. At a guess, she was perhaps in her middle forties—a sturdy woman and no beauty with her strongly featured face and short, straight black hair. She was regarding him with interest, even curiosity, and instantly that peace of spirit gave way to resentment against the person who had destroyed it.

"What do you want?" he asked harshly.

"Nothing, personally," she told him coolly. "But you left some of your property in Mrs. Watchett's shop and she asked me to give it to you so that you wouldn't worry that you'd lost it."

And she held out his note-case.

"Good lord!" John felt in his inner coat pocket and it was empty. "Yes, it's mine." He came towards her, crossed the narrow plank gangway—and belatedly remembered his manners. "Thanks," he said reluctantly. "Extremely careless of me. I'm very much obliged to both you and Mrs. Watchett."

"Not at all." She regarded him gravely. "And please, don't feel that you're under any obligation to me. I was coming down here anyway. I'm your next-door neighbour," with a jerk of her head towards the *Pride of London*.

"Oh yes?" Deliberately John made the two words sound as lacking in interest as possible. He could have cursed himself for having given her this opportunity to scrape acquaintance!

"Yes." There was amusement now in the dark eyes which had a shrewdly penetrating quality about them. "No need for alarm, Mr. Lindsay! Returning your wallet was a purely disinterested kindness with no strings attached. I value my own inviolability far too highly to want to trespass on yours—or anyone else's, for that matter!"

With a casual nod of farewell, she turned and walked back to her own craft with a confident, unhurried step which conveyed unmistakably her complete mental tranquillity.

And that was something John had completely lost in the engagement. He was fuming! An infuriating woman! In the space of a few minutes she had put him in her debt, had laughed at him—and had made him feel that he was behaving boorishly.

"Oh, confound the woman!" he muttered under his breath, and went into the galley to throw together the odds and ends of food he had collected for his first meal aboard. It was then he discovered that he had forgotten to buy any salt.

It took the best part of a week to master the essential mechanics of living on his own in the long-boat.

The first lesson he learned was the most important of all—what he didn't do himself wasn't done at all. And while, manlike, he could shut his eyes to a certain amount of dust here and there, other jobs, some of them none too pleasant, couldn't be neglected without penalty. At first it seemed a waste of time to heat water in order to wash up after each meal—far more sensible to save up and do the job once a day. But that, he discovered, only made it more difficult, especially where pots and pans were concerned. Besides, there were the flies—

He had not thought it necessary to make his bed properly each day. Surely just to plump up the pillows and heave the bedclothes more or less into position was sufficient—but that, he found, was not so. One or two restless nights convinced him of that. The bottom sheet became runkled up and the bedclothes wouldn't stay put—

Then there was the question of the water supply. True, there were adequate tanks on the craft and a stand-pipe reasonably near on the bank. But to fill the one from the other meant at least a dozen trips backwards and forwards carrying a couple of pails. It was both laborious and uncomfortable, for it required skill if one wanted to avoid spillage and consequent soaking of clothes and shoes. And the fact that his neighbour, with the aid of a sort of primitive milkmaid's yoke, performed the same task without difficulty, did nothing to decrease his sense of frustration.

It was all such a waste of time! For months past he'd had the bare framework of the play he intended to write clear and precise in his mind. All he had to do was clothe it in words. And words kept bubbling up into his consciousness—but always at the time when he was occupied with one of the wretchedly mundane jobs. Worse than that, by the time he was free to get them down on paper, the brilliance of inspiration had gone and what he wrote seemed second-rate and lacking in impact.

He was driven to working out a system. The household chores *must* take second place to his writing. There was only one way to make sure that they did. However disinclined he might feel, they must wait until he had already written himself out. Then inspiration was far less likely to visit him. He learned, from sheer necessity, that plates and pots and pans, if submerged in cold water, could safely wait without disaster.

But there was still shopping to do, and that meant observing other people's times. Thanks to the little refrigerator, he could, he had thought, cut down to a single trip a week—except for the question of milk. Even with a refrigerator, he doubted if it would keep that long. Besides, there wasn't room for more than a couple of pint bottles.

He almost wished he'd agreed to let Sid Watchett deliver whatever was necessary—but not quite. He'd seen Sid just once—and he *was* a gangling, goggled-eyed youth. Inquisitive, too, like his mother.

Besides, the fewer people who visited his retreat the better. To have a neighbour was bad enough, though he had to admit that, to use a favourite phrase of his old nannie, she did keep herself to herself. An artist, apparently, though whether amateur or professional he neither knew nor cared. At least her work absorbed her. He had seen her literally start inches from her little stool when a cow in a nearby field had given vent to a sudden bellow.

So, taking it by and large, life settled into a satisfactory rhythm and he found that he had not been mistaken. By sheer luck he had found ideal conditions for producing what, without vanity, he knew was good work. He had never been so happy in his life or so absorbed. But that was his trouble. It was all very well working out a system, but if one had reached a place where words were coiled up like a spring in one's brain, just waiting to be released, it was so easy to forget everything else.

That happened one day when, having got up early and without stopping even for breakfast, he had worked at white heat for hours on his first act of the play. Then, suddenly, he had remembered that he ought to get in supplies. He was out of tea, out of milk and very low on both bacon and eggs—his main standbys. And he'd got to see that chap Mangell about a new container of Calor gas.

He looked at his watch. Twelve o'clock—and, confound it, early closing day! He'd have to get off at once or go on very short commons until the next day. He pushed his chair back savagely, collected a carrier bag from the galley and went up on deck. That was when, for the first time, he realised that it was raining, not heavily, but with dreary persistence.

In a thoroughly bad temper he hunted out his mackintosh and set off. In an hour's time he returned in an even worse one. It hadn't seemed worth while getting the car out seeing that it was such a short distance that he had to go, but that had been a mistake. The rain had come on more heavily and, never a man to wear a hat if he could avoid it, his hair was soaked and streams of chilly water were running down inside his collar. Shivering, he planned to have a good stiff toddy when he got back and wished to goodness that, by the simple method of turning on taps, he could have a hot bath—and with a groan, remembered that he couldn't even have a cold one unless he filled the tank.

It was the last straw. He gained the comparative comfort of the galley, dumped the carrier bag and was just going to pick up the two pails when something caught his eye.

Last night he had worked so late that he had turned in without doing his day's washing up. He had dunked it in a bowl in the little sink and had left it. Now the bowl was empty and what had been in it, was dried and neatly stacked on the draining board. What was more—he sniffed experimentally—there was an unmistakable smell in the galley. Within the last hour someone had cooked bacon and eggs there.

Clearly he had entertained a visitor unawares. But who? Not his next-door neighbour whose name, he had been gratuitously told by Mrs. Watchett, was Miss Alice Coates, though she preferred to be known just as Miss Alice. No, not her. She might, just conceivably, have seen him go off and have been sufficiently curious to pry. She might, with that appalling sense of superiority possessed by so many females, have done his washing up for him. But she certainly wouldn't have cooked a meal for herself—

A tramp, then? No, he might have stolen food but certainly wouldn't have washed up. With a shrug, John temporarily dismissed the problem. The most important thing was to get himself into dry clothes. As for the water, that could wait. He'd enough for the day if he was careful.

He took off his mackintosh, hung it up where it could drip in safety and made for the cabin. Passing through the sitting room, he glanced at the table and saw to his relief that the papers on it were just as he had left them. Then he went into the cabin—and came abruptly to a dead stop, his jaw dropping.

There, lying on his bed, fast asleep, was a girl. Her fair hair was spread all over the pillow—*his* pillow—and she had pulled the coverlet roughly over herself.

For a moment John was too astounded to do anything but stare incredulously. Things like this just didn't happen—

But evidently they did, and indignation surged up. The cheek of it! To steal his food and then calmly to take possession of his bed!

He took a couple of quick strides and catching hold of her shoulder, shook it energetically.

"Wake up, Goldilocks!" he requested harshly. "The big bear has come home!"

Possibly that fitted in with her dreams, for without opening her eyes she made a petulant little movement as if to free herself from his grasp. So he shook her again.

"Wake up!" he ordered more loudly.

This time he got results. The girl's eyes opened. For a moment she lay still, half way between sleep and consciousness. Then, with a horrified gasp, she propped herself up on one elbow.

"Oh, my goodness!" she ejaculated. "This is the last thing I meant to happen! What must you think of me?"

John didn't answer immediately. Waking up, the girl had added still another shock to those she had already dealt him.

With fair hair like hers he would naturally have supposed, had he given the matter a thought, that her eyes would be blue. They weren't. They were green.

Then, because her pale cheeks were suddenly flooded with colour while her free hand clenched tightly, he realised that she was genuinely frightened at her predicament—or else she was a superb little actress. Well, he'd soon find out. And if she was scared, she had only herself to thank for that!

"Get up," he ordered harshly.

Obediently she turned back the cover and swung her legs on to the floor, scuffling her feet into the shabby sandals that he hadn't noticed until then.

She stood up—a tall girl and slim to the point of thinness. Her clothes, a creased and shapeless cotton dress topped by a woollen cardigan, were old and as shabby as the sandals. But she had recovered her poise by now. The green eyes met his unwaveringly.

"This way," he said curtly, and led the way to the day cabin. She followed meekly enough, but he took the precaution of placing himself between her and the door to the deck. "Sit down." And when she had done so, he sat down opposite her. "Now, if you'll be so good, may I have an explanation?"

"I truly didn't mean to go to sleep," she told him earnestly. "Only, when I'd made the bed, it looked so comfortable, and I was so tired—" her voice trailed away as if, even after her stolen rest, it was still almost too much effort to talk.

John's hands moved impatiently.

"Not just that. The whole business. Why did you come on board at all? And why did you steal my food?"

"Because I was hungry as well as tired," she explained, answering the second question first. She paused and then in a flurry of words: "I wouldn't have done it—honestly

15

I wouldn't—but I was *desperate*. You see, I had to stop—oh, hours ago—for petrol—"

"Oh, so you've got a car!" he interrupted. "Where is it?"

"In that field the other side of the hedge just by the old barn."

"Well, go on!"

"Well, when I decided to stop to have something to eat I couldn't find my purse. It wasn't in my handbag and it wasn't anywhere in the car. I suppose I must have dropped it at the garage."

There was a decided tremor in her voice, but John hardened his heart.

"Do you really expect me to believe that tarradiddle?" he asked sceptically.

"Why not?" Her head came up defiantly and John found her defiance far more attractive than her earlier pathos. "It was careless of me, I know, but things like that do happen if one has—has other things on one's mind—"

He looked at her sharply. She couldn't possibly know of his own carelessness in leaving his wallet on Mrs. Watchett's counter, but unknowingly she had got under his guard and much as he resented it, he had the honesty to admit to himself that he was hardly in a position to take her to task for a similar fault.

"So you came straight down here and helped yourself?" he suggested,

"Oh *no*!" she denied. "It wasn't like that at all. I didn't even know that there was a canal here, let alone boats. No, I simply turned down the lane because it looked quiet and I wanted to park somewhere and try to think what I could possibly do. You see, I started before breakfast—and I hadn't slept much and I knew it just wasn't safe for me to go on driving. So I drove into that field and hunted through everything I'd got with me to see if there was anything I could sell—and there wasn't. Then I saw the boats. I wondered if perhaps there might be someone who—who would help me, but there was no one about—" again that quaver in her voice. "So then—I—I took the law into my own hands. Oh, I know I shouldn't have done it, but truly, I was at the end of my tether and—and I did wash up and make the bed as a sort of payment—"

"H'm!" John considered. Yes, there was something, though not much, in that. "All right, we'll call it quits up to that point. But only on condition that you tell me the whole story. For instance, who are you? What's your name?"

She hesitated momentarily. Then—

"Rosamund Hastings."

He shook his head unbelievingly.

"Oh no—your real name, please!"

"But that is my real name," she insisted.

"I don't think so. You hesitated before you told me," he pointed out.

"I know I did. I was wondering if it would be a good idea if I made up a name. Then I decided that it might be inconvenient and too difficult to remember, anyway," she explained ingenuously. "So I told you my true one. Really I did."

Well, true or not, she'd stick to it, of course! He let it go.

"And where do you live?" he asked instead.

For answer she pressed her lips firmly together and shook her head vigorously.

"No? In other words, you're a runaway. Borstal?"

"Certainly not!" she denied indignantly.

John shrugged his shoulders.

"Sorry—but how could I know? After all, you *are* light-fingered, aren't you?"

"I don't suppose you'll believe it, but I've never done anything like that in my life before today," she told him earnestly.

"I'll have to take your word for it," he retorted ironically. "All right, not Borstal. Then where? From school?"

To his surprise, a change came over the serious little face. The lips curved in a provocative smile, the green eyes sparkled with amusement.

"How old do you think I am?"

He shrugged his shoulders.

"Fifteen—sixteen, perhaps."

"I'm twenty-three."

17

"I don't believe it," he retorted flatly.

The smile vanished and she sighed deeply.

"You haven't told me what your name is, but I know what it ought to be—Thomas! You seem utterly incapable of believing anything!"

"Now look here, young wonan—" he stood up, towering over her. "I've had enough of your impudence! What's more, I don't care whether you're telling me the truth or not. But one thing is very certain. Whether you're fifteen or twenty-three, you can't stay here! Is that clear?"

"But what shall I do?" she asked, her face starkly white. "Where shall I go?"

"That's for you to decide," he told her inexorably, "since you insist that you're of an age to run your own life!"

"But—" she began.

John interrupted her ruthlessly.

"Now listen, Rosamund Hastings, you're not getting easy money out of me! Understand? But what I will do is this—I'll pay the cost of a telephone call to anyone, a relative or friend, whom you believe will help you out of this jam—provided that I see and hear you make the call. Well?"

Again that stubborn look marred what was, he had to admit, quite an attractive face—if you happened to like a pink and white complexion, golden hair—and green eyes. For his part, he didn't.

"No," she said unequivocally.

"No?" He shrugged his shoulders. "Just as you like! But if that's your line, then off you go—at once!"

She stood up and without protest walked steadily to the cabin door. He watched her go in a mood partly of satisfaction that he was getting rid of her and partly of annoyance at having been forced into such an invidious position at all.

Suddenly an idea occurred to him.

"Wait a minute! It must have been raining when you got here, yet your clothes aren't wet. You must have had a coat or a mackintosh. Where is it?"

"In the galley on the hook on the inside of the door," she told him in a voice completely devoid of expression.

"Well, get it," he ordered grimly. "I don't want you to have any excuse for coming back!"

"You needn't worry, I wouldn't come back if I was dying!" she declared passionately, and dashed into the galley to emerge struggling into a mackintosh as unprepossessing as the rest of her clothes. "Would you like me to turn out the pockets in case I've stolen anything?" she demanded belligerently.

He ignored that, contenting himself with standing, arms folded, while she negotiated the narrow plank gangway. Then, involuntarily, he took a step towards her. The rain had made the wood slippery and just as she was about to step on to the bank, one foot skidded and she almost fell.

But John's intervention was unnecessary. At that precise moment Miss Coates emerged through the little gate in the hedge, unceremoniously dropped the parcels she was carrying and was in time to keep Rosamund from falling.

"That was a nearly!" she remarked cheerfully. Then, anxiously: "My dear, you're crying! Have you hurt yourself?"

"N-no," Rosamund stammered. Then she pulled herself together. "No, I'm quite all right, thank you very much."

"But you're not, my child," Miss Coates insisted. "Now, tell me what's wrong and we'll see what we can do about it!" And putting a protecting arm round the slim, shivering figure, she shot an unmistakably accusing look at John.

"Not what you're quite evidently thinking, madam," he was stung to retort. "I have not inveigled her here and I have not assaulted her! On the contrary, she came of her own free will and without my knowledge or consent. In addition, she had helped herself to some of my food, her excuse being a cock and bull story about having lost her purse! If you'll take my advice, you'll send her packing, as I've done!"

"But I'm not willing to take your advice," Miss Coates replied blandly. "Any more than you, I'm sure, would accept mine! Good afternoon, Mr. Lindsay. And now—" she smiled reassuringly at Rosamund, "let's go to my boat and share a cup of tea, shall we?"

John watched them go as they turned their backs on him and made for the *Pride of London*.

It would have been very natural if his principal feeling had been one of relief at having got rid of his incubus. But it was nothing of the sort. He was keenly aware of a sense of perplexity.

As Rosamund turned her back on him he was convinced that he'd seen her before, though where and when he had no idea. Oh, absurd! If that was so then surely he would have remembered her face, and he hadn't. But there was something about her walk—elegant to the degree that she seemed almost to float along, despite the roughness of the towpath. And the poise of her head—

No, he couldn't remember, and after all, what did it matter? Whether Miss Coates allowed herself to be imposed on by the girl or not, he would take good care that he wouldn't be further involved!

But it was vexing that several times that day—and afterwards—his thoughts turned involuntarily to the perplexing half-memory.

"Now, you sit down while I get tea, my dear," Miss Coates said cheerfully. "No, I don't need any help and you certainly need to relax! Sit down in one of the armchairs and try to think of nothing at all!"

Thankfully Rosamund sat down. That was easy enough, but to think of nothing—that was impossible! Too much had happened since she had started out so hopefully that morning.

She had laid her plans so carefully! Aunt Ruth, proprietress of one of London's most exclusive dress salons, had gone to Paris for a week, leaving Rosamund in charge and with urgent instructions to make absolutely sure that every dress they had designed and created for one of the biggest weddings of the season was absolutely perfect. In fact, everything went without a hitch, and in the evening Rosamund rang her aunt up at her hotel and reported to that effect.

"And I had quite a long talk afterwards at the reception with Mrs. Castleford," she went on to say. "You know, the wife of the American financier. They expect to be over here for three months and I think she was genuinely interested. In fact, she asked me to make an appointment for you to see her next week."

"Why me?" Ruth Hastings asked sharply. "Why not you, since you made the contact?"

"Because she's the sort of person that doesn't think she's getting her money's worth if she isn't looked after by the head of a firm," Rosamund explained, and instantly wondered if that didn't sound too glib.

But Ruth accepted it without question, gave a few details of her own activities since she had left home and then asked suddenly—almost suspiciously :

"What are you going to do tomorrow with the salon closed?"

"I've been thinking about taking a run into the country," Rosamund replied. "I could do with a breath of fresh air. It's stifling in London."

All of which had been absolutely true—but it wasn't the whole truth. She had said nothing about the shabby second-hand car she had bought or of the cheap clothes so different from the ones she usually wore. And most important of all, she had said nothing of her determination never to live or work with her aunt again. There was no point in doing so. She had tried so often to make her aunt understand how much she hated the life she was leading with all its cloying luxury, the over-heated, over-perfumed salon and the shallow, greedy women who patronised it, but without success. Aunt Ruth simply couldn't or wouldn't believe it.

To Ruth Hastings, her achievements in the world of fashion were all-satisfying. She revelled in success and the knowledge that she had fulfilled the ambitions which at one time had seemed so out of reach. She really enjoyed the work, too, and was completely blind to the fact that not all people are made in the same way. Of course Rosamund must feel as she did, and into the bargain, think herself lucky to benefit by someone else's efforts instead of having to drudge through all those years of alternate hope and despair.

Rosamund sighed. You couldn't convince a person like that that you *wanted* to make a personal effort, wanted, most desperately, to do your own thing even if you weren't quite sure what that was.

So, in the end, she'd decided that there was only one

thing to do—go away and stay away until Aunt Ruth had to accept her decision.

The most important thing, of course, was to avoid a confrontation, and in order to do that, she had gone to extreme lengths. She had drawn quite a large sum of money from her bank account, sufficient to last long enough not to need to draw any more until Aunt Ruth was convinced. Even though it was most unlikely that the bank would divulge to her aunt where a cheque had been drawn, she wasn't going to take even that small risk!

And now all her plans were wrecked by her own stupid carelessness. Without money what could she do except crawl back abjectly, convinced of her own stupidity and probably never again finding the courage to make the break.

She was not sorry when Miss Coates came back with an attractively laid tea-tray. For a little while she could try to forget her troubles and respond to the kindness that she was receiving.

Over the teacups Miss Coates did her best to put her visitor at her ease. She described life on the long boat with enthusiasm and not a little humour, poking fun at herself for the mistakes she had made at first. To her own surprise, Rosamund found herself compelled to smile and even laugh once or twice.

It was not until the tray was carried back to the galley and between them the washing up was done that her hostess asked what Rosamund had realised must be the inevitable question.

"Now, my dear, will you tell me all that you care to about yourself?"

Put that way, Rosamund found it easier to explain what had happened than she had when John Lindsay had crossed-questioned her. She was franker, too.

"Mr. Lindsay accused me of being a runaway. He thought—" she smiled faintly, "that it might be from Borstal—"

"How stupid of him," Miss Coates said unflatteringly. "Quite apart from anything else, he had only to look at your hands. I doubt very much if a Borstal girl would have such beautifully manicured nails as you have!"

"Oh!" Rosamund gave a little start and looked frightened. "I didn't think of that—how stupid of me!"

Miss Coates made no comment, but she stored the remark up for future consideration since she felt that it could be interpreted in more than one way.

"Go on, dear," she encouraged.

Rosamund drew a long breath.

"He was wrong about Borstal or that I had run away from school. But he *was* right about me being a runaway." She paused, looking doubtfully at Miss Coates.

"But you don't want to tell me why or from what?" Miss Coates suggested. "Now listen to me, Rosamund. All of us need to escape from something or somebody at some time or other in our lives. Sometimes it's a wise thing to do, sometimes not. *I* think I'm wise in spending as much time as I can down here. You see, I don't like limelight very much and I detest being lionised—"

"Oh!" Rosamund leaned forward. "Why, of course, I should have remembered before. You're the artist who painted that lovely portrait of Her Majesty the Queen!"

"And a most enjoyable task that was!" Miss Coates nodded. "None the less, it had the effect of putting me in the public eye, which was advantageous in a financial sense, but—" she made a little grimace. "Perhaps it sounds rather affected, but to do decent work, one *has* to belong to oneself, and beyond a certain point too much publicity makes that impossible. So, except when I'm actually working on a portrait, I rusticate down here and paint watercolours of birds and water scenes. So far, though I've earned the name for being eccentric, no one has discovered my hideout—and I sincerely hope they never do!" And she looked gravely at Rosamund.

"No one ever will from me," she promised earnestly. "And thank you for trusting me, Miss Coates." She stopped short, feeling embarrassed.

"But though I've told you my secret, you'd still prefer not to tell me yours? All right, I accept that, but I would like you to answer one or two questions. For instance, are you married?"

"No, I'm not," Rosamund met her eyes squarely. "Nor have I done anything against the law. It's just that—" she paused and then took the plunge. "You run away from lots of people. I'm running away from one. Someone I both live and work with. I—I've already told her several times that I want to break away and make a fresh start on my own, only she doesn't understand—"

"Probably doesn't want to," Miss Coates suggested dryly. "I've met that sort. They see other people only as adjuncts to their own lives—most exhausting. Makes you feel absolutely drained of all personality."

"You *do* understand," Rosamund exclaimed gratefully. "But do you see that because it *is* just one person, I don't want to say who it is?"

"Yes, I see that," Miss Coates nodded, wondering whether the girl realised how much, in spite of her caution, she was actually giving away. "All the same, isn't there a possibility of quite reasonable enquiries being made, possibly by the police? After all, when an attractive girl just vanishes into the blue—"

"I left a letter which explained everything very clearly," Rosamund assured her. "And I don't think my— she would like the sort of publicity that an enquiry would bring—"

"Probably not," Miss Coates agreed. "Well, that's all right, then! Now, let's be practical. About your purse. Do you remember the name of the garage where you got your petrol and where it was?"

"I didn't notice the name and I'm not very sure of where it was. Marlborough was the last big town I'd gone through. It was some miles beyond that and it was on an open stretch of the road and on my side of it. Not very big, but very well run."

"Not, by any chance, by a very cheerful little man with a shock of red hair? It was! Oh, splendid! I often stop there myself. What's more, I'm pretty certain I've still got a bill somewhere for a small repair he did for me once. I'll hunt it out and then we'll go to the village and ring through. I'll go and hunt that bill at once—and there's a letter I want to write to my next-door neighbour. No, not Mr. Lindsay. On the other side, the *Rosebud*. His name is Robert Dexter. Another runaway, when he can manage it! I won't be long."

She went through to her sleeping cabin, found the bill without difficulty and then took a writing case from a drawer. For several moments she sat, frowning thoughtfully. Then, rapidly, she wrote :

"Dear Rob,
I don't know if you're planning to come down here this weekend, but if you possibly can, please do.
Something has happened which I find both startling and astonishing and I want to know whether you agree with me.
I don't think you'll feel you've wasted your time, but I must warn you that if you think as I do, you will be in for a shock. But please don't show it—that's important.
I'm sorry to be so mysterious, but you must judge for yourself.

Yours,
Alice."

CHAPTER TWO

ROSAMUND waited anxiously while Miss Coates made the telephone call.

"Tom? Oh, good! Look, Tom, a young friend of mine—a fair-haired girl in a rather battered blue mini car—stopped at your garage this morning for petrol. She thinks she may have dropped her purse—she did?" Miss Coates made a thumbs-up sign to Rosamund, standing outside the telephone kiosk. "Splendid! Well, look, it's rather late now to come to collect it. Tomorrow? About lunch time? Right! What? Yes, we'd like that! Thank you very much, Tom."

She rang off and came out to join Rosamund, beaming all over her pleasant face.

"Yes, you did drop it there, just as you got back into the car. But Tom didn't see it until you'd started off, and though he shouted to you, you didn't hear. He's put it in his safe. I told him we'd pick it up tomorrow."

"O-oh!" Rosamund breathed a deep sigh of relief.

"Yes, you've been lucky," Miss Coates acknowledged. "Tom is as honest as the day. And his wife is a delightful girl—a first-class cook, too. Which reminds me, Tom asked me if we'd have a meal there as their guests and I said we would. All right?"

"Yes, of course," Rosamund's eyes sparkled. "You know, when I was there this morning there was something cooking which smelt quite heavenly—something with onions in it. It made my mouth water and I almost asked if I could have a meal there, only—" the sparkle faded, "I wanted to get on—"

"Well, we'll make up for it tomorrow," Miss Coates promised. "And now we'd better get back. It was fortunate for us that the rain stopped long enough for us to get here, but the clouds are blowing up again."

Neither of them spoke much on the way back, Rosamund because the sense of sheer relief obsessed her to the exclusion of everything else, Miss Coates because she was genuinely glad that Rosamund had been proved to have told the truth and far from displeased that her own perspicacity had assured her that it would be so.

When they reached the gate in the hedge leading to the canal, they had a brief glimpse of John. He was swabbing down the deck and might or might not have seen them, but certainly he let go of his mop and vanished inside with considerable speed.

Miss Coates gave an unregenerate little chuckle which made Rosamund turn and look enquiringly at her.

"Just I was thinking how pleasant it will be to inform that young man that I was right and he was wrong!"

"About me telling the truth?" Rosamund asked, and when Miss Coates grinned and nodded, she looked doubtful.

"But is it worth worrying about?" she asked. "I mean, it wasn't only a question of my purse. I did do other things that annoyed him. I took his food and went to sleep on his bed and even though he hadn't locked up, from his point of view—"

"Are you defending him, by any chance?" Miss Coates interrupted in surprise. "Because, if so, I consider that uncommonly generous of you. He behaved like the oaf I'd already found him to be."

"Yes—well, perhaps he did. But I've been wondering—he looks like somebody with a chip on his shoulder. So perhaps he's had good cause not to trust anybody. And in any case, he was quite right about one thing. It *was* impossible for me to stay here."

"True," Miss Coates agreed absently, her mind suddenly off at a tangent.

For the first time she was reminded that many a love story has begun with conflict between the two people concerned and that almost invariably innocent bystanders were apt to get caught up in the maelstrom. She sighed. She liked what she had seen of Rosamund and she had her own reasons for being resolved to stand by her. All the same, it seemed likely that this summer the tranquillity of mind which she was accustomed to find here might be difficult, if not actually impossible, to come by.

Robert Dexter arrived during Saturday morning. He was a man in his early fifties and despite the fact that he was wearing extremely informal clothes, Rosamund's first impression of him was one of essential spruceness. For one thing, old though they were, it was evident that his clothes had been personally tailored. His brown hair, only lightly flecked with white at the temples, was short and well brushed. He wore a small Vandyke beard trimmed with professional skill and his hand, when Miss Coates introduced them and he took Rosamund's in his, was warm and firm. In fact, she took an instant liking to him and as their eyes met she smiled with instinctive friendliness.

Dr. Rob—which was how Miss Coates had introduced him—smiled responsively and his grasp of her hand tightened very slightly.

"I'm very glad to meet you, my dear!" he told her, and the way in which he said it convinced her that it wasn't just an empty, conventional remark. He really meant it, and even in that brief space of time she knew that she had made a friend.

"Well?" Alice Coates demanded.

The sun was shining gloriously now and freshened by the rain earlier in the week, hedgerows and flowers were more beautiful than ever.

But the two old friends, sitting together on the deck of the *Rosebud,* were barely aware of their surroundings.

Rosamund, thinking that they might enjoy their own company better if she was not there, had made the excuse of shopping to go to the village. Almost immediately Miss Coates had left her own craft to visit Dr. Rob.

"The likeness is undeniable," he said slowly. "And of course, the eyes—" He paused. "Tell me what you know about her, Alice."

"Not very much," she acknowledged regretfully. "She's far from being communicative. But what I do know all fits in. For example, she tells me that she's twenty-three, and though I don't know exactly when her birthday is, any time during that year would make it possible."

"True enough," Dr. Rob acknowledged. "What else?"

"Only odds and ends that I've pieced together," Miss Coates explained. "But of course it's possible that, having already jumped to a conclusion, I'm *making* things fit that really don't. So check on my reasoning very carefully, Rob!"

"I don't know that I'm the best person to do that," he said a little wryly. "You see, I *want* your conclusions to be right! Still, go ahead."

"Well, after the initial shock of realising the likeness, I looked out for anything she said or did that was in any way revealing. She admitted to me that she had run away from—somebody, but even before that I had thought it more than probable. You see, these days, most girls use make-up. Rosamund doesn't. Yet her nails are most exquisitely manicured. Now, those two things contradict one another. Nails like that *go* with make-up—quite a lot of it, in my opinion. But to stop using it is the best disguise a woman can adopt. I'm quite sure that nobody who knows her with it would recognise her as she is at present."

"Not even with those eyes?" Dr. Rob suggested, shading his own eyes with his hand. "They're very unusual, you know."

"Yes," Miss Coates acknowledged. "They are, of course. But if I'm right about the make-up, then she would certainly use eye-shadow—probably green. But quite likely, just because green eyes are so unusual, most people, unless they were face to face with her, would conclude that her eyes were no more than greenish-blue, and that she was deliberately emphasising the green to make a gimmick out of the unusual. You see what I meant when I said I was trying to make things fit," she added wryly.

"Well, as a mere man, I don't feel I can criticise your reasoning. I'm frankly out of my depth. But your suspicions were at least confirmed by her own admission later. Let's go on from there."

"I'll try to remember as nearly word for word as I can," Miss Coates promised, and after a brief interval, with her eyes fixed unseeingly ahead of her, she delved back into the recent past.

Dr. Rob listened attentively, once or twice looking at her with keen, half-closed eyes as she made some point or other. "So we know that she's doing work that she doesn't enjoy and is both living with and working for a woman who can see no other point of view than her own."

"You're quicker on the uptake than anyone else I know, man or woman," Miss Coates declared appreciatively. "I suppose it comes from sorting the grain from the chaff when your patients tell you their symptoms! Anything else?"

"By the way in which Rosamund referred to the *wrong* sort of publicity, it surely means that there is a *right* sort. In other words, that good advertisement is essential to—whatever sort of activity is involved." He looked questioningly at his companion, who nodded without speaking. Clearly that was not the only conclusion she wanted him to draw.

Dr. Rob pursed his lips thoughtfully.

"Yes. You made a correction in repeating something Rosamund said. First of all, you reported her as having said that she didn't think *her*—and then altered it to *she*. Whose correction, Rosamund's or yours?"

"Hers."

"H'm! '*I don't think my*—' Now, what did she nearly say? It would fit in if it was some group name for a special type of relative, wouldn't it? I think we can dismiss the possibility of it being 'mother'. There is a certain sentiment about avoiding such criticism. So—an older sister, do you think?"

"Possibly," Miss Coates admitted, but without enthusiasm.

"But that doesn't fit into your pattern?" Dr. Rob smiled faintly. "Cousin? Or aunt?"

"It could be," Miss Coates said, still in that non-committal way.

"But you're still determined not to put ideas into my head?" Dr. Rob touched her hand gently. "You're a woman in a thousand, Alice. In such circumstances most members of your sex would resent me doing any thinking of my own, because a woman's intuition is never at fault!"

"It isn't very often," Miss Coates said dryly. "Well, what next?"

"Well, next, my dear, is that you're withholding a vital piece of information, aren't you?"

"Am I?"

"Oh yes, that is if you know it. What's the child's surname?"

"Hastings," Miss Coates said briefly.

Dr. Rob stood up and walked to the side of the boat. His back was towards Miss Coates, but she could see that he was gripping the rail so tightly that his knuckles stood out white. Her eyes very tender, she waited in silence for him to speak.

"So it would seem to be possible that your little waif is—my daughter!" he said at length in a deeply moved voice.

"That's how it seems to me," Miss Coates said unsteadily. "Of course, it's not absolutely conclusive—"

"It's sufficiently conclusive to warrant me making enquiries," Dr. Rob asserted grimly. "And that I intend to do without delay!" And for emphasis, he lifted one hand and brought it down resoundingly on the rail.

"You mean—you'll question Rosamund?"

He thought that over for a moment, then turned and came back to his chair.

"No, not in the first instance. I want the child to get to know me better and, if possible, to like me before she's told—if, indeed, there's anything to tell. I've got to face it, Alice, there may not be. Which is another reason for saying nothing to Rosamund at this juncture."

"Yes," Miss Coates nodded. "All the same, Rob, in your heart of hearts you do more than hope it's true, don't you? You think it very likely is!"

"Yes, I do," he said slowly. "There's too much coincidence otherwise. Besides, this could be history repeating itself!"

He slumped in his chair, his hands in his pockets, deep in thought. Miss Coates waited patiently, wondering if he was going to take her into his confidence, and made up her mind that much as she longed to know just what he meant, if he preferred not to, she would respect his reticence. But suddenly, and to her, surprisingly, he said:

"How long have we known one another, Alice?"

"Since we were children. We've always been good friends."

"Yes, always," he agreed. "And yet I've never told you much about my married life, have I?"

"Not very much," she replied evenly. "But then our work lay in such different spheres. It was almost inevitable that we should drift apart. But I did meet Celia, you know. We met by chance in Regent Street, and you introduced us. I've never forgotten what she looked like—I remember thinking that I'd never seen a lovelier face and that I'd love to paint it. In fact, when I got back to my studio, I did a painting of her from memory. I still have it."

But she didn't tell him just why she had painted it—to be a reminder of her own folly. Even now, after so many years, she felt that agonising pang when she had seen the lovely girl he had fallen in love with. No wonder, once he had met her, he had forgotten his old friend's plain face! No, not forgotten. They were still the best of friends—but Celia was still enshrined in his heart.

"I'd like to see it some time, if you'd let me," Dr. Rob said quietly. "Particularly now, to make a comparison." He was silent for a moment, then, almost as if he was thinking aloud: "She was very lovely—and very young and inexperienced. As for me, I was a bumptious young cub!"

"Rob, you were never that!" Miss Coates disclaimed indignantly.

"Oh yes, I was, my dear! I had an extremely good

opinion of myself. I'd got on very well and I put that down entirely to my own brilliance instead of realising that I had incredible luck. The right opening always seemed to turn up at just the right time for me—"

"Perhaps it did—but only because you were the right man!" she insisted.

Dr. Rob smiled rather wryly.

"You always were a partisan where your friends were concerned, weren't you? Well, we won't argue about that, though my mentality at the time played a large part in the break-up of our marriage."

"It did break up?" This was news to Miss Coates. "I knew, of course, that you were in America when she died, but I had imagined that you were there only temporarily—that you thought you'd gain useful experience—"

"You were quite right. But that wasn't the only reason." He leaned forward, his hands dangling loosely between his knees. "The break was already imminent before I left and I, in my high and mighty way, thought that a temporary separation might bring Celia to her senses. But I'd reckoned without her sister—"

"Ruth Hastings," Miss Coates supplied quietly.

He looked at her sharply.

"So you knew that! How?"

"Because even then she was making quite a name for herself in the world of fashion," Miss Coates explained. "Not my world, of course—I've never met her. But very certainly an increasingly important person to more than one of my women clients. That's the worst of painting women. They will chatter so when one wants to concentrate," she added in parenthesis.

"Poor Alice!" Dr. Rob said absently. "But if you've never met her, you wouldn't appreciate what a dominant personality she had. She was, and I suppose still is, a brilliantly clever woman at her job. In addition, she and I had one thing in common—we were both ruthlessly ambitious! In an incredibly short time she progressed from being a very humble worker employed by a London couturier to being his chief designer—there was even talk of a partnership to come, so Celia told me. She, at that time, was modelling for the same firm and I gathered that quite a lot of Ruth's success was due to the fact that Celia displayed her creations to such advantage."

"I can well understand that," Miss Coates said gently.

"Yes, indeed. But Ruth never gave credit to anyone else, even a close relative, although subsequent events proved that she knew it well enough." He paused and sighed. "You know, Alice, it's one of the tragedies of life that something in a woman that attracts a man may, after marriage, be the very thing that irritates him."

"I don't think that's an exclusively male failing," Miss Coates told him. "I've known cases—still, that's by the way. Go on, Rob!"

"Celia was lovely enough to turn any man's head. She had in addition a look of exquisite fragility that made an irresistible appeal— Rosamund has that same look, though I hope that in her case—"

"That she has something of you in her as well?" Miss Coates supplied gently as he paused. "Don't worry, Rob, she has! Courage—and spirit. She's already shown that."

"Courage and spirit," he repeated. "Yes, that's what was lacking in Celia, poor child! She had to have someone to lean on, and inevitably Ruth made capital of that. But she overdid it. She not only overworked Celia, she dominated her to the point where she couldn't call her soul her own, and though Celia was really unhappy, she was quite helpless. That was where I came charging into the picture!" He laughed bitterly. "In my arrogance, I saw myself as a knight errant! *I* would rescue Celia from her bondage. We would get married and then Ruth would have to be more reasonable! I wouldn't listen to Celia's doubts. We were going to get married and that was that! She gave in—good lord, there wasn't much to choose between Ruth and me when it came to bullying the poor little soul. But I, of course, did it from the highest of motives! Well, we were married very quietly one morning, had lunch together and then went off to our different jobs. When I got back to my uninspiring lodgings, Celia was already there—in floods of tears. You see we—or rather I—had assumed that Ruth would appreciate that she hadn't sole claim on Celia now and would be less demanding. It hadn't occurred to me that she'd sack Celia out of hand. But that's what happened, and there we were, entirely dependent on what I earned as a houseman—which wasn't much for two to live on! It was a pretty bleak outlook."

"But surely Celia could have got a similar job elsewhere?" Miss Coates suggested, barely hiding her indignation.

"No. Ruth had seen to that. Celia had a contract which stipulated that she mustn't work for any other similar firm in London, and since I was based on London, what was there to do about it? If she worked somewhere else, we might just as well not have been married! As regards any other type of work—Ruth had taken care that she simply hadn't any abilities which would have made that possible. So there we were, hard up, living in squalid circumstances and rapidly becoming disillusioned, the pair of us. Quite apart from my determination to get on—doubled now that I had Celia to provide for—my work *was* demanding. Not only did I have to be away from home for long hours but there was also the fact that I could get caught up in an emergency. It's like that in a hospital and one has no choice but to get on with it. But it was all new to Celia. She felt neglected and she was bored beyond words. There wasn't enough money to spare for outings and there she was stuck in those ghastly lodgings with nothing to do. Small wonder that she felt I'd let her down. Not, of course, that I admitted it. I told her that she ought to have known what marrying a doctor meant—and that I'd no choice but to work hard in the hope of promotion since I'd got her to provide for as well as myself. She cried, poor child, and that made me impatient. I said a lot more things that I've bitterly regretted since."

He fell silent and Miss Coates stared straight ahead of her. She couldn't bear to see that regret that was even now, she knew, written on his kindly face.

"Then one day when I came home she was tremendously excited and gay. Ruth had been to see her. There was a big dress show coming off the next day and the model who had taken Celia's place had gone down with appendicitis. Would Celia take her place—but of course, only temporarily. There was no promise of future work—Ruth was too clever not to make that clear! But I saw it

34

for what it was—the thin end of the wedge that she intended to drive between Celia and me. I told her that and she shrugged her shoulders. I'd blamed her for being a burden on me and so how could I object now that she had got a chance of earning some money?"

"Which, of course, was unanswerable," Miss Coates commented. "And naturally, there were more offers of work?"

"Oh yes. Occasionally at first but with increasing frequency. Then I had the offer of this post in America. I was determined to take it—and to take Celia with me, but she refused, point blank. She simply didn't trust me. I'd let her down once, how did she know that I wouldn't do it again? Suppose something went wrong in America? We argued—quarrelled, and in the end I gave my ultimatum. She could come or not as she chose, but either way I intended going to America."

"But still she wouldn't?"

"No, she wouldn't. I might have persuaded her, but not with Ruth in the background, frightening her—and offering her the old job back again. So that was the end of it. She went back to live with Ruth and a month or so later I left England. I went to see her the night before and asked her for the last time to change her mind—she could have followed me over there. But it was no good." He sighed heavily. "That was the last time we saw one another, and though I wrote several times, she never replied."

Silence fell between them. Then Miss Coates said slowly :

"Yes, I do see what you mean, Rob, about the possibility of history repeating itself. Substitute Rosamund for Celia in what you've told me and it fits perfectly—except that Rosamund isn't married. She told me so herself."

"I'm glad of that. It puts me in a stronger position for dealing with Ruth," Dr. Rob said grimly.

"Yes, I suppose so." Miss Coates frowned consideringly. "Rob, how did you hear of Celia's death?"

"From Ruth. And there was no doubt but that it was the truth. She enclosed the certificate."

"Did she!" Miss Coates sat suddenly erect. "Rob, what was the cause—"

"Not childbirth," Dr. Rob had no difficulty in reading

her thoughts. "Influenza—there was a lot about just then."

"But that doesn't mean that she couldn't have had a child," Miss Coates argued eagerly. "But surely she'd have let you know, either before or after Rosamund was born!"

"She may have done, but if so, I never received the letter. There again, Ruth may have intercepted it." Dr. Rob stood up and paced up and down the deck. "What I must discover is how the child was registered at birth— also, more than likely, by Ruth. Was it under her correct name, if she is my daughter? Or under Ruth's? After all, Rosamund gives her name as Hastings. Ruth may have said that she was her own illegitimate child—"

"Yes, that's a possibility, I suppose," Miss Coates admitted. "Even so, there's Rosamund's likeness to Celia, particularly her eyes. That would want some explaining because, as stepsisters, there was no tie of common blood between Celia and Ruth."

"Yes, there's that," Dr. Rob agreed. "Then, speaking from memory, I think Celia died at a private address. I can verify that when I get back to town. It's important, of course, because in all probability, Rosamund was born in the same district, though not necessarily at the same address. That will help to limit the scope of the search. That, and the date of her birthday."

"I'll find that out somehow," Miss Coates promised, and stood up. "She's just coming through the gate, Rob," she warned. "Pull yourself together, my dear, or she'll guess that something has happened—and we don't want her to be afraid it's about her and take flight!"

"No, indeed!" Dr. Rob agreed fervently, as he, too, watched the approach of the slender figure. He slipped his hand under his companion's arm and pressed it gently. "I shall never cease to be thankful that she's fallen into your kind hands, Alice!"

Without speaking, Miss Coates returned the pressure.

Then, acknowledging Rosamund's blithe wave of the hand, they went smilingly to meet her.

Rosamund dangled her bare feet over the bank opposite the *Pride of London*, and decided that she had never been so blissfully happy in her life before or known such peace of mind. Even the erratic tapping of John's typewriter so near at hand didn't worry her. Why should it? He, presumably, was enjoying what he was doing and in her present frame of mind Rosamund was prepared to extend toleration, if not liking, towards any of her fellow beings who contrived to live their lives as it suited them—that was, so long as they didn't hurt anyone else in doing so.

Her smooth forehead puckered. *She* was living her own life, but in doing so she was certainly upsetting Aunt Ruth. She was truly sorry about that, but how could she avoid it? Just supposing she had not run away, what hope of compromise could there have been? Aunt Ruth's attitude where the Salon was concerned was so very definitely: *"All or nothing!"* Rosamund knew only too well that no matter how forcefully she had stated her case or how glibly Aunt Ruth had promised that things should be different and agree to make fewer demands on her in future, that state of affairs wouldn't have lasted. Sooner or later, enthusiasm would have run away with her aunt and they would have been back where they were before.

She was quite sure of that, for she knew beyond doubt that even after reading that letter which had been very difficult to write, so plain-spoken was it, Aunt Ruth still didn't blame herself for what had happened.

Her aunt had not written to her, of course. That was impossible since no one connected with her old life knew where she was. But Ruth had contrived to send her a message, none the less. Every possible day since she had read the letter she had put an appeal in the personal column of the *Daily Telegraph*. It read :

"Rosamund darling, come back to me! All forgiven, no recriminations, R.H.*"*

Perhaps the appeal in the first part of the message might have made Rosamund weaken. But the last sentence was an unmistakable warning. There would be a prodigal's welcome for her and however little Ruth might actually say, in her heart, she would blame Rosamund, not herself for what had happened.

So there it was. You might regret causing distress to

someone else, but when you were convinced that what you had done was both right and necessary, you had to go through with it.

The week that she had spent with Miss Coates—or Miss Alice as she preferred to be called—had only served to strengthen that belief. It would hardly be possible to live in closer companionship with a person than in the comparatively restricted confines of the boat. Yet never once had Rosamund felt any sense of intrusion of her own personality. Nor, in addition, had she felt any uncomfortable obligation for the hospitality which had been so freely given.

You could hardly have two people less alike than Miss Alice and Aunt Ruth, and yet they had some things in common. Each did work which they loved and did it with great skill. And in each case, they were dependent on the approval of other people for their success. But there the likeness ended. Of course, Miss Alice didn't need anyone to help her do her work, whereas Aunt Ruth did. But it was something which went deeper than that. Something in the basic nature of the two women, though just what it was, Rosamund couldn't decide. The nearest she could get to it was that Miss Alice was essentially a *giver*, while Aunt Ruth was a *taker*.

All the same, one mustn't accept too much generosity when it seemed most unlikely that there would ever be any opportunity of making a return in kind. Of course, there was the question of the domestic chores which Rosamund had taken over, but that was only a very small thing, particularly as, though she was in a position to pay for her keep, Miss Alice refused point blank to allow her to do any such thing.

"Nonsense, child," she had said emphatically when Rosamund had broached the matter. "You're doing the jobs for me which I frankly dislike, and because of that, I've more time to do the work I enjoy—and for which, by the way, I shall be paid!"

Which Rosamund knew was true, yet it didn't altogether satisfy her.

"Miss Alice, why are you being so good to me?" she asked wonderingly.

38

Miss Alice looked up from her little sketch block and smiled.

"For a variety of reasons, my dear. At first, because you were in distress and it seemed to me that I could and should help you. Then, because I've grown fond of you. And finally—" she paused to concentrate on her delicate brushwork. "Finally," she said deliberately, "because you remind me of—someone I once knew."

"Do I? Had she got peculiar eyes like I have?" Rosamund asked with interest.

"Your eyes aren't peculiar, my dear. Just rather unusual," Miss Alice told her firmly.

And it was not until now that Rosamund realised that her question had remained unanswered, but of course, it wasn't of any real importance.

But she had let her thoughts slide away from making plans for her future, and really, it was too glorious a day to think of anything except *here* and *now*. She wriggled a little nearer the edge of the canal bank and dabbled her feet in the warm water. A brilliant Red Admiral butterfly settled momentarily near to her hand, and a kingfisher flashed like a living jewel from one side of the canal to the other. It was heaven! She could have stayed here for hours, but the chiming of the church clock in the village reminded her that it was time for tea. Regretfully she stood up, walked up to the lock and crossed the canal by the narrow bridge which was part of the lock gates.

She was smiling with the sheer joy of being alive on such a day as she passed the *Seven Stars* and it was only at the last moment that she saw John had left his typing and was now on deck.

It was rather an embarrassing situation for Rosamund. She had only seen him at a distance since the day when he had so unceremoniously bundled her off his boat and she had no idea whether Miss Alice had carried out her intention of telling him that the purse had been recovered.

The smile faded from her face. His back was towards her, so it might be possible to pass without him seeing her. She hoped that it would be. It would save any further chance of unpleasantness.

But she was unlucky. More than once during the day the pollen-laden summer air had made her sneeze. It did so again with no warning whatever just as she came up to the *Seven Stars.* It wasn't a very loud sneeze, but it was enough to make John turn sharply. What was more, when he saw who it was, he came across his gangway and stood blocking her way along the path.

Rosamund stood still. She knew quite well that it would be impossible to dodge past him. There simply wasn't room, and John would certainly stay just where he was until he had said whatever was in his mind. All her earlier happiness evaporated. Was he still angry with her and was he going to make more trouble? She didn't want him to. She wanted to be friends with everybody in this little paradise into which she had strayed. But while it took only one person to pick a quarrel, it took two to make a friendship.

She waited in silence for him to speak, her grave eyes on his face—and then saw with relief that though he, too, looked very serious, he didn't look angry.

"I—I'm glad we've met, Miss Hastings," he announced with a diffidence which Rosamund found more surprising than anger would have been. "I—I owe you an apology. You see, I've been informed that you told me the truth about your purse—"

"Oh, please!" Rosamund said quickly, finding to her own surprise that though she was glad he knew she hadn't lied to him, it gave her no pleasure at all for him to have to eat humble pie. "I've realised since that you weren't to blame for thinking what you did. It must have sounded a most unlikely story."

"It shouldn't have done to me," John insisted, evidently determined to make a good job of it. "Not seeing that only a few days earlier, I left my wallet in the village general store!"

"Oh—I don't know," Rosamund said consideringly, her fair head on one side. "It must have seemed just too much of a coincidence, almost as if I might have heard of that—Mrs. Watchett *is* such a chatterbox—and decided that I might as well try it on!"

"You know, you're heaping coals of fire on my head," he told her wryly. "Because, until this moment, such an idea hadn't occurred to me. No, I was just flaming angry—"

"At having other people's problems thrust upon you when you'd just got everything nicely settled so that you could get on with your work in peace?" Rosamund suggested as he paused.

"That was just it," he replied eagerly. "Although—" dubiously, "put into so many words it sounds rather egotistic, doesn't it?"

"Not if it's a question of—of self-preservation," Rosamund said with so much conviction that John, she saw, looked at her with very lively interest.

"You know, that sounds as if you know what you're talking about—as if you've experienced the same sort of thing yourself!"

"Does it?" Rosamund asked lightly. "Well, I suppose everyone does at some time or other! And please, don't worry any more. After all, there was no harm done."

"But no thanks to me," John pointed out grimly. "What would you have done if Miss Coates hadn't happened to come along just at that moment?"

Involuntarily Rosamund shivered and though she did not realise it, there was a strained look in her face which spoke for itself. It was a question that she had more than once asked herself—

"I honestly don't know," she confessed.

"No, and nor do I. A pretty girl on her own with no money—I could at least have given you a pound or two without being so infernally cocksure and superior!"

He was angry now—but with himself—a very different state of affairs from the way he had been at their first meeting.

"Well, I'm glad you didn't lend me any money," Rosamund declared stoutly. "I shouldn't have got to know Miss Alice—or Dr. Rob—and they are such dears!"

"I thought he looked rather pleasant," John acknowledged, "but she's something of a dragon, isn't she?"

"Is she?" Rosamund suddenly dimpled. "I wonder what makes you think that?"

"My guilty conscience, I expect," John admitted wryly.

Rosamund laughed. She couldn't help it. He looked so like a small boy caught scrumping apples. Then her face grew serious.

"Actually, she's the most tender-hearted person I've ever met," she said softly. "And I can never repay her for the way she's taken me under her wing. But that, you see, is the very reason why—"

"Why she had it in for me," John finished. "She thinks of me as a wolf who threatened her ewe lamb!"

"Well, perhaps," Rosamund conceded. Then, as she heard the church clock strike the quarter hour: "Goodness, I must rush! I'm going to be late making tea as it is." She hesitated and then took the plunge. "Mr. Lindsay, won't you have tea with us so that you can get to know Miss Alice properly?"

"Shall I be welcome?" John asked doubtfully.

"Oh yes," Rosamund told him serenely. "She much prefers living at peace with people, and if you come with me, she'll know that everything is all right." The mischief danced in her eyes again. "I can promise you that the dragon won't breathe fire at you."

"In that case, I'd like to come," John said simply, and clearly meant it, although he would have been hard put to explain how it came about that his original intention of keeping his neighbours at arm's length now seemed both short-sighted and unnecessary.

Miss Alice didn't breathe fire when she saw him approaching, but she was surprised. She had already appreciated that though Rosamund had plenty of spirit, she was none the less essentially gentle by nature. That being so, no doubt she'd be able to forgive this young man for his harsh treatment of her, but surely they wouldn't be on the friendly terms they obviously were without his co-operation.

However, neither of them gave any explanation of the new state of affairs and Miss Alice had no intention of asking any questions. None the less, when Rosamund had left them to get the tea, she surveyed the unexpected guest with an artist's shrewd eyes.

Now that his face was not marred by that angry expression, she saw that he was really quite good-looking though not conventionally handsome. His features were good—clean-cut and well proportioned. His chin was, perhaps, rather noticeably strong, but his mouth was sensitive. It made rather a pleasant combination, she thought. And he looked you straight in the eyes.

"Do sit down, Mr. Lindsay," she said pleasantly.

For a moment or two there was silence. Then their eyes met and they both smiled. With relief John knew that there was no need for explanations or apologies. This was a fresh start.

Rosamund came back to find them deep in conversation.

"And you're finding this a good place for working?" Miss Alice was saying.

"First class," John replied enthusiastically. "Though that doesn't mean I haven't struck snags—"

"Yes?" Miss Alice encouraged.

"Yes. You see, I've had my plot in mind for months. But when it came to turning it into people, I knew that there was something wrong. The result just wasn't convincing. At first I thought I'd have to change my plot to suit my characters. Then, this afternoon, I realised that it was the other way round. I'd been so in love with my plot that I hadn't given sufficient thought to just what sort of people would behave and react in a realistic way in such circumstances. They just didn't come off the paper!"

"So?"

"Heroic measures! I'll have to re-write everything I've done." He sounded surprisingly cheerful in the circumstances. "The girl in particular—"

At that moment Rosamund came out with the laden tea-tray and as John jumped up to take it from her, something in his expression made Miss Alice wonder.

She had more than once visited the *Seven Stars* the previous year when Charles Thomas had been working there and now she visualised the layout of the day cabin.

The table at which John must almost certainly work was just under the big window that overlooked the canal bank. Rosamund had been sitting on the bank most of the afternoon.

Was there any connection between those two facts and his new conception of the girl of his play?

If so, Rosamund would naturally be entirely unaware of the influence she had had. But John?

Had it seemed to him to be a matter of inner vision—or

had he known that he was drawing from life? Even more important than that, if he had realised it, had it been personally significant to him?

Miss Alice gave herself a mental shake. Really, she was behaving like a hen with one chick! For all that she knew, the girl of the play might be a thoroughly undesirable character and not in the least like Rosamund. In any case, young people of today felt themselves to be completely competent to manage their own affairs! She must remember that!

She gave her entire attention to pouring out the tea. None the less, it was impossible not be aware that they seemed to have a lot to say to one another—

How could she help wondering *if* anything came of it, would it simplify life for Rosamund or complicate it still further?

And what would Rob feel about it?

CHAPTER THREE

"MISS ALICE, I'm getting *fat*!"

Miss Alice looked up into the pretty, dismayed face and smiled reassuringly.

"Not exactly fat, dear. You'd have a long way to go to get to that state! But I think you have put on a little weight—and very well it becomes you! When we first met you looked as if a puff of wind would blow you away."

"Yes, but, Miss Alice, one simply can't afford to be fat in my—" Rosamund stopped short. She had so very nearly said more than was wise, even where Miss Alice was concerned. That final word had been *job*, and there were only a comparatively few occupations to which the remark really applied. The stage, perhaps, or film acting. But certainly the world of fashion doesn't tolerate bulges! "I mean," she went on hurriedly, "if I'm not careful, none of my clothes will fit me, and think how expensive that will be!"

It sounded very lame to her own ears, but Miss Alice accepted it without comment.

"I'll have to take more exercise—and not eat so much," Rosamund lamented. "And it's awful to confess, but I do enjoy my food so much!"

"Not awful in the least," Miss Alice told her briskly. "Just natural, particularly at your age. In fact, to most people, eating is one of the natural pleasures of life. It needs to be since it's essential to life and health. Think how awful it would be if we found it so disagreeable that we had to force ourselves to eat! But you know, I wouldn't have said that you have a very big appetite. In fact, I would go so far as to say that if, before you came here, you ate less than you do now, then you weren't having enough. Or, of course," she added thoughtfully, "it could be that the circumstances in which you eat now are different—"

"What do you mean?"

Rosamund was conscious of the sharpness of her voice and knew that once again she had been incautious. She waited breathlessly for Miss Alice's reply.

"Simply, my dear, that you're living in much healthier conditions than it's possible to in London with its overcrowding and its polluted air. And our meals here are very leisurely and regular affairs. I expect that you, like most girls who work, had only a limited time to gobble down anything so long as it was quick to eat. Or even that you went without anything at midday if you wanted to do any shopping."

Unconsciously Rosamund drew a sigh of relief. It was all in such general terms that it could apply to any girl—

"Yes, that happens sometimes," she admitted. But not because she wanted to do any shopping. Because Aunt Ruth lost all sense of time and the need to eat if work was pressing. And she expected everyone else to show the same devotion. That sort of situation had been happening with increasing frequency lately. Indeed, it was one reason why—but Miss Alice, she suddenly realised, had evidently said something more for she was waiting expectantly.

"I was woolgathering, I'm afraid," Rosamund confessed. "Would you mind saying it again?"

"It wasn't all that important. Just that I'm going into

45

Bath this morning and I wondered if you'd like to come too?"

Rosamund considered.

"I would love to see Bath, some time," she said at length. "I've never been there yet—in fact, I've hardly been anywhere. But there are several things I really ought to do."

"Not housework?" Miss Alice asked quickly. "I don't want you to feel tied down, dear, particularly on a lovely day like this!"

Rosamund smiled at her with very real affection.

"I don't feel tied in the least," she said earnestly. "In fact, I've never felt freer in my life. But no, it isn't housework. It's just that I must look through my clothes to see if I can let them out a little. This waistband is really uncomfortably tight. And then I thought I'd go for a good long walk. That ought to help!"

"So it might," Miss Alice agreed placidly.

"All the same, I don't mind housework," Rosamund went on reflectively. "Oh, I know, some of it's dull and even disagreeable at times and you have to do the same thing over and over again. All the same, it does turn a house into a home, doesn't it?"

"If you don't overdo it," Miss Alice suggested dryly. "A woman who is over-houseproud is a menace to both the comfort and happiness of her entire family!"

"Yes, I expect so," Rosamund agreed, and then, hardly realising that she was speaking her thoughts aloud, she went on dreamily: "It must be wonderful to have one's own home and family—"

"And a husband?" Miss Alice teased gently.

"Well—yes. Only not just as a means to get a home of my own. I don't want to marry anyone unless—unless he matters so much that it wouldn't matter if we had to live in one room or in a palace!"

Miss Alice laughed.

"I wouldn't be surprised if you didn't find that there are problems in either. But you've got the right idea and you'll make out all right. He's going to be a lucky man, Rosamund!"

"But there isn't anybody—I mean, I was just talking in general terms," Rosamund explained in alarm.

"Of course. So was I," Miss Alice said absently as she checked through the contents of her handbag and made a few additions to it. "Now, is there anything you want me to buy for you in Bath? Cosmetics—anything like that?"

"No, thank you," Rosamund said so definitely that, seeing Miss Alice's slightly quizzical expression, she added hurriedly : "I suppose it does seem a bit odd that I don't use make-up, but it seems so out of place here—"

"Yes, I suppose it does, really," Miss Alice agreed. "Well, I think that's all. I'll be off now."

Rosamund watched her go with a sense of relief of which she felt ashamed. It didn't seem right to feel one must be on one's guard with anyone who had been so incredibly kind to her as Miss Alice had been, and yet she felt she must be. Miss Alice never asked inquisitive questions, but Rosamund knew that more than once she had been perilously near to giving more information about herself than she had meant to—almost as if she had been deliberately lured on to thin ice.

"But that's nonsense!" she told herself sturdily as she watched Miss Alice pause to exchange a few words with John. "She's far too nice a person to do that sort of thing. It's me! I don't think I'm really a deceitful sort of person and I just forget to be careful. I wish I felt I could tell Miss Alice everything. I would if only I wasn't such a coward! But I'm still too much afraid of Aunt Ruth to risk the possibility of anybody linking me up with her! If she suddenly turned up here and told me I'd got to go back with her—" She drew a long, shuddering breath at the thought and something of the brightness of the day vanished.

She went into her cabin and began, aimlessly, to turn over the clothes she had brought with her. They weren't very inspiring and she quickly saw that, being off the peg and cheap at that, they had been cut from the minimum amount of material and that the seams and turnings would allow for no letting out. She bundled them all back into the wardrobe-cupboard with a little sigh. Just for a moment she felt that it would be fun to wear the sort of clothes she used to—

But the sigh turned into a chuckle. All those immaculately tailored trouser-suits, the delicate materials of dresses and negligées—why, besides looking out of place here, they wouldn't last five minutes! A few grassy stains on dungarees or easily washed frocks didn't matter, nor did brambles and briars do much harm to her bare legs that wouldn't heal in a few days, but Aunt Ruth's exquisite creations—!

All the same, something prompted her to study her face far more closely than usual in the rather spotty mirror. She'd never really liked using the heavy make-up Aunt Ruth insisted on, but now she felt that just a little, perhaps—

It was then, for the first time, that she realised how brown her skin was compared with what it had been and that the natural colour in her face and particularly lips was brighter than it used to be. Perhaps, after all, she didn't need make-up!

Anyway, John didn't seem to think so, for when she walked past the *Seven Stars* his greeting was extremely flattering even if he sounded slightly surprised.

"Hallo, you're looking remarkably attractive this morning, Rosamund! What's happened? Been left a fortune?"

"No, just I feel absolutely fit and flourishing," she told him gaily. "Partly because it's such a lovely day and also because I'm afraid Miss Alice is right—I am all the better for having put on some weight, even though all my clothes are getting tight!"

John inspected her critically.

"You don't look like a heavyweight to me even so," he remarked. "Just—" his hands moved expressively, "pleasantly curvaceous!" and he laughed. "Now I've made you blush—I didn't think girls could, nowadays! Come and have some coffee?" he added coaxingly. "Just to show you're not cross with me!"

"I'm not cross, truly," Rosamund told him. "But I really mustn't have extras like that or I shall get *huge*! Actually, I'm going for a good long walk—and I've brought just two apples with me—that's going to be my lunch!"

John groaned.

"Sooner you than me! I like my grub! Well, I hope you enjoy yourself! If you come back in a fainting condition, I'll cook you—bacon and eggs!"

She flashed a reproachful look at him and then asked impulsively:

"Why don't you come too? You don't get very much exercise—"

"Not get exercise!" He was really quite indignant. "What do you call humping buckets of water and doing housework and cooking and washing-up and going shopping—besides— " he ran his fingers through his hair until it stood on end, a note of irritation crept into his voice— "I simply must get down to that damned play! It's holding out on me!"

Rosamund didn't answer immediately. John rarely talked about his work and she wasn't sure what was the right thing to say. Ought one to be sympathetic or en-encouraging—either, she thought, might be rather irritating.

"You see," John went on bleakly, "it's too long! And I can't boil what I want to say down to the length it will have to be—at least, not without leaving out what I feel are some of the best lines I've written! Oh well, there it is! My problem, not yours! Off you go and enjoy yourself."

"I wish I could help," Rosamund said wistfully.

John looked at her curiously.

"Bless you, poppet, I believe you mean that!" He sounded as if he was really touched. "But I'm afraid it's a one-man job—and I'm the man! So off you go before I'm tempted to down tools and come with you!" He blew her an airy kiss and vanished into the day cabin.

There was a happy little smile on Rosamund's lips as she began her walk. What a different sort of person John had turned out to be from what she had thought he was when they had first met! Even the fact that he was in trouble with his writing didn't make him turn into that scowling, unfriendly person that he had been then.

Not for the first time she wondered not only what had brought about the change but why he had been like that at all. There had been something very wrong, though just what she had no means of knowing, for John was as reticent about himself as she was about herself. Not that it really worried her. John, she was quite certain, was thoroughly nice. She simply couldn't imagine him doing anything underhand or dishonest. So, as long as he was happier now, why worry? So she didn't—at least, not about that. Only about John's present problem. If only she could help him over that!

Deep in thought, she walked along the path up to Yeoman's Lock, crossed the bridge and paused to pass the time of day with the lock-keeper's wife, a plump, cheerful woman, busy kneading a batch of bread-dough.

"Going for a walk, are you, miss? And a very nice day for it, too! But you didn't ought to be alone, not a pretty lady like you! Isn't there a nice gentleman somewhere to keep you from being lonely?"

It was said in such a friendly way that it was impossible for Rosamund to take offence even though a knowing jerk of the head in the direction of the long-boats made it clear that the speaker had John in mind.

"Oh, I shan't be lonely, Mrs Bunce. I've got a lot to think about—" she said cheerfully, but that didn't satisfy Mrs. Bunce.

"You don't want to do too much thinking, not at your age," she disapproved. "What you ought to be doing is having a good time while you can! It doesn't last long, you know. Once you get married and the children come—" she shook her head, but looked so contented that Rosamund laughed.

"Well, you don't look as if you've found it too depressing," she commented.

"Ah, but then I've always had to work hard," Mrs. Bunce explained. "Right from a girl. Mother died and I was the eldest of five—but you, miss—" she shook her head reproachfully. "If you don't mind me saying so, you don't look as if you could stand up to much in the way of hard work!"

This was so obviously another feeler for information that Rosamund decided it would be wiser not to linger.

"Oh, I'm stronger than I look," she said lightly. "And now I really must get on with my walk or I'll have no time left!"

"Drop in on your way back and I'll have a hot loaf ready for you," Mrs. Bunce offered cordially.

Though the mere thought of hot home-made bread made Rosamund's mouth water, she was on the point of explaining that she was trying to lose weight when it occurred to her that John would certainly enjoy the treat, and accepted the offer gratefully.

An hour and a half later she was back at the Lock, very hungry and very tired. The apples she had taken with her didn't even take the edge off her appetite and she hadn't taken into consideration that she wasn't used to walking any distance. It was rather disturbing. Perhaps, after all, Mrs. Bunce had been right and she wasn't as strong as she had thought, though goodness knew, she'd worked hard enough until now! Aunt Ruth had seen to that! But of course, it had been a very different sort of work.

"A hot-house plant, that's what I was," she thought regretfully. "Too used to going even the shortest distance by car! Well, I'll just have to get into training, that's all, because I'm not going to miss half the fun in life because I'm so feeble!"

There was no sign of John when she reached the *Seven Stars*, but with Mrs. Bunce's lovely crusty loaf as an excuse, she crossed the gangplank and went in search of him. He was in the day cabin, sitting at the table. It was covered with sheets of paper and John, looking thoroughly gloomy, was stirring them up with one hand as if he was in despair of finding anything worth keeping among them.

"Hallo." He looked up, but there was no welcome either in his face or in the way he spoke. "Back again?"

"Yes," Rosamund said briskly, determined not to be put out by his lack of enthusiasm. "And I've brought this—" she put the loaf down on the table. "I'm being absolutely crazy after what I said about losing weight, but I'm *starving*, and I'm going to have some of it to eat now for my lunch! Will you go shares so that I don't have a chance of eating too much?"

"I don't honestly think I want—" he paused and gave his whole attention to the loaf. "It looks and smells good, doesn't it?"

Ten minutes later they were sitting companionably side by side on deck, eating hunks of bread—John had insisted that you didn't cut slices off a loaf like that. You just pulled pieces off. Then you put lashings of butter on and topped up with cheese.

With amusement that had an odd thread of tenderness in it, Rosamund found that she needn't have worried about putting on weight because, though he didn't seem to realise it, John was greedily tucking into the lion's share. And for the first time in her life she discovered how satisfying it is to see a man enjoying his food, particularly when one has been the means of providing it. And, of course, when one happens to be—interested in the man concerned.

They finished the meal with coffee, talking in a desultory way for a time, and then fell silent until suddenly John said bitterly :

"It's no damn good, Rosamund ! I might as well tear up everything I've written ! Going through it this morning, I realised that it's not only too long. There are far too many characters. It's clumsy, unwieldy—utterly impossible !"

Rosamund leaned forward and disentangled a stem of grass from the buckle of her sandal with quite unnecessary care and without looking at him, she asked tentatively :

"John, what made you decide to be a playwright?"

He shrugged his shoulders.

"An exaggerated opinion of my own cleverness, I suppose"

"No, I didn't mean what made you decide that it should be a *play*?"

"Because I—here, what are you getting at?" he demanded suspiciously.

Rosamund hugged her knees and rested her chin on them.

"Did you see Frederick Dane's play 'Guessing Game' last winter?"

"As a matter of fact, I did. But what's that got to do with it?" John asked impatiently.

"It might have quite a lot," she answered seriously. "So please, John, tell me what you thought of it."

"Oh—I don't know." He frowned as if making an effort to remember. "Yes, I do. It hung together all right and yet by the end of the first act I began to feel—" he paused, the frown deepening.

"Yes?" Rosamund urged encouragingly.

"As if—somehow or other, I had missed something vital," he said slowly. "Something that would have made the situation—and the cast—seem real. As it was, they were only two-dimensional."

"Yes," Rosamund agreed eagerly. "That was just how I felt! And it made me wonder if the book from which the play was written was as wonderful as I'd thought. So I read it again. And it still was."

She felt rather than saw that John had grown very still and tense and she waited, holding her breath.

"What are you trying to tell me, Rosamund?" he asked at last in a queer, strained way.

"Just that I don't think a really first-class book will of a necessity make an equally good play." Purposely she spoke slowly, deliberately, so that he had time to realise that every word she said was important. "There's so much more *room* in a book than there is in a play, isn't there, because there isn't the same time limit. And when I real 'Guessing Game' again. I discovered that what they'd done was just to use the *bones* of the plot, highlighting the essential points. But, to me, what they had left out was what made the book live," she explained earnestly.

"Do you mean you think that I—" he began slowly, and stopped short.

"It's cheek of me to suggest it, seeing that I don't know a thing about it," she said diffidently. "But do you think perhaps it's possible that really it's a book, not a play, that you've got in your mind?"

It was so long before he answered that Rosamund was convinced that he thought she was not only cheeky but stupid.

Suddenly he stood up and pulled her to her feet. For a moment they stood face to face, their hands still linked. Then he bent his tall head and very gently kissed her on her soft pink mouth.

"Bless you, Rosamund!" he said huskily, and without another word, turned and strode into the day cabin.

Rosamund watched him go, her fingers gently touching the lips he had just kissed. Then, feeling as if it must all be a dream, she took the coffee cups into the galley and cleared up the debris of their meal. When everything was done to her satisfaction, she went out on deck again and tiptoed to the door of the day cabin. She need not have been cautious. John was far beyond the state where extraneous noises could disturb him. Already he had reduced his scattered manuscript to a neat pile, and with occasional references to it, he was writing, writing, writing as if his life depended on it.

Perhaps it did, Rosamund thought—that creative part of him which, denied, would mean that he wouldn't be able to live his life to the full. And that, she thought passionately, was what she wanted most for him—fulfilment and, wonder of wonders, she had already played a part, however small, in helping him to achieve that.

Contentment filled her—a contentment of a sort so deep rooted that, inexperienced as she was where men were concerned, she knew instinctively could mean only one thing. She loved John. And she always would.

"No, no luck at all," Dr. Rob confirmed glumly. "Not even though you were able to let me know the date of her birth. How did you manage to get that, by the way? You didn't ask her outright, did you?"

"No, you asked me not to, so I resorted to devious means. You know, Rob," she added wryly, "I'm getting all too good at that sort of thing! I think I must have a naturally criminal mind."

"Most women have," Dr. Rob told her matter-of-factly. "They're convinced that the means are justified by the end—if it benefits someone near and dear to them."

And to whom did that refer? Miss Alice wondered. To Rosamund or to himself? She had no intention of asking.

"Well, be that as it may, I needed to make an application for a new passport and I took care to fill in the form in front of Rosamund. I made some stupid remark about my age—that when one gets to a certain age one ought to be excused from revealing it and that I did my best to forget my birthdays now. Then I said something about that not being the case where she was concerned and wondered if her birthday was sufficiently near at hand for us to have a party. And she told me when it was. July the twenty-third, as I told you."

"There was no hesitation in telling you?" Dr. Rob asked quickly.

"None whatever. But later on, after I'd rung you up to give you the date, she told me something that I found very interesting. She's never had a passport, Rob. Never been out of the country, in fact."

"In other words, has had no need to produce her birth certificate on that account," Dr. Rob said reflectively.

"Or, I think, on any other," Miss Alice suggested. "You see, I've watched carefully and I'm quite sure that the name Dexter means nothing personal to her as, surely, it would do if she knew that it and not Hastings is her true name."

"Yes, seems sound reasoning," Dr. Rob agreed. "Which suggests that Ruth has taken care she doesn't see her birth certificate because she was registered as Rosamund Dexter—"

"And *is* your daughter."

"It's a bit more evidence to support its probability," Dr. Rob said judicially. "But still not proof. And that I feel I must have before I claim Rosamund!" He beat his hand emphatically on the wooden arm of his deck chair.

"Just what have you done so far?" Miss Alice asked.

"Made a thorough nuisance of myself at Somerset House," Dr. Rob told her grimly. "I've had them search every district near to the address where Celia died, with no result at all. Which makes it clear that Rosamund was born outside that area. But where, where? Think what it means in London alone. It's like hunting for a needle in a haystack!"

Miss Alice was silent. Personally she had come to the conclusion that Rob might be mistaken in deciding not to take Rosamund into his confidence, but the decision was for him to make, not her.

"It's terribly discouraging," she said at length.

"It is, indeed," Dr. Rob agreed grimly. "So discouraging that I decided to make a more definite approach."

"You mean—tell Rosamund?"

"No, not that. Tackle Ruth herself."

"Oh, Rob!" It was impossible for Miss Alice to hide her dismay.

"Not wise, you think? Perhaps not, but in the circumstances, inevitable. In fact, I felt that so very strongly that I went to see her yesterday."

"And—?" eagerly.

"I might have saved myself the trouble. I was told that Ruth has had a nervous breakdown, is in a nursing home and is allowed no visitors."

Miss Alice looked at him sharply.

"It might be true, you know. She must be a very busy woman and not as young as she was. Besides, to a woman of her type, Rosamund's defiance must have come as a very real shock. All the same," she added shrewdly, "you don't believe it, do you?"

Dr. Rob shrugged his shoulders.

"It may as you say, be true. But on the other hand, she must be perfectly well aware that she has put up the one type of obstacle between us which I can't possibly override. It wouldn't be ethical."

"But that means you think she knows that you and Rosamund—No, that's impossible, Rob! How can she possibly connect you with Rosamund's disappearance?"

"I don't say that she can. But I do say that since she has never let me know of Rosamund's existence, she must always have been afraid that we might meet by accident—as, indeed, we have. So now, isn't it at least possible that she's wondering if that has happened and decided to manoeuvre herself into a position where I can't get at her to ask awkward questions?"

She didn't answer and after a moment he went on:

"I know what you're thinking, Alice. That even if she didn't really connect Rosamund's disappearance with me, she certainly will do so now! She'll feel that it's surely too great a coincidence that I turned up demanding to see her at this particular time. I'm afraid that's true." He stirred restlessly in his chair. "Yet is it such a very big risk? No one but my secretary knows where I am when I come down here and she also knows that the job wouldn't last five minutes if she gave me away! Still, just to make sure, after this weekend, I'm not coming down here for a bit. Indeed, I shan't be able to. I've had an invitation to lecture in America and frankly, I can't refuse it. It's not only that it's an honour, but I'd give offence to some very good friends."

"How long will you be away?" Miss Alice asked, her heart sinking uncontrollably. She had a conviction that the next few weeks were going to prove very important in the lives of the man beside her and the girl who had come so suddenly and unexpectedly into their lives.

"I'll be back in three weeks," Dr. Rob told her, and

frowned. "It means, of course, that I won't be able to make any more enquiries—but apart from that, will it really make much difference in the long run—that is, if you are staying on down here and will let her stay with you?"

"Yes, to both questions," Miss Alice said slowly. "But you must remember, Rob, that whatever Rosamund may choose to do, I've no authority over her at all."

He looked at her sharply.

"You've got something particular in mind, haven't you?" he asked.

"Yes, I have, Miss Alice said unwillingly. "Though I don't like telling tales out of school. It's simply that she and John Lindsay—" she indicated the *Seven Stars* with a jerk of her head—"have got very friendly this last week."

"No more than that?"

"At this stage, no, I don't think so." Miss Alice chose her words with considerable care. "But there's something about Rosamund—a sparkle a—a sort of inner light which might mean she's falling in love with him. It's difficult to explain just what I mean, but you must judge for yourself. They went into Bath together, but they'll be back for tea."

"H'm!" Dr. Rob's frown was almost a scowl. "What's your opinion of the young man, Alice?"

"I like him," she said unhesitatingly. "I think he's got a temper and is capable of being very moody—in fact, I know he is. On the other hand, he strikes me as being both clean and honest. But really I don't know a great deal about him. In fact, Rob, he's as reticent about his past as Rosamund is about hers!"

"Is he, indeed!" Dr. Rob exclaimed grimly, and then laughed. "You know, Alice," he said wryly, "Rosamund being reticent about her past simply seems to be natural and reasonable in the circumstances. But where this young man's concerned, I'm inclined to jump to the conclusion that he's got something shady to hide. In fact, with very little encouragement, I could play the heavy father to perfection! Perhaps it's just as well that I'm going away for a time. I might be tempted to interfere and precipitate something that otherwise might never happen. All the same—" his voice grew very tender—"keep an eye on my girl for me, Alice!"

"I'll do that," she promised gruffly, near to tears.

The warm summer days flitted past, one much like the other and, to Rosamund, all quite perfect. Every night, before sleep engulfed her, she would live over again the day that had just passed. The pearly morning when, disturbed by the clamouring bird song, she had gone out on deck to breathe the chilly, sweet-scented air. The simple, everyday tasks that she performed so effortlessly because she was so preoccupied thinking of the exquisite magic that had come into her life. And that, of course, meant that she was thinking of John. She knew now beyond all doubt that she loved him, and she was daring to hope that he was beginning to love her.

He sought her company, talked much more freely about his book with frequent references to the part she had played in finding the solution to his earlier problems. All that would have been wonderful by itself, but there was much more to it than that. The little silences that fell between them had a significance at once sweet and disturbing. The way he looked at her when he didn't think she was noticing and the way in which his hand so often touched hers. Surely all that added up to one thing—he loved her even if, as yet, he didn't realise it. But soon he would, and in the meantime she was content to wait in her world of dreams and hopes.

Only one thing troubled her. Sooner or later she would have to tell him more about herself—in fact, in view of his obvious interest in her, it surprised her that he had not already begun to ask questions, and oddly enough it didn't occur to her, as it had done to Miss Alice, that John himself was extremely reticent about *his* past.

Her concern was not whether John would be able to understand her genuine desire to get away from the hot-house existence of the past. It was the sort of life which, she was quite sure, would be repugnant to anyone of John's simple tastes. None the less, the fact remained that she had been used to luxurious surroundings such as, she knew, he couldn't offer her. He had been quite frank about that.

"I'm living on the small income I get from money which my mother left me," he had explained. "I plan to make out on that until—*if*—I sell my book."

"You will," Rosamund told him with serene conviction.

He gave her an enquiring look.

"What makes you say that so positively?"

"It's rather difficult to explain," she confessed. "But I think you—tell me, John, sometimes when you read through what you've written, do you just *know* it's good—and you can hardly believe that you've written it?"

"Yes! Even to the point of hardly being able to remember that I did write it! The old subconscious, I suppose. But how did you know?"

"It shows in your face—a sort of satisfied but awestruck look. I'm explaining very badly," she apologised, seeing how startled he looked.

"No, you're not, my dear! You're making me understand just how well *you* understand. It's as if you've read my thoughts! Tell me more about myself."

"Certainly not!" she refused mischievously. "You might get too vain—"

The colour surged up into her cheeks as she realised what John would read into that, and panic-stricken, she turned and fled. John didn't follow her, but as she reached the sanctuary of the *Pride of London* she couldn't resist the temptation to look back. John was standing just where she had left him. He was smiling and as she watched, he lifted his hand and blew her a kiss. For a moment Rosamund hesitated. Then she made a similar gesture and spent the rest of the day in such a bemused frame of mind that Miss Alice gave up any attempt at conversation. She understood what that head-in-the-clouds state meant. Rosamund *was* in love with John.

Miss Alice sighed. Perhaps it would be all right. Very often the two people most intimately concerned were the best judges of that despite the doubts of older folk. None the less, her promise to Dr. Rob to look after Rosamund for him was, if not a burden certainly a very real anxiety.

During the next week, Miss Alice had to go to London to see a prospective client. She was considerably put out about it.

"Wasting this lovely weather going to town," she grumbled. "It will be hot and smelly and extremely tiring."

59

"Do you *have* to go?" Rosamund asked sympathetically.

"I'm afraid so. You see, the lady in question is regarded as a great beauty, but that isn't enough, you know, to guarantee that there is anything I can really paint! Oh, one can make a charming map of perfect features, of course, but that's not the same as painting a portrait that *lives*. So I owe it to her and to myself to make sure that I can get something out of her. If I don't feel I can, thank goodness I've got to the stage where I can afford to turn work down if I think it's necessary. And since I've already got grave doubts in this case, I've no choice but to find out, face to face."

"She won't like it if you do refuse," Rosamund commented. "I mean, people who are very, very beautiful so often do expect to have their own way, don't they?"

"They do," Miss Alice agreed drily, not very much surprised at Rosamund's appreciation of such a situation. She could well imagine that the child had come across many such women in her aunt's salon! "Now, I expect to be home in the late afternoon—I certainly intend to get away as early as I can. Are you sure you'll be all right? John won't be here either for part of the day, you know, so you'll be all alone."

"Of course I'll be all right," Rosamund assured her confidently. "And John won't be away so very long—only an hour or so, he thinks. He's going into Bath to get his signature witnessed on some papers, that's all."

She didn't sound in the least curious as to what the papers were, Miss Alice noticed. Of course, they might simply be that John had told her already, but somehow Miss Alice didn't think so. It was, she thought, far more likely that it simply didn't occur to Rosamund to question anything John did or said. Which was natural enough when one was in love, but whether it was wise or not was another question.

As soon as both Miss Alice and John had left, Rosamund became very busy. She had made up her mind that this was an ideal opportunity for doing various jobs without making a nuisance of herself. Neither Miss Alice nor John seemed to think it necessary to do more in the way of cleaning than to flick round with a duster and mop the bits of floor that showed. Rosamund had different ideas.

She worked quickly because she knew that John would be back just as soon as possible and her plans took in the cleaning of the *Seven Stars* as well as of the *Pride of London*. She did John's boat first because she wanted to make sure that she had finished before he got back. That way, although he was sure to tell her that she shouldn't have done it, it would be too late to argue!

However, he still hadn't arrived by the time she had finished, so she returned to the *Pride of London* and set to work, though without the same enthusiasm. It was an extremely hot day, the sun, by now, was high in the sky and there wasn't a breath of wind. Rosamund decided that she had taken on rather too much and catching sight of herself in a mirror, saw that unless she wanted John to see her looking an absolute sketch, she'd have to leave the rest for another day. There were smears of dirt on her face, her hair, damp with the heat, was sticking to her head in streaky strands and how she wanted a bath, or at least a shower!

But she had only got as far as putting away her cleaning materials when she heard footsteps outside on the deck.

"Is that you, John?" she called out, wishing devoutly that she'd stopped work a quarter of an hour earlier. "I won't be long—I'm just tidying up—"

But John didn't answer, though he must have heard her, and after a moment or two, convinced that something must be wrong, she went out to investigate.

And there was, indeed, something very wrong. For it wasn't John. It was her aunt, Ruth Hastings, who stood within a few feet of her.

CHAPTER FOUR

WHITE-FACED, Rosamund stared incredulously at her aunt.

"How did you—how did you—?" she stammered.

"Find out where you were?" Ruth smiled derisively. "Oh, that was quite simple!"

That wasn't true, but she was convinced that the more she could impress upon Rosamund that she had not only been stupid to run away but also far from clever in covering her tracks, the easier it would be to regain her hold over the girl. But she had no intention of telling Rosamund just how she came to be here. That would mean telling her something which she sincerely hoped Rosamund hadn't already found out.

It had not needed Dr. Rob's attempt to see her to suggest to Ruth that he might be involved in Rosamund's disappearance, for it never occurred to her that she would take the risk of leaving the security she had always known if she hadn't some definite haven available.

But if, by chance, Rosamund had met her father, and as Ruth had always feared, he had appreciated the significance of her striking likeness to his dead wife, then there was the answer! And the most likely one.

But it hadn't been quite as straightforward as that. Ruth felt it was reasonable to assume that if Rosamund had gone to her father, then she would no longer be in London. Much as she detested Dr. Rob, she didn't underrate his brain. He'd be quick to realise that she wouldn't let Rosamund go without a struggle and so he would bundle the hysterical little fool out of the way to some place or other where she couldn't be easily found.

But that might be anywhere! It would be like looking for a needle in a bundle of hay! Or would it? Ruth had always been on the alert at any chance mention of Dr. Rob's name. Now she recalled a conversation between two of her clients which she had overheard. It was to the effect that he had some retreat out of London to which he went as often as possible at weekends. Just where it was was apparently a jealously guarded secret for which the two women had a simple, and to them, an obvious solution.

"A woman," they agreed with meaningful nods of their heads. "Someone he can't acknowledge publicly—"

Ruth didn't care what the reason was for the secretiveness. All she cared about was *where*? She acted promptly. Apparently Dr. Rob rarely had a professional appointment after lunch on Friday. She would have him watched and followed.

And she was lucky. The weekend when Miss Alice had

summoned Dr. Rob was the first occasion on which her watchdog was on duty. His report gave Ruth all the information she needed for it even included an unmistakable description of Rosamund.

That she had had to delay her visit until now had been annoying but unavoidable. Her doctor had insisted that the cause of the periodic bouts of pain she was experiencing must be investigated at once. Annoyed, as only a person who has never known bad health can be in such circumstances, Ruth had agreed to go into a nursing home. The verdict—she had insisted on being told the absolute truth—was unequivocal. The condition of her heart was such that, at the best, she could not expect to live much more than a year—and then only if she lived a quieter, less demanding life. But she had little use for life on those terms and she ignored the warning.

"Easy?" Rosamund repeated, and shook her head emphatically. "No, it couldn't have been. I didn't tell anyone where I was coming. I didn't even know myself until—" she stopped short, deciding that the less she told her aunt the better. "So how *did* you find me?"

"Does that really matter?" Ruth asked with a shrug.

Ruth would have given a lot to know how that unfinished sentence was to have finished, but she had no intention of asking. Even in these few minutes she had discovered that there was a radical change in Rosamund. She had been startled, but she hadn't been scared by Ruth's unexpected appearance. That was clear from the mulish obstinacy of her expression and the defensive way in which she stood blocking the doorway.

Ruth sank down in one of the deck chairs. She was tired and that wretched pain was beginning to make itself felt, but not for anything in the world would she have confessed to either. One didn't dominate people by parading one's own frailties.

"What matters," she went on dogmatically, "is that I *am* here and that you are coming back to London with me!"

"No," Rosamund contradicted quietly but very firmly.

Ruth regarded her thoughtfully. She sounded completely sure of herself. There must be someone backing her in her rebellion. An idea occurred to her.

"This man, John," she said curiously. "Are you living with him?"

The bright, angry colour flamed to Rosamund's face, but she knew that she must not lose her temper. That would only give Aunt Ruth the advantage.

"No," she denied briefly.

Ruth believed her. Rosamund, she knew, was not naturally a liar. Besides, she had complete faith in her own ability to detect a lie.

"No? Then who are you staying with?"

"With an artist—a lady—" Once again Rosamund left her sentence unfinished and shook her head. "No, Aunt Ruth, I'm not going to tell you anything else. What I do is my own affair, and though I'm sorry if it annoys you, I've got to make you understand that it's not your concern at all. Please do accept that—and the fact that in no circumstances will I ever come back to work for you or live with you! That's finished completely."

Almost Ruth gave up. Despite Rosamund's almost uncanny resemblance to her mother, there was something of her father in her, too. His obstinacy, his inability to see anything except from his own point of view—

Her father! Had Rosamund and Dr. Rob discovered one another? Surely, if they had, Rosamund would have been told the whole story and would have used it to justify herself. But she hadn't and Ruth was puzzled. Rob simply couldn't have missed the likeness.

And, of course, he hadn't, but he wanted to make quite sure of his facts before he claimed his daughter. That was why he had tried to see her—and how lucky she had been that his visit had coincided with her stay in the nursing home!

But in that case one had to accept it that Rosamund coming to this out-of-the-way spot where she was bound to meet her father was sheer coincidence, and that Ruth found disconcerting. It was as if a stronger force than herself was playing a part! She discarded the idea impatiently.

"Now, don't waste any more time," she ordered imperiously. "Get your things together—"

"No!" Rosamund squared her shoulders and met her aunt's eyes squarely. "You've got to understand, Aunt

Ruth, that I'm not coming either now or at any other time!"

Suddenly the pain took command and it was all that Ruth could do to keep from crying out. Strangely, it didn't occur to her that if she had, if Rosamund knew, she would almost certainly have given in out of sheer pity. But at least it could be said for Ruth that she was as hard to herself as she was to anyone over whom she had authority. For a moment or two her hands gripped the arms of the chair until her knuckles were white. Then, as the pain receded a little, she spoke in almost her usual manner.

"You must be crazy!" she announced with conviction. "With me you've got prospects that most girls would give their eyes to have! I—I won't be able to keep on indefinitely, and then you will take over the Salon."

"But I don't want to, Aunt Ruth," Rosamund insisted earnestly. "I know it means a great deal to you, but it doesn't to me."

"But why not, Rosamund?" For the first time there was something like a plea in Ruth's voice.

Rosamund hesitated and then shook her head. She knew only too well why she had to make this stand and she had tried more than once to explain to her aunt, though always without success. That, she felt, might be because, however strongly one may feel, it is never easy to tell someone that they themselves are to blame for your actions. Now she must tell the brutal truth or, once again, fail to be convincing.

"Go on," Ruth said ironically. "Don't trouble to spare my feelings!"

"I don't find—" Rosamund began, and started again. "To me, it isn't a satisfying job. It's all so artifical and—and shallow. And so are so many of our—of your clients."

"They pay well," Ruth commented laconically.

"I think that's just it," Rosamund said eagerly. "They've got lots of money and they think that's everything. Oh, I know what you're going to say—" as Ruth's lips parted. "That there are very few things that money can't buy. But I think the things it can't buy are the most important ones."

"Such as?"

"Love, loyalty, common honesty," Rosamund explained diffidently, well aware that she was making no impression whatever. "Aunt Ruth, you *do* know what I mean! You know as well as I do how vain and silly so many of the women who come to the Salon are! And I'm so tired of having to flatter and fawn on people like that as if they were something special and wonderful! It's—it's degrading!"

"What a shocking little prig you are, Rosamund!" Ruth exclaimed irritably. "Let me tell you, my dear, if it wasn't for these women whom you despise so, you would have had to go without a lot of the things you've taken for granted all these years!"

"I know," Rosamund admitted distastefully.

Ruth's eyes narrowed. This was going to be more difficult than she had expected. But not impossible, of course.

"And that is all?" she asked indifferently.

"No," Rosamund said slowly. "There are other reasons. One is that I want to be myself. I can't go on making the Salon my whole life. I want to be free at least sometimes to have interests of my own." She paused. "That's one thing. The other—"

"Yes?" Ruth encouraged drily.

"The other is—"

"Well?" impatiently.

"Oh, Aunt Ruth, you must surely know!" Rosamund protested. "The Salon is such an unhappy place! Behind the scenes, I mean. Everybody grumbles and quarrels and gets upset—don't you realise that I've been spending half my time to help people and smooth things over! And I can't stand any more of it! I simply can't!"

Ruth didn't reply. She knew just how much truth there was in what Rosamund said, and though even to herself she wouldn't admit that her own aggressive, domineering manner was at the bottom of the troubles, she did acknowledge that Rosamund had got a knack of soothing frayed nerves and keeping the peace. That, in fact, was one of her biggest reasons for determining to take Rosamund back with her.

"So you see, Aunt Ruth, I *can't* come back with you,"

Rosamund went on, her face tense at the mere thought of doing such a thing. "I truly think I should be ill if I did! And now—if you'd like it, I'll get you a cup of tea, and then you must go, please."

Ruth stood up.

"Tea!" she almost spat the word at Rosamund. "Do you think I'll accept even a cup of tea at your hands after this? I've more pride than that! No, if that's how you feel, you're no use to me! With all these high-falutin' notions of yours you'd be more trouble than you'd be worth! I've no wish to have my clients upset by your offensiveness, and that's what would happen, sooner or later. So just consider this—if you don't promise to behave and come with me now, you don't come at all! I've finished with you! Is that clear?"

"Quite clear," Rosamund said steadily, thankful that at last her aunt understood that she must accept the situation.

But Ruth hadn't finished yet. Deliberately she looked Rosamund over from head to foot; a look that took in tousled hair and smudged face, bare suntanned legs and work-stained hands. A look that made Rosamund feel as if something in her had withered and left her defenceless.

"You arrant little fool!" Ruth said, the very softness of her voice making it all the more venomous. "I can almost find it in my heart to be sorry for you—but not quite! Your hypocrisy revolts me too much for that!"

"I'm not a hypocrite," Rosamund was stung into protesting.

"No? Then how would you describe someone who doesn't practise what they preach?" Ruth said contemptuously. "All this talk of yours about loyalty and honesty—it means absolutely nothing! It's no more than an excuse for your selfishness—"

Rosamund's heart sank. She had been too quick to imagine that she'd won the battle. She should have known that Aunt Ruth didn't give up so easily! What was more, what was coming now was going to be more difficult to combat than anything that had gone before. Instinctively Rosamund braced herself and deliberately took the war into the enemy's country.

"As your employee I've always been completely loyal to your interests, Aunt Ruth," she said steadily. "Though, as you know quite well, I've wanted to stop working for you for some time. Even so, perhaps I should have given you formal notice that I was leaving—or else have forfeited a month's salary. But as you haven't paid me yet for the last two months, I don't really think you have much cause for complaint on that score!"

Inwardly Ruth raged at being put in the wrong in this way and knowing that there was little if anything that she could say in her own defence, promptly changed her tactics.

"I consider that a very debatable statement," she declared with a dismissive gesture of her hand. "What I was thinking of is our personal relationship. I wonder—" she paused and seemed to consider what she was about to say very carefully. Then, with added emphasis, she went on : "Yes, I do indeed wonder, Rosamund, if you realise just how much you have cost me in happiness as well as in money!"

Rosamund, out of her depth, stared at her aunt dumbly. She had never known just how it had come about that Aunt Ruth was her guardian, for the few questions she had found the courage to ask were invariably ignored. Now, it appeared, she was going to be told—

"Your mother died when you were only a few months old," went on the cold, relentless voice. "She died completely penniless. I had the choice of putting you into a Home or looking after you myself. Like a fool, that was what I did. It wasn't easy. At that time I was earning only a small salary. I'd never been able to afford more than just about the bare necessities of life. Now I had to provide for you as well. Not just ordinary expenses, I mean. I had to pay someone to look after you so that I could work. I soon found that I couldn't make ends meet. So I worked harder. I took on an evening job as well as my day's work—"

The short, staccato sentences beat like hail on Rosamund's brain and by their very brevity, brought conviction. She swallowed convulsively, unable to speak, waiting for what was still to come. And Ruth, quick to see that she was making an impression, invented a story on the spur of the moment which, she was sure, would tip the scales in her favour.

"Then I met a man who wanted me to marry him. But, as his wife, I'd have to travel all over the world with him, never staying more than a few months in any one place. So I refused him. Not on my own account. I'd have enjoyed that sort of life. But for *your* sake, Rosamund. You needed a settled home and I decided that it was my duty—" Momentarily her face was convulsed with an expression which was an extraordinary mixture of bitterness and triumph. "So I gave up my chance of happiness."

"I—I'm very sorry, Aunt Ruth," Rosamund whispered. "I had no idea—"

"I didn't want you to have," Ruth told her bleakly. "I made the decision, not you. But I had thought that the natural affection you would surely have for me would make a sufficiently strong bond between us to repay me for what I had sacrificed. However—" she shrugged her shoulders in a fatalistic gesture— "it seems that I was wrong!"

Rosamund felt as if actual prison bars were closing round her. Her hands came up in an instinctively defensive movement as if to hold them off. Then she asked the question which she had never before found the courage to ask.

"My—my father?" she spoke the unfamiliar word with difficulty. "Am I—am I illegitimate?"

For the briefest moment Ruth hesitated. Then she shook her head.

"No. Your parents were married. But that made no difference. Your father deserted your mother less than a year after they were married. I believe he went abroad—certainly she never heard from him again."

"But he knew about me coming?" Rosamund whispered.

"To my certain knowledge, your mother wrote several times to tell him of your birth. I know that because I posted the letters myself."

"I—see." Rosamund's hands dropped limply to her sides. "Is—is he still alive?"

So Rob hadn't told her that he was her father!

"So far as I know he is," she shrugged indifferently. "But I haven't set eyes on him since he left your mother."

She held her breath. Had she worn Rosamund's resistance down to breaking point or were there to be any more awkward questions?

Apparently not. Rosamund's whole body seemed to sag and her wide eyes held the haunted look of a bird mesmerised by a snake.

"Well?" Ruth asked. "Now that you know the truth, are you going to repay the debt you owe me or do you prefer to admit that you *are* a wretched little hypocrite? It's up to you!"

"I—I—" Rosamund moistened her dry lips with the tip of her tongue.

"Rosamund! Hi, Rosamund, where are you?"

At the sound of John's voice hailing her blithely from the towpath, Rosamund came to life. She darted across the little deck and the narrow gangplank, straight into John's arms, and as they closed protectingly round her, she clung to him, sobbing like a frightened child.

"Darling, darling, what is it?" he asked urgently, and then, realising that she was beyond speech, his arms tightened. "Listen, Rosamund, listen! Whatever is wrong, you're safe now! I'll see to that! But try to tell me—"

Rosamund was still shaking violently, but she made a valiant attempt to control herself.

"My—my aunt," she whispered. "She—she's been trying to make me go back to London with her—and I can't, John, I can't!"

"Then you shan't, sweetheart," John told her matter-of-factly. "Come along and we'll tell her so!"

But Ruth had followed Rosamund and now, from the slight advantage of the gangplank, she looked down at them, her calm apparently unruffled.

"For your own sake, young man, I really do advise you not to interfere," she said coolly. "Rosamund is a very naughty girl, you know!"

Rosamund felt John stiffen.

"No, madam, I know nothing of the sort," he retorted coldly. "And please don't trouble further to convince me that you're right. It won't get you anywhere."

Ruth sighed and shook her head.

70

"How persuasive a pretty face can be!" she mocked. "Even when it could do with a good wash! Now, do be sensible! I know my niece better—" and bit her lip as she saw John's face harden. Stupid of her to make the mistake of trying to ridicule him in his own eyes! Clearly he had far too good an opinion of himself for that to produce results. "I don't think you understand the situation, Mr.—?"

"John Lindsay," John supplied automatically.

Ruth bent her head graciously.

"Mr. Lindsay. Thank you. As I was saying, I don't think you understand the situation. Rosamund has behaved very foolishly and inconsiderately. Indeed, most people would say that I'm being extremely silly in giving her another chance. However, that's just what I am doing! I'm willing to overlook—"

"No!" Rosamund said breathlessly. "No, *no*!"

Ruth felt a sudden stab of pain. Her air of patience, so deliberately assumed, snapped abruptly.

"Oh, for heaven's sake, Rosamund, stop this nonsense! Of course you're coming back with me—*now*!"

"No," John told her very quietly. "She's doing nothing of the sort. Rosamund is of age. Consequently she has the right to make her own decisions. That is definite and final!"

Ruth glared at him.

"If you don't stop interfering—" she threatened.

"But I have every right to interfere," John assured her a convincingly vibrant note in his voice. "Rosamund and I are engaged. Now do you understand? We're going to be married!"

Ruth had gone, but not before she had fired a parting shot. To Rosamund she enlarged on her earlier threat.

"From now on, no matter what sort of trouble you get yourself into, don't expect that I'm going to help you out! Do you understand? I've finished with you!"

To John she spoke with pitying contempt.

"You don't, of course, know what you're taking on, Mr. Lindsay. Well, you'll find out! Because Rosamund won't remain satisfied with love in a cottage—or on a barge—for very long. She'll soon be whining for the comfort and luxury she's always been used to when the initial glamour wears off, as it always does. A pity you're not a rich man, you know. If you were, your marriage could well be a success. As it is—" she shook her head. "Not a chance! Not, of course, that in your present besotted state you believe that. But remember, you have been warned!"

Over Rosamund's bent head John watched Ruth walk slowly along the towpath to vanish through the gate in the hedge. There was a peculiar expression in his eyes, part apprehension, but to a far greater degree of determination. But when Rosamund lifted her head from his shoulder, she saw nothing but kindness and strength there.

Tentatively she sought to free herself and instantly John let her go.

"Well, that's that!" he announced cheerfully, and then, as Rosamund didn't reply, he went on matter-of-factly: "I suggest that we indulge ourselves in Miss Alice's inevitable panaceas for all ills—a cup of tea! After that we'll talk things over."

Suddenly tongue-tied now that she and John were alone, Rosamund nodded in silence and ran quickly up the gangplank.

"I'll just tidy up first—" she said breathlessly, and hurried to her cabin.

Quickly she washed her face and hands, combed her hair and then stood hesitating over the choice of a dress. Not that there was a very large or inspiring selection. But there was one dress, a bluish-green which she knew suited her fair colouring better than anything else she had. Usually she kept it for special occasions—well, wasn't this a *very* special occasion? Of all times, didn't she want to look her very best?

She slipped into the dress, slid her feet into more attractive sandals and then, all ready to face up to John, she suddenly lost her self-confidence.

John had told Aunt Ruth that they were going to be married, but had he really meant it? Wasn't it much more likely that he had said it on the spur of the moment because he realised that it was the one argument which would checkmate Aunt Ruth?

She drew a deep breath. She knew that she loved John, but not that he loved her, and just because he'd come to her rescue so unhesitatingly didn't mean that she had any right to keep him to his word. She'd got to make him understand that—it was only fair.

She walked through to the galley and found John already there, just about to pour boiling water into the teapot. He looked up with a grin as she came in.

"I'm quite domesticated, these days," he remarked proudly. "Pop up on to the deck and I'll bring the tray."

Rosamund understood. That light, easy manner was, she felt sure, meant to put her at her ease, but it had the reverse effect. To her it meant just one thing—that without embarrassing her by putting it into words, John was telling her that there was nothing for her to worry about—that nothing that had happened need be taken seriously.

They drank their tea in a silence which seemed to Rosamund to grow more oppressive with every passing moment, yet it was beyond her power to break it. But John, though not exactly scowling, certainly looked worried. Supposing that he had already guessed that she loved him ! She *must* take the initiative—

"Another cup?" John asked abruptly, and when she refused : "Then shall we talk things over?" he suggested.

"John—" She saw that he looked taken aback at her urgency and it needed all her courage to go on. "Before you say anything, I want to tell you that I—I think it was quite wonderful of you to come to my rescue the way you did, but of course, I quite understand—"

"Just what do you understand?" John asked grimly.

"Why, that you—you only said—what you did to stop Aunt Ruth—"

"Now, let's get this straight," John insisted. "Do you mean that you think I said that we were going to get married simply to get the better of that objectionable aunt of yours?"

"Yes," Rosamund said miserably. Then, with suddenly upflung head : "Yes, of course," she told him resolutely.

In one swift, decisive movement John stood up, scooped her from her chair and held her so close that she could feel the pounding of his heart. His lips sought and captured hers with ruthless, passionate fervour.

"You little idiot, does that suggest that I was pretending?" he demanded savagely. "Does it? Or this—?"

Again his mouth claimed hers, and stirred to the very depths of her being, Rosamund knew that her dreams had come true. John loved her! She need not be afraid to show her own love—

Time stood still for them—

"And now," John said at last in a voice shaken with feeling, "will you kindly tell me why you did your best to scare the daylights out of me? Do you know you almost convinced me that—you didn't care?"

"Did I?" Looking up into his adoring eyes, her own glinted with mischief. "Well, it didn't seem to—to—"

"To cramp my style?" John suggested wryly. "Don't you understand, Rosamund, I was desperate! You seemed to be slipped away from me and I—" he left the sentence unfinished, but his lips sought hers again, not in passion now but as if he was seeking reassurance and comfort.

And in that brief moment of time it seemed to Rosamund that she was given a complete and awe-inspiring understanding of what love between a man and a woman can and should be. It was not simply a matter of romance, wonderful though that was. It was something much deeper and more enduring than that. It was the sharing of life in every respect, the desire to stand between the loved one and pain or danger. It was the knowledge that two imperfect human beings can make mistakes and yet forgive and start afresh. And perhaps, most important of all, it meant that there are times when even the strongest natures are vulnerable and need to know that they do not stand alone.

With utter conviction that this was one of those times, she put a hand on either side of John's face.

"John, my own dear, I love you so much," she said with passionate tenderness. "Now—and always. Believe that, for it's the truth."

And gently she laid her soft lips against his.

When Miss Alice returned she was, as she had anticipated, hot, tired and frankly, in none too good a temper. None

74

the less, absorbed though she was in her own discomforts, she was quick to guess what had happened. True, John and Rosamund were simply sitting side by side on the deck, but before they had noticed her, she had realised how deeply absorbed they were in their conversation and as she got nearer and they jumped to their feet to greet her, she saw the unmistakable, glowing happiness in their faces.

"It's happened," she told herself helplessly. "They've told one another—this really is the last straw! What on earth do I do now? Oh, Rob, how I wish you were here!"

"Dear Miss Alice, you do look tired," Rosamund said sympathetically. "Do sit down while I get you some tea. Everything's ready so it won't take a minute!"

"Thank you, I'll get it for myself," Miss Alice said gruffly, and turned her back on them, ashamed at her apparent ungraciousness, but feeling that she must have a few minutes to herself to think over this new situation.

When she had gone, John and Rosamund looked at one another in consternation.

"I've never seen her like this before," Rosamund whispered, anxious not to be overheard. "What can be the matter?"

"She's pretty shrewd. I imagine she guessed about us," John frowned as he spoke.

"But how can she have done?" Rosamund protested. "I mean, we were only talking—"

John's expression softened as he put a finger under her chin and tipped her face up.

"Yes, my love, just talking. But possibly you don't realise that your eyes are like stars, and there's a sort of radiance—"

For a moment they forgot Miss Alice and then John said uneasily:

"All the same, supposing she did guess, why should it have upset her, as it evidently did? I mean, why should she object? And in any case, what business is it of hers?"

"None, really," Rosamund admitted. "Only she's been very good to me and I think she's really fond of me as I am of her. I think, perhaps, she feels sort of responsible for me—"

"Well, if she does, while I'm sure she'd be much more pleasant about it than your aunt was, she still mustn't be allowed to interfere," John started forcefully. "Rosamund, you won't let her, will you?"

"No, John," she promised gravely. "Neither Miss Alice nor anyone else."

"Good!" He spoke emphatically, yet his expression was one of preoccupation. "You know, Rosamund, I think it might be a good idea if we—"

At that moment Miss Alice returned and it was clear that she had regained her usual poise.

"Sorry I was so shrewish," she said cheerfully. "But I really was feeling at the end of my tether."

"Yes, of course," Rosamund began, and then, as John took her hand in his, she looked at him enquiringly.

"I think we'd both like Miss Alice to be the first to hear our news, wouldn't we, Rosamund?" And when Rosamund nodded, he turned smilingly to Miss Alice. "Rosamund has promised to marry me, Miss Alice! Will you give us your good wishes?"

Miss Alice looked from one face to the other. How happy they looked and how confident! Well, that was only right, of course. To start their life together full of doubts and fears would be both unnatural and disastrous. Yet she herself could not feel entirely at ease. Had they really had time to know each other? And wasn't that important, too?

Besides there was very definitely a protectiveness in John's manner towards Rosamund which made her feel instinctively that something had happened during her absence—something unexpected and possibly alarming— which might have precipitated matters. Or was she imagining things? Wasn't it only natural for a young man who was deeply in love to want to cherish the girl who had promised to entrust her life to him?

"I do, indeed, wish you both every happiness!" she said with a sincerity all the more genuine because of her unexpressed doubts. "Now, and for the rest of your lives!"

She kissed Rosamund affectionately, patted John's shoulder in a friendly way and then remarked that if they didn't mind, she'd like to have a little rest before it was time to think about the evening meal.

A little smile played round Rosamund's lips as she watched her go.

"What a pet she is!" she murmured softly.

"What?" John asked in a preoccupied way.

"Well, perhaps she does want a rest, but I think she was being tactful because she must know that we'd rather be alone!"

"Yes, I suppose so," John agreed, but something in the way he said it made Rosamund look at him quickly.

"What is it, John?" she asked anxiously.

He hesitated for a moment. Then he laid a hand on either of her shoulders.

"Rosamund!" He spoke tensely, imperatively. "You do trust me, don't you?"

"Yes, John," Rosamund said unhesitatingly.

"Then—" his grasp of her shoulders increased to almost painful intensity— "will you marry me at once—without telling anyone, even Miss Alice?"

CHAPTER FIVE

"BUT can we do that?" Rosamund asked. "I thought one had to wait quite a long time—weeks—before it was possible to get married."

"So it is, if it's a matter of having banns read," John explained. "But it's also possible to be married by licence and then there's only a very short delay—a matter of a few days, I think. But I'll have to go to London to find out the exact details. But if it is possible—will you, Rosamund?"

"Of course!" she said unhesitatingly.

John took her arm in his arms and as he looked down into her candid trusting eyes, a little muscle flickered at the corner of his mouth.

"Bless you, darling," he whispered fervently. "I swear you shan't regret it!"

"Of course I shan't," Rosamund said confidently.

"And—and I'm so glad you've suggested it, John. I shall feel so much safer, married to you!"

"Yes, that's just it," John agreed. "Once we're married, nobody and nothing can ever come between us!"

"That's how I want it to be," Rosamund sighed contentedly. "Actually, I think Aunt Ruth must realise by now that there's nothing she can do, but once we're married I shan't even have to worry that she might still try. I shall just hide behind you, John, and feel perfectly safe."

"I hope you'll always be able to say that!"

Rosamund's happiness was suddenly dimmed. There had been something disturbingly sombre about the way in which John had said that. It was as if, despite his determination, he wasn't entirely confident.

"John, it's not only because of Aunt Ruth that you're worried, is it?" she asked gently. "Because you don't have to be, you know. I mean, I think Miss Alice might try to persuade us to wait because she feels we haven't known each other long enough—"

"Has she said so?" John asked sharply.

"No, she hasn't," Rosamund admitted. "But all the same, I do think she feels like that—"

"You're quite sure you're not just assuming that because really you yourself feel it's true?" John asked searchingly.

Unconsciously Rosamund squared her shoulders as if to resist a threat she could sense but not understand.

"I'm quite sure, John," she said simply. "To me, all that matters is that we know we love one another. We'll have the whole of our lives to discover the rest, and I'm not frightened of the prospect. It sounds like—like heaven!"

With a queer, strangled exclamation, John caught her to him.

"You wonderful girl!" he said fervently, and then, as she smiled tremulously up at him: "That's why I've got the jitters! I can't believe my luck! You're so wonderful that the mere thought of ever losing you—"

She felt his body shudder against hers and knew that his fear went even deeper than she had at first thought. There *was* something—but it was for John to tell her if he wanted to. If not, then she would just keep on loving and trusting him until his fear left him—

"You're not going to lose me, John, I promise," she vowed.

To her relief, the black mood seemed to fall from John like a discarded cloak. His thoughts turned to the practical aspects of the situation.

"Tomorrow—" he began, and stopped short, looking over his shoulder at the door through which Miss Alice had gone. "Rosamund, walk with me up to the *Seven Stars*. I'd rather not risk any chances of being overheard—"

"That's better," he said a few minutes later when they reached his boat. "Now then, tomorrow I'll go up to town and make enquiries about the licence. I think there may be some residential qualifications required about at least one of us, but in all probability I can comply with them. Then I'll phone you—oh, damn it, I can't, of course. Well, in that case, I'll give you a number and you can phone me there at some definite time. All right?"

"Yes, I'll go into Bath to do some shopping," Rosamund planned. "And it will sound convincing because it's true."

"Convincing?" he repeated sharply. "To whom? Miss Alice again? But, darling, we've decided, haven't we, that it isn't really her business."

"I know, John," Rosamund agreed quickly. "But don't you see, whether it is or not, there's far less chance of her asking awkward questions if I volunteer a reason before she has time to ask them?"

"Something in that," John admitted. "On the same principle, I'd better give a reason for going to Town. And as it happens, it will also be a perfectly true one. Rosamund, I've had what may turn out to be very good news. I didn't tell you in case nothing came of it—but I sent my first chapter to a firm of London publishers last week together with a short précis of the rest of the book. And this morning there was a letter waiting for me at the Shop from them. They want me to go and see them to discuss it—hey, steady on! You almost had me off my feet!"

For Rosamund had flung herself into his arms and was hugging him with shameless delight.

"Oh, *John*!" she was bubbling over with enthusiasm. "How wonderful! How absolutely wonderful!"

"Well, it may be," he admitted cautiously, though he returned her embrace with fervour. "But we mustn't build too much on it yet. There may be snags. All the same—" he drew a deep, satisfied breath— "what a day! To know that you're going to marry me and that there's at least a chance for the book—"

"I'm glad you put the two events in their right order," Rosamund said demurely.

John gave her a little shake.

"You vain little minx!" he said with mock severity. "All the same, I'm willing to pander to your vanity still further! I admit that in any case I would have been pleased about the book. That's no more than natural. But cross my heart, Rosamund, it's sharing the news with *you* and knowing what it may mean to us—" he finished his sentence with his lips on hers.

A little later, Rosamund decided that she must go back to the *Pride of London* to prepare the evening meal.

"Will you have it with us?" she asked as, reluctantly, John let her go.

He considered.

"No, I don't think I will, if you don't mind. Actually, I want to read through what I've already written so that it's fresh in my mind. Particularly the précis. I'm not altogether satisfied with it. There are several situations that need expanding and it might be a good idea if I were to give them a bit more thought so that I can come up with the answers to any questions that might be asked. Provided, of course, that I can concentrate to that degree!" He touched her bright hair with gentle fingers. "You're a considerable distraction, sweetheart, as well as an inspiration!"

Rosamund laughed softly.

"That sounds rather a contradictory statement! And I'm not quite sure which I prefer to be! But I do know one thing for sure—I mustn't get between you and your work because it *is* you and I don't want you to be any different. No, John darling, let me go now," as his arms reached out for her again. "I shan't be very far away, you know!"

He watched her go, and once again he was struck by the familiar elegance of her walk as he had been on the day that they met. And again he was convinced that he *had* seen her before in different circumstances somewhere, but again, for the life of him, he could not remember where.

Oh well, one of these days they must compare notes and see if it was possible that they had met.

In the meantime he really must get down to work.

Fleetingly, as he sat down at his work table, it occurred to him that neither Rosamund nor her aunt had given any hint as to what their work was. A little bit odd, perhaps—

Oh well—he dismissed it with a shrug of the shoulders—it wasn't of any importance since, for Rosamund, that was all past history. He began to re-read what he had already written and was quickly absorbed in the world of his own invention.

Miss Alice heard the news of John's summons by his possible publisher with a generous enthusiasm that made Rosamund feel rather guilty.

"You see, it isn't only that I appreciate what this could mean to your joint future, but also because it always delights me when someone with a creative gift receives the encouragement that makes all the hard slogging they've done seem so very well worth while! I know. I went through it myself. And though John's gift and mine are totally different, they have this in common—we both do creative work. Something we spin out of our entrails as a spider does its web. Do you understand what that means, Rosamund?"

"That it's part of you," Rosamund said seriously. "And so you've *got* to do it because, if you don't, it would be like making a perfectly well person being made to live the life of an invalid. You wouldn't be *whole*."

"Yes, that's just it," Miss Alice agreed, but she wondered a little. Was what Rosamund had just said the outcome of an understanding deeper than one would expect from a young girl who was outside the charmed circle to which John with his writing and she with her painting belonged? Or was it just the repetition of what

John himself had already explained? A little of both, perhaps, but at any rate, the child did understand, which augured well for their future together. She realised that Rosamund was speaking again and gave her all her attention, though the topic had now changed to a less important one.

"I'm thinking of going into Bath tomorrow," Rosamund said so casually that, again, Miss Alice wondered a little. Wasn't it just *too* casual?

"Oh yes?"

"Yes. It's an opportunity, while John's away, to do a few odd bits of shopping and I thought I might have my hair shampooed. It's getting a bit dry with all this sunshine. Of course—" Rosamund felt that she was gabbling a bit now and that it all sounded artificial, but she ploughed on—"I may not be able to find a hairdresser with any free time, but I'll just have to take a chance."

"Quite," Miss Alice said equably. "In other words, you don't really know how long you'll be."

"No, I don't," Rosamund only just suppressed a sigh of relief at the easy acceptance of her announcement. "But I'll start off as early as I can so that I'm not too late back. Is there anything you want me to get for you while I'm there?"

"I don't think so, dear. In any case, you'll have your hands full getting through everything you want to yourself, won't you?"

Rosamund looked at her quickly. It was the most natural remark in the world and yet some quality in the way in which Miss Alice had spoken suggested that she suspected there was something more to the trip than a mild shopping spree.

"Or else it's that I feel mean at deceiving her," Rosamund wondered uncomfortably. "I wish I could explain—but it just isn't possible—and it isn't as if we're doing anything *wrong*—"

Having reassured herself on that point, she went to the galley and began preparations for the meal which, fortunately, was a simple one, for she only gave half her mind to her work.

But how could she help that when John was occupying all her heart and a large part of her thoughts? The incredible wonder of it! He loved her. And that wasn't all. He trusted her. He must do, for the beastly things Aunt Ruth had said about her hadn't made any impression at all on him! How *heavenly* life was—and it was going to be even better, for in a few days' time she would be John's wife! Happiness bubbled up in her and she began to sing softly to herself for the sheer joy of living.

Miss Alice heard the blithe little song and momentarily the tears sprang to her eyes. It was such a young sound and so confident—indeed, with all her heart she *did* wish them well, particularly this girl that she had taken under her wing. For her, she wanted happiness and security—all the good things of life. And much as she liked John, she wasn't entirely sure that Rosamund had made a wise choice—

She pulled herself up with a jerk.

"I'm an old fool," she told herself severely. "I'm being possessive, that's the trouble! I don't want her to fly away yet and so I'm inventing reasons why it would be better that she didn't. But it's no use. Once people grow up, they have to take their chance and there's nothing one can do about it. Thank goodness, there's no talk about them getting married yet! That really *would* have worried me!"

"Yes, we can fit you in this morning, madam," the receptionist told Rosamund. "One of our ladies had to make a last-minute cancellation, but I'm afraid it's not for another hour and a half—?"

"That will do beautifully," Rosamund assured her. "It will give me time to do some shopping."

"And your name, madam?"

"Hastings. Oh, will you tell the assistant who will be looking after me that my hair is very dry so that she'll know what sort of shampoo to give me?"

"Certainly, Miss Hastings. At eleven-thirty, then," the receptionist smiled, and Rosamund went out into the sunny street feeling that this was quite evidently going to be her lucky day.

The feeling was intensified a little later when she found just the dress she was looking for. One couldn't really say that it looked particularly like a wedding dress, yet its white simplicity struck a note which seemed just right to

Rosamund. She smiled as she looked at her reflection. John, she thought, would like it, though Aunt Ruth, if she were to see it, would probably dismiss it as a rag!

The thought of her aunt made Rosamund remember all the fashionable weddings which the Salon had dressed—the silks and laces, the embroidery—the yards and yards of tulle and the way in which even the plainest girls seemed to blossom into something like beauty in their bridal finery.

Yet she had no envy for any of them, for after all, none of them had married John! She bought another two dresses, one blue, the other green, cotton. Just the thing for a honeymoon on a barge! She completed her purchases with a pair of white shoes with silvery buckles and then went back to the hairdressers.

The assistant who looked after her did her job well, but she was something of a chatterbox and Rosamund wasn't sorry when she was left to herself under the drier. Content to let her thoughts drift happily, the time passed quickly and with ample time to spare before she rang John up, she stopped for a thoroughly feminine lunch of a poached egg, fruit salad and coffee. Then the Abbey clock struck the hour and it was time to phone John. She dialled the number he had given her and his voice answered immediately.

"Rosamund darling!" There was a lilt in the way he said it which told its own story. Everything was all right! So she was not surprised when he went on: "It's all set! No difficulty at all. I've got the licence and we can be married in any church we like right way!"

"Oh, John!" Rosamund was half laughing, half crying with happiness. "How wonderful!"

"Isn't it?" he agreed. "So—when, darling?"

"Whenever you say," she told him unhesitatingly.

"Bless you!" There was a caress in his voice and her heart swelled with tenderness. "Then how about Thursday?"

"Perfect!" she sparkled.

"And where?" he went on.

"I don't mind, John. Just so long as we do get married!"

"We'll do that all right," he assured her confidently. "Now, how do you like this idea—I'll be home tomorrow and then, on Thursday morning, we'll start off very early and drive until we find a nice old village church we like the look of. Then we'll rustle up the Rector and persuade him to do the job—"

"Persuade?" Rosamund said quickly.

"Well, it's going to be very short notice—he may have other engagements," John explained.

"Yes, of course. I hadn't thought of that." She hesitated momentarily. "John, what are we going to do about Miss Alice? I mean, we can't just vanish without giving her some explanation, can we?"

"No, I suppose not," he admitted reluctantly. "But we did decide that we wouldn't tell anybody, didn't we? And anyhow, we'll be coming back the same day—look, I tell you what, we'll tell her that we're going off for an all-day picnic and not to worry if we're late getting back. How's that?"

"Yes," Rosamund agreed, relieved. "And we'll have a picnic and that will make it true!"

John laughed softly.

"You're a truthful little soul, aren't you?" he said, and then, with sudden earnestness: "You don't know how much that means to me, Rosamund! Don't ever change, will you?"

"No, I won't," she promised seriously. "Oh, John, I am happy!"

"So am I!" And then, rather ruefully: "But I'll be even happier if my interview this afternoon is satisfactory."

"It will be," Rosamund assured him serenely. "I'm quite, quite sure it will be. Don't you realise, our star is in the ascendant? Nothing *can* go wrong!"

"Hey, keep your fingers crossed when you say that!" John advised, and Rosamund was not quite sure whether his alarm was genuine or pretence. "You don't want the gods to be jealous, do you?"

She laughed confidently.

"That's just superstition," she scoffed. "You'll see—and now I must ring off, John. Somebody is waiting for the phone. Goodbye, darling. I'll be thinking of you all the time and wishing you luck!"

"That should do the trick if anything will!" John said gratefully. " 'Bye now, darling! See you tomorrow!"

There was a little smile on Rosamund's face as she left the telephone box. It was so wonderful to feel that John relied on her and turned to her for reassurance. And equally wonderful, that for the rest of their lives, she would have John to rely on.

She walked to the car park where she had left her car and putting her purchases carefully on to the back seat, began her homeward journey. When she reached the village, she stopped outside the shop and went inside to ask Mrs. Watchett if there were any letters for Miss Alice.

Mrs. Watchett, engaged in cutting up a side of bacon into joints, wiped her hands on her voluminous apron and reached behind herself to the shelf where letters to be called for were put until they were claimed.

"Two, miss." She inspected first one and then the other so earnestly that Rosamund began to wonder if she had X-ray eyes and was able to read the letters through the envelopes without opening them. Then, reluctantly, she doled them out to Rosamund. "And one for you, miss," she added unexpectedly, reaching to the little shelf again.

"For me!" Rosamund was too much surprised to hide the fact, and Mrs. Watchett's eagle eyes raked her mercilessly.

"Miss Rosamund Hastings," she pronounced. "That's you, isn't it?"

"Oh yes," Rosamund confirmed, her heart sinking. She knew that it could only be from Aunt Ruth because no one else knew where she was, and a glance at the neat, angular handwriting told her that she was right.

"Nothing wrong, is there, miss?" Mrs. Watchett asked, agog with curiosity. "You look quite pale."

"I always do when it's very hot," Rosamund said mechanically. "Thank you, Mrs. Watchett!" And made her escape.

She drove down the lane and turned into Joblings' field. There, in the lee of the old barn, she picked up her letter from the seat beside her, but even then she couldn't find the courage immediately to open it. Then, with sudden resolution, she tore the envelope open and took the letter out. After all, no matter how unpleasant

86

she might be, what real harm could Aunt Ruth do now?

She began to read:

"Dear Rosamund,
"Clearly, you're not such a fool as I thought you were. In fact, I congratulate you on a campaign very cleverly planned and skilfully executed."

Rosamund paused, frowning. What on earth was Aunt Ruth talking about? A campaign? It didn't make sense. She read on:

"However, a word of warning. Your young man, tired of the sort of popularity which his money brought him (particularly among his girl-friends) vanished from his usual haunts a few weeks ago. Just how you managed to run him to ground I don't know, but to represent yourself as a damsel in distress while keeping your knowledge as to his identity to yourself was really clever. I'd be proud to have thought of it myself."

Rosamund shook her head impatiently. Really, Aunt Ruth must be crazy! But, horribly fascinated, she read on:

"And here I would like to say that I bear you no grudge for having represented me as the bad fairy. Your act was quite brilliant—he didn't have a chance!

"But that warning I spoke of—no man likes to know that he's been made a fool of by a woman, so take care that your knight errant never discovers how clever you've been. He wouldn't forgive you, believe me! And if, at times, you find it boring to keep on playing the beggar maid to his King Cophetua, remember that there are and always will be plenty of women only too eager to step into your shoes!

"Every good wish for your future success.
                    Ruth Hastings."
"P.S. Of course, you'll come to me to be dressed."

Rosamund folded the letter with hands that would shake, despite her conviction that Aunt Ruth had made the whole thing up just to create trouble.

John, wealthy, and herself a fortune-hunter! What utter rubbish! It wasn't worth another thought.

Then, as she put the letter back into its envelope, she saw that there was a slip of paper still in it which she had previously missed.

She took it out and caught her breath.

It was a photograph, obviously cut from the pages of a glossy society periodical, of a young man incredibly like John. For a moment the picture blurred dizzily. Then, forcing her eyes into focus, she read the caption below it.

It *was* John.

"John Lindsay, only son of the late Gordon Lindsay. Mr. Lindsay, whose tragic death occurred recently when piloting his Pippet IV plane, was, of course, a financier of international repute. John ('Johnny' to his friends), a popular young man with a gift for enjoying himself, is, needless to say, regarded as one of the most eligible bachelors of the day."

"No!" Rosamund whispered through dry lips. "*No!*"

She couldn't think clearly.

John—her John—wasn't a poor man with a purpose in life as he'd led her to believe. He was rich. He had so much money that he didn't need to work. He was the masculine version of the shallow, idle women who patronised her aunt's salon—a playboy.

And he had lied to her. Deliberately misled her. Why, why, *why?*

The word hammered relentlessly in her brain. There must be a reason—

She turned again to the letter.

"—tired of the sort of popularity which his money brought him—"

Yes, that must surely be the answer. And how understandable that made everything! Why, there might even have been a girl to whom he had been attracted only to find that she was interested not in him but in his money. Certainly Aunt Ruth more than hinted at that.

Small wonder if he had been disillusioned and had sought sanctuary in a different world where he could be a different person. Small wonder, too, that he had deliberately given the impression of being a comparatively poor man or that, at first, he had been so suspicious and unfriendly. He simply couldn't believe in basic decencies like sincerity or integrity.

But he did now. He believed in her love for him.

Her forehead puckered in perplexity. Her first impulse was that she must assure him that she didn't want to be rich. That she, too, had run away from a life as superficial and unsatisfying as his own had been.

If John had been immediately available that, she knew, was what she would have done. But he wasn't here and he wouldn't be until tomorrow. Inevitably, she began to question whether impulse was her best guide.

Of only one thing could she be absolutely certain. The criterion which must guide her decisions was that she must do whatever was best for John. And that could surely only mean that his new-found faith in humanity and himself mustn't be destroyed, least of all by her.

Again she consulted the letter.

"No man likes to know that he's been made a fool of by a woman."

Well, she hadn't made a fool of John. She did truly love him and money didn't enter into it—except from the point of view that she'd rather they didn't have too much of it.

But would John credit that? Would he be able to? Wasn't it too big a risk for her to take?

She drew a deep breath and made up her mind. She would say nothing at all about the letter, either now or in the future, even though she would so desperately prefer to have no secrets from John. But honestly, what satisfactory alternative was there? Trying to put herself in John's place, she decided that there wasn't.

Very well, then, she would destroy the letter and say nothing about it. But even so, she could see that there were dangers in such a course.

For one thing, there was Aunt Ruth. Supposing she was ever able to convince John that he had been a victim of, to use her own words, a skilfully executed campaign? Unconsciously, Rosamund shook her head. That was unlikely in view of that very typical P.S. Aunt Ruth saw her chance to make something out of the situation and she didn't hesitate to make use of it. It was something unpleasantly like blackmail, but at least Rosamund could be quite sure that she would never risk imperilling the possibility of making money!

The other, far greater and more personal danger lay in herself. Every instinct she had, everything in her nature, made her want to be absolutely honest with John. But when, sooner or later, he told her of his wealth, she would have to act a lie—and keep on acting it. She'd have to seem convincingly surprised, and she didn't trust her own histrionic capabilities sufficiently to be sure that she could carry it off. And that would spell disaster.

But as quickly as it had returned, the temptation faded. *Her* mind would be at ease if she told the truth, but how about John's?

Vividly there returned to her mind that moment of understanding which she had had on the day when John had told her of his love—that love wasn't only a question of romance. It was, among other things, the desire to stand between the person you loved and pain or danger. John was still too vulnerable, too sensitive for her to risk endangering his newly found self-confidence.

Her mind finally made up, she rummaged in her handbag for a flat packet of matches. Then she got out of the car, tore the letter and its envelope into shreds and set fire to them.

John's photograph? She hesitated, unable to bring herself to destroying that. She tore the caption carefully off and added that to the little blaze. She waited until nothing but black ash remained, and even that she stamped into further nothingness.

The photograph she put into her handbag.

They drove for over an hour before they found just the right church. They saw it from a high level road and simultaneously they exclaimed: "That's it!"

It was old and weathered and it had a look of permanence that delighted them both. And it was tucked into a green valley beside a sparkling little river. Perfect!

What was unmistakably the Rectory stood just by the church. It was large and square and just a little bit shabby and it was set in a garden which was obviously someone's pride and joy. Flowers and shrubs burgeoned as if they liked growing there.

"It looks just like a Rectory ought to look," Rosamund remarked contentedly. "I'm sure the Rector will be just right, too!"

But it was actually the Rector's wife whom they saw first. She was kneeling beside a border that she was weeding and she, too, had that indefinable air of gentle shabbiness. She wore a big, floppy-brimmed hat which had seen better days and a big hessian apron. Like a true gardener her earth-stained hands were bare of gloves.

She looked up with a smile as Rosamund and John came towards her.

"I'm afraid my husband is out at present," she told them. "Can I do anything for you?"

"Well, actually, we want to get married," John explained, smiling in response.

"How nice!" The Rector's wife beamed at them and got to her feet with so obvious an effort that John put out a helping hand which she accepted gratefully. "Thank you so much. It's this wretched arthritis, you know. I get stuck in one position and then I creak like a rusty gate when I try to move. That's better!" She straightened up. "Now then, you want to get married. Well, I don't suppose my husband will be long. He's over at the church with his warden."

"Splendid!" John said heartily. "Then, if you don't mind coming with us, the Rector can marry us and you and the warden can be the witnesses!"

"Oh, but, my dears, it's not as easy as all that!" the Rector's wife said sympathetically. "It takes time, you know. Banns have to be read—"

"Not for us!" John declared triumphantly. "We've got a licence."

The troubled look faded and the kind old face beamed again.

"Have you? How exciting! Francis will be interested. Usually it's banns here, you know, and sometimes it's just a little bit embarrassing. The girls will giggle so! Only nerves, of course, but sometimes it makes one wonder if they realise what a tremendous step they're contemplating. Now, will you sit on that garden seat—it's quite clean—or come into the house while I make myself presentable? You'll stay out here? Right! I won't keep you waiting long."

She was as good as her word. In a very short time she was with them again wearing a different dress, old but well polished shoes and with her hair tidy and her hands clean.

"Now, my dear, if you'll just zip up my top six inches," she requested, turning her back to Rosamund. "I never can manage to do it myself. That's it! Now, come along—"

The church was as right inside as it was out. Its pews were carved and were mellow with age and elbow grease. The memorial tablets and the two big family tombs spoke of the many generations who had brought their joys and sorrows here. And the altar flowers were fresh—

"I'm so glad—I did them again this morning," the Rector's wife whispered. "That's what's so nice about the summer—we're never short of flowers to bring here."

They found the Rector in the vestry. He was a tall, scholarly-looking man whose face had the benign expression of a medieval saint and, like his wife, he too beamed when he heard why they had come to him.

"Yes, indeed, I will marry you," he agreed, and studied the licence which John handed him with almost boyish enthusiasm. "How very interesting! It's a long time since I saw one of these—quite ten years, I should think. You remember, my dear. That very nice couple who arrived in the middle of a snowstorm."

"Yes, I remember." The Rector's wife nodded. "They wanted a quiet wedding because they thought people might be amused at them falling in love so late in life. Actually, they needn't have worried. Most people are really very kind. They don't laugh when they see real happiness!"

"Indeed, no," the Rector agreed. "Now, I'll call Budge—"

And so they were married in the quiet church, with sun pouring through the windows and the birds singing outside—

"To love, cherish and to obey—"

The old, familiar words took on a new and vital meaning. This was for always—

Out in the sunshine again, they said good-bye to the kindly couple, refusing an invitation to stay for lunch, but promising to come back and see them quite soon. Then they were on the open road again, very silent and perhaps a little shy of each other. But as Rosamund's right hand cradled her left one with its bright new ring, John laid his hand over both of hers and no words were necessary.

They found the ideal spot to stop for their picnic, high on a hillside with miles of unspoilt countryside surrounding them. The crusty new bread and cheese they had bought at a village shop was sheer ambrosia as the canned, rather warm drinks were so much nectar—life was wonderful! They could not tear themselves away from that enchanted spot.

Then, reluctantly, they knew it was time to turn back. They made sure that they had left no litter and went back to the car. John opened the door for Rosamund, but just as she was getting in, her foot turned on a loose stone. She made a grab at the door frame to save herself from falling—and dropped her handbag.

It flew open as it hit the ground and its contents were scattered far and wide.

"Golly, why you women carry all this junk about I can't think!" John announced, as he began to pick up the bits and pieces. "Anybody would think you—"

Abruptly, he left his remark unfinished and stood erect. He was staring at a small piece of paper that he had picked up.

Then he looked at Rosamund and her heart froze, for his eyes, bleak and hostile, were the eyes of a stranger.

CHAPTER SIX

"SO you knew all the time!"

"No, John, no, *no*! It wasn't like that at all!" Rosamund heard the rising note of hysteria and struggled for self-control. She faced John squarely. "I didn't know until the day you were in town," she insisted—and read cynical disbelief in his stony eyes.

"Really? Then why didn't you say anything about it to me when I got back?"

"Isn't it rather—why have you never told me?" she suggested sadly. "Didn't you trust me?"

"If I didn't—" John began, and stopped short. "All right, go on! Let's hear your version, but I warn you, you'd better make it convincing!"

She knew that she was battling against tremendous odds—that John, in the past, had been so badly hurt that now he was already condemning her out of hand. John who, such a short time back—she swallowed convulsively.

"Well, go on!" the harsh voice ordered.

"Aunt Ruth wrote to me. She enclosed the cutting—"

"Which I recognise as having been taken from a periodical that was published nearly six months ago!" John commented ironically. "Are you trying to tell me that since she paid her visit, she just happened—by pure chance, of course—to come across it? Oh no, Rosamund, you'll have to do better than that!"

"If I were lying to you, I'd probably have thought up a more convincing story," Rosamund retorted spiritedly. "But this happens to be the truth, so there's nothing I can do to make it more plausible!"

A muscle flickered faintly at the corner of John's mouth and Rosamund felt a momentary hope. Had she made an impression, however slight, on his impregnable mistrust? But if so, he gave no further indication of it. Simply, he waited in silence for her to go on.

"She said some pretty beastly things," Rosamund ploughed on desperately. "She, of course, assumed that I already knew—"

"Why 'of course'?" John asked in an abstracted way as if it wasn't really of much importance.

"Because she's got that sort of mind. It just wouldn't occur to her that there could be any other explanation. She thinks people will do anything for money—"

"I appear to have done her an injustice," John commented. "She evidently has a very sound knowledge of the world and its ways!"

Momentarily Rosamund sagged against the car, her eyes closed.

"John, what's the use?" she asked hopelessly. "It doesn't matter what I say. In your heart you've condemned me already."

He gave no sign of having heard, but stood there, rock-like, so close yet miles away—

In desperation, she tried again.

"What really matters is why I didn't tell you, isn't it? It was because I felt I understood why it could hurt you so. You see, long before I had Aunt Ruth's letter, I'd realised that—that something had happened which—which made you want to make a fresh start—"

"How could you know that?" he demanded sharply. "I said nothing—"

"No, that was just it," Rosamund explained eagerly. "Except for referring once to your mother, you never spoke of yourself or your family—nothing."

"Nor, for that matter, have you told me much about yourself," he reminded her.

"I know," Rosamund nodded. "And that was why I felt I understood. I didn't want to talk about my past, either. I just wanted to forget it. You see, I ran away from Aunt Ruth because I couldn't bear the life I was living with her. I didn't only live with her. I worked with her as well. I could never be myself—"

"Your aunt—" John interrupted with a faint gleam of interest. "Just what is her job—and yours?"

"She runs a very exclusive dress salon," Rosamund told him. "And she was training me to take her place later on."

"Ah, now I remember!" he exclaimed. "I was sure I'd seen you somewhere before! I got dragged to a dress show and you were modelling some of the clothes. I didn't remember your face—it was the way you walked that stayed in my mind."

"Yes, I did some modelling," Rosamund agreed. "But not lately. I've been understudying Aunt Ruth—seeing clients and helping them make their choice."

"It doesn't sound very onerous," John remarked with a shrug.

"It can, in fact, be very tiring, particularly with clients who can't make up their minds. But it wasn't just that. It was—oh, the whole atmosphere! The triviality of it all— the sort of women I had to deal with—greedy and shallow—"

"And rich?" John suggested drily. "I suppose, in fact, you were jealous of them!"

"No." She shook her head. "Not that. Just—exhausted by it. All I wanted was to get away from it all and make a fresh start. I tried to make Aunt Ruth understand, but it wasn't any good, so in the end I just walked out."

"And what's the moral of this pathetic little tale?" John asked sardonically.

"Just that—because of the way I had felt, I guessed that for some reason or other, you'd felt the same way," she explained. Then, with sudden impatience, she caught him by the arm and shook it.

"Oh, John, don't shut your mind against me! Please, please believe me!"

He looked at her with lacklustre eyes.

"You know, I almost might—but for one thing," he said slowly.

"What?" Rosamund asked eagerly.

"There's altogether too much coincidence about the whole thing!"

"Coincidence?" Rosamund repeated. "But coincidences do happen!"

"Oh, to be sure they do," he agreed. "But when they come as thick and fast as all this—well, really, you can hardly wonder if my credulity is strained to breaking point!"

"What coincidence?" Rosamund challenged.

"Oh, must we? All right, if you insist! Coincidence number one—" he ticked off on one finger. "You just *happened* to choose *my* boat for your opening gambit although there were two others to choose from—"

"Yours was nearest to the gate," Rosamund reminded him.

"So it was! All right, we'll let that go. However, number two—you tell me that you ran away from your aunt, by which I presume you mean me to understand that you didn't tell her where you were going. Right? Then how do you explain that she found you with apparently little difficulty?"

"I don't know," Rosamund admitted flatly. "I asked her, but she wouldn't tell me."

"But to me it's perfectly understandable," John told her, his lips curling derisively. "Your aunt's visit was all part of the scheme—a put-up job. The idea was to convince me that you were in trouble."

Something snapped in Rosamund's mind.

"I think Aunt Ruth put it rather better in her letter," she said in a brittle voice. "*She* referred to me as a damsel in distress and you as a knight errant!"

Again the muscle twitched at John's mouth.

"Ah yes, that letter! It should make interesting reading! Let me see it—it might even convince me that you're telling the truth!"

"I can't," Rosamund said miserably. "I burnt it."

"What a pity!" John mocked. "Your one piece of evidence—and you destroy it!"

"John, stop it! Stop it at once and listen to me!" In sheer desperation, Rosamund stamped her foot in its pretty silver-buckled shoe.

Her peremptoriness startled him, for she saw that though his eyes were still hostile, she had at least gained his whole attention.

Time seemed to stand still and to Rosamund it seemd as though her brain had stopped working as well. What could she say to him that she hadn't already said—what was there left that would convince him?

Then, as if she was listening to someone else speaking, she heard her own voice saying very clearly and deliberately as one might speak to a little child or a sick person:

"John, I'm not going to defend myself any more, because it's no good—it only makes you doubt me all the more. I'm just going to tell you one thing. I married you because I loved you. For no other reason. And I shall go on loving you, whether you can believe it or not. That's all!"

She turned away blindly from him and got into the car to sit very still, staring straight in front of her.

For what seemed like an eternity John stood motionless. Then with a sudden, violent movement, he tore the photograph he still held into fragments and flung them from him. Then, grim-faced, he walked round to his side of the car, got in and started up.

It was a silent journey and if John drove with a sort of determined recklessness, Rosamund was hardly aware of it. She had a strange sensation of utter emptiness as if all thought, all feeling, had been blotted out. She wasn't herself any more. She was just the hollow husk of a girl who, so short a time ago, had experienced the fullness of life.

And John? She had no idea what his thoughts were and, strangely, little curiosity. She knew now that what she had previously only partly sensed was true. Before he had ever met her, some experience had so poisoned his mind that he had lost faith in *himself*. That was the real trouble and that was why he couldn't believe that her love for him was genuine. Nor could it be otherwise until, somehow, the poison was expelled. And that was something that John must do for himself. There was no way in which she could help—except, of course, to go on loving him—

Quite suddenly she was stirred from the grey mist that enveloped her.

"John, aren't we going in the wrong direction?" she asked warningly. "Too far south?"

"We would be—if we were going back to the *Seven Stars*," he agreed. "But we're not."

"Not going—" she faltered uncertainly.

"No. You see, I seem to remember that, not so very long ago, I promised to endow you with all my worldly goods—"

"Oh, John!" she protested despairingly.

"So," he went on as if she hadn't spoken, "why shouldn't I start doing that right away? We're going to Lindacres which, in case you've forgotten, is the house that my father built in Hampshire some ten years ago. You'll like it, I'm sure. It's built in the grand style—practically every bedroom has its own bathroom, there's a ballroom, two swimming pools, one under cover, and magnificent gardens and hothouses. Father used to use it for his really big parties—"

He went on talking, but what he said made no impression on Rosamund. One thought only echoed and re-echoed in her numbed brain.

She had failed, utterly, hopelessly. Failed to regain John's trust, failed even to persuade him to give her a chance and so failed in her battle to give their marriage any hope of fulfilment.

"You're not very enthusiastic!" John's reproachful

voice cut through her nightmare. "Would you perhaps rather go up to my—sorry, *our*—London flat? Or the villa at Cannes? Or perhaps a cruise? That might take a little time to organise, but it wouldn't really matter, would it? You could spend the time buying clothes—"

Rosamund's hands, clenched together in her lap, turned white at the knuckles, but she didn't speak. She'd said she wasn't going to try to defend herself any more and somehow or other was going to stick to that. She mustn't let him goad her into argument—

"Or perhaps," went on the mocking voice of the stranger who had been John, "you'd prefer that we went back to the *Seven Stars*? In the hope of convincing me that you really do prefer the simple life, you know?"

In her mind's eye, Rosamund saw a picture of the *Seven Stars* and its setting—the tranquil water, the flowery hedges and the birds singing in a blue sky. But even more vividly she recalled the peace and happiness of the place and the friendliness she had been shown there.

Her hand moved in sharp protest.

"No! Not there. Not now!"

"No? Just as you like. Then we'll make it Lindacres, shall we?"

"I don't think, really, it matters where we go," Rosamund told him quietly. "I leave it to you."

John didn't answer, but his foot came down more heavily on the accelerator. He drove for the best part of an hour and then, for no apparent reason, stopped on the crest of a hill. Rosamund, roused from her apathy, turned to look at him questioningly.

John pointed down to the valley.

"As a sentimentalist, I thought you'd like to have your first glimpse of your new home," he explained. "Charming, isn't it? So simple and homelike!"

It was surely the least apt description of Lindacres that there could be!

Glaringly white in the bright sunshine, it sprawled incongruously in grounds that were outstandingly beautiful. It was angular, clumsy and pretentious. To Rosamund it also looked oddly self-conscious as if it knew that it didn't really belong in that delightful setting.

"No, I'd hardly call it charming," she said consideringly. "I think functional is the word I'd use to describe it. Built for a special purpose and probably quite satisfactory from that point of view. As to it being homelike—it could be, of course, because being a home doesn't depend on any particular building but on the people who live in it."

John laughed shortly.

"You're right about it being functional. But if you can turn that soap-works into a home, I'll—" he left the sentence unfinished to go on in a puzzled way: "What the deuce is going on down there? There's a coach just drawn up at the front door and another one following it. And they're both full of people—children—masses of them!"

"Could it be a fête of some sort?" Rosamund speculated without much interest. "Do you lend the grounds for that sort of thing?"

"I think so, sometimes, though I can't say I know much about it. But it can't be that. It's too late in the day for people, particularly children, to be arriving for a thing like that. Besides, there'd surely be marquees or tents if it was a fête. There always are. Oh, confound it, perhaps, after all, we'd better go up to town—"

"No, we can't do that," Rosamund declared decisively. "If it isn't a fête, then it must be an emergency of some sort, and we must see if we can help."

John, startled not only by her earnestness but also by her evident concern, looked at her sharply, and then without comment started the car up again.

When they reached the wide open gates of Lindacres it became clear that Rosamund was right—there was some sort of emergency, for a policeman was posted there. John pulled up as he came towards them.

"What's up?" John demanded.

"A fire at the Greystoke Orphanage and they're bringing the kids here," the policeman explained briefly. "I must ask you to move on, sir, you're blocking the entry. No, you can't go in!" he laid a heavy hand on the side of the car as if to detain it by force. "It's not a peepshow, you know!"

"Don't be a fool, man." John said crisply. "It happens to be my property! I'm John Lindsay."

"Sorry, sir," the constable apologised, taking his hand away. "I didn't know. I'm new in this district—"

John accepted the explanation with a nod and continued along the well-kept drive. On either side of them were immaculately kept lawns that were broken at intervals with glowing flower beds and low-growing shrubs. It was, perhaps, rather formal, but none the less very beautiful, yet neither John nor Rosamund had a look to spare for them. They were motivated by a common urge to get to the house as quickly as possible.

A little spark of hope flamed in Rosamund's heart.

"At least we're sharing something," she exulted. "Perhaps—"

But after that, she had no time to think of anything but the contretemps into which they had so suddenly and unexpectedly become involved.

Pandemonium reigned! Children, both boys and girls, milled in and out of the house, completely out of control, shouting and screaming with excitement. There didn't seem to be anyone in charge of them.

"This won't do!" John declared wrathfully. "I don't mind coming to the rescue, but I'm damned if I'll stand— there *must* be someone in charge! Follow close behind me, Rosamund, and we'll see if we can wade through these brats—"

He succeeded in clearing a way into the huge hall, but here the commotion, if possible, was even worse. The children, most of them sitting disconsolately on the floor, were younger than those they had already encountered and they were frightened and unhappy. Most of them were sobbing uncontrollably and several had flung themselves face down in a state of near-hysteria. And still there seemed to be no one in charge.

Grim-faced, John made his way to the preposterously ostentatious staircase at the foot of which was an outsize metal gong. Seizing the stick, he began to beat an imperative and noisy tattoo on the gong.

The effect was instantaneous and dramatic. As if by magic the hubbub stopped and even the older children crowded silently in from the garden to see what it was all about. Even more, two startled women shot out of a room which opened off the hall. One was elderly. Her grey hair was dishevelled and her distracted air gave the impression of a hen that is convinced someone is going to rob her nest. The other was very much younger, at the outside not more than twenty-two or three. She had a pretty little face that looked as if it was made for smiling, but at the moment it was preternaturally serious and concerned.

"Well, really!" the older woman snorted indignantly, her hand on her heart. "As if we haven't enough to put up with already—"

"Are you in charge of the children, madam?" John demanded, ruthlessly cutting across the fluttering complaints.

"Yes, I am!" The elderly voice assumed a rather incongruous note of authority. "And whoever you are, I must really ask you not to make a nuisance of yourself. Everything is difficult enough—"

"And will become rather more difficult still if you don't even try to keep these little hooligans in order! Because unless you do, I'm going to turn the whole lot of you out, lock, stock and barrel! And if you question my authority for saying that, the answer is that this is my house and you are here without my permission!"

It was brutal, but it was effective. The mouth of the older woman opened and shut like that of a stranded fish, and if there was the hint of a grin on the younger one's lips, she quickly suppressed it.

But now, Rosamund saw, John was at a loss to know what the next step was—and small wonder. This was essentially a woman's problem.

"Is there a housekeeper?" she murmured, and saw the relief in John's face as he nodded. "If you'll send for her, I think she and I might put our heads together—"

He accepted the suggestion without comment and was about to go off in search of the housekeeper when a dignified presence made itself felt at the top of the staircase. In her trim black dress and immaculate white collar and cuffs, to say nothing of her air of authority, this could only be a housekeeper of the most competent type.

"Really, Miss Fletcher, I should have thought—" she began coldly, saw John—and they had another near-hysterical female on their hands. "Mr. John!" she exclaimed in dismay. "I had no idea—of course, if I had, I'd never have agreed—though the children had to go somewhere and both the Rector and the doctor thought—"

"All right, Mrs. Brickwell," John interrupted briskly. "I fully appreciate that this is the only house for miles around big enough to cope with the situation. My dear—" he turned formally to Rosamund, "this is our housekeeper, Mrs. Brickwell. Mrs. Brickwell, my wife."

If the housekeeper had been startled by John's unexpected arrival, she was completely flabbergasted by his announcement. Her mouth was slightly open and she breathed heavily as she came slowly down the stairs.

Rosamund had a strange sensation of change in herself. She was not the cool, businesslike self that she had been in London. Nor the self she had become when she had gained her freedom and happiness. Nor even the broken-hearted self of the last few hours. She had become a blend of all three.

Here was a practical problem to be tackled, but she would do it for love, not money. And her own grief should help her to understand other people's distress. Mrs. Brickwell, she reasoned rapidly, had been forced by circumstances into an extremely invidious position, and now, because of John's sudden appearance, had been caught in the very act of having assumed an authority which was not hers. Nor, it was clear, had John's acceptance of the situation entirely reassured her.

It was more than a possibility, too, that there was at least a degree of antagonism between the housekeeper and Miss Fletcher. Each, used to giving orders, would resent the presence of the other and would be convinced of her own superior claim to having the last word.

It was the sort of situation which had more than once occurred in the Salon, and there was only one way out of such an impasse. A third person whose authority neither contestant would dispute must take command. And she knew quite well who that person was at this moment. Not John because, as a man, he would be at a disadvantage dealing with two women. Herself.

And so, by the time Mrs. Brickwell reached the hall, Rosamund was there to greet her.

"How do you do, Mrs. Brickwell?" she asked, holding

out her hand. "I'm so glad we've arrived in time to be of help!"

Rosamund had been careful to speak pleasantly, but she had also taken care to speak with confidence. One had to at times like this, even if one was shaking in one's shoes. People didn't, in her experience, accept authority unless it was made clear to them that one took it for granted that they would. And to her relief, Mrs. Brickwell proved to be no exception to the rule.

"Indeed, madam, you could not have arrived at a more opportune moment," she declared with a baleful glance in Miss Fletcher's direction. "Really, we're all at sixes and sevens. I hardly know which way to turn—"

"A very difficult situation," Rosamund agreed briskly. "And naturally, the children are alarmed and excited. Fire is a terrifying thing."

"Yes, indeed, madam," Mrs. Brickwell answered meekly, evidently realising that she had been firmly told that allowances must be made, but in such a way that she had not lost face. "I expect you'd like to know what arrangements have already been made—"

"Yes, we would, wouldn't we, John?"

She turned to him and saw a look on his face that she had never seen there before. The grimness had gone, though there was no suggestion of amiability. Simply, it was an intent, preoccupied look as if his own thoughts were of more absorbing interest than the chaos around him.

"John—!" she gave his elbow a gentle nudge.

"Oh yes! Of course! Arrangements." He came back to earth with a start. "The children will have to spend the night here, I suppose—"

"Will you discuss just what's to be done with Mrs. Brickwell?" Rosamund suggested. "I want to have a word with Miss Fletcher—something must be done to amuse those children! How many are there, Mrs. Brickwell?"

"About fifty, so I've been given to understand."

"Good lord, only fifty!" John ejaculated feelingly. "I'd have said nearer five hundred! Yes, by all means try to organise them a bit, Rosamund. Absurd to have sent even fifty with only two adults in charge!"

Rosamund made her way over to where Miss Fletcher,

with singular incompetence, was trying to quieten the children nearest to her, some of whom were still in tears, though others had got over their fears sufficiently to have become obstreperous. But while Miss Fletcher was really quite hopeless, Rosamund noticed that the younger woman was making a better job of it, though clearly she realised how inadequate an effort it was, for she smiled ruefully at Rosamund.

"If only we could get them all into the garden where there's more room," she said under her breath. "But—" and she glanced significantly at Miss Fletcher.

Rosamund nodded encouragingly, but she didn't stop. It was Miss Fletcher whom she had to persuade and cajole and, as a last resort, coerce. But it wasn't going to be easy. Miss Fletcher was probably only too well aware of her own incompetence and would all the more resent— and possibly fear—having her authority undermined.

"I am Mrs. Lindsay," Rosamund explained, and added sympathetically: *"What* a responsibility for you, Miss Fletcher!"

"I don't mind responsibility," Miss Fletcher insisted in an aggrieved voice. "If only I could get some co-operation!" And she in her turn shot a malevolent look across the hall! Yes, decidedly, there had already been trouble between her and Mrs. Brickwell!

"Yes, indeed, we must all pull together in an emergency like this," Rosamund said briskly. "I think, if you'd give me some idea of just what has happened so far, and what damage has been done at the Orphanage—" she suggested, hoping that Miss Fletcher would feel that here, at last, was someone who was willing to be genuinely co-operative—by which, of course, she meant helpful without being self-assertive.

It appeared that the fire had started in the kitchen of the Orphanage—an old brick building with timber floors and staircase—and had got a good hold before, by chance, it was discovered since the last evening meal had been served and the clearing up done.

"And it spread with such terrifying speed," Miss Fletcher explained agitatedly. "We had only just time to get the little ones—who, of course, were in bed—out before the staircase was involved." She shuddered. "It's terrible to think what might have happened——"

"How thankful you must be that it didn't," Rosamund interjected fervently. "Now, I gather that the kitchen will be completely out of action. Is there any hope of beds and bedding being salvaged?"

There appeared to be some doubt about that, at least as regarded the dormitories above the kitchen. For the others, on the far side of the house, there appeared to be some hope. Indeed, Miss Fletcher explained, the men had gone back in the coaches to see what they could get.

"Which men?" Rosamund asked.

"Two of our resident masters and another who lives in the village. And two of the outside staff here," Miss Fletcher explained. "And really," with a glance at her wrist watch, "they are taking their time about it!"

"It's probably not an easy job if the staircase has gone," Rosamund suggested. "But I don't suppose they'll be long now. In the meantime——" she glanced round the cluttered hall and decided that she'd allowed Miss Flecher sufficient rope—"you'll be anxious to have the children safely out of the way before they start carrying things through. Otherwise, some of them might get hurt. I expect you'd prefer them to be out in the garden, wouldn't you, Miss Fletcher?"

And with only a token bleat that the grounds were so large that the little ones might get lost, Miss Fletcher agreed that that was what she'd like—but of course, she hadn't liked to suggest it.

"The last thing I want is for us to be a nuisance to you," she explained virtuously.

It was nearly midnight when John and Rosamund finally got rid of the last of their guests. Tim Ferris and Owen Weeks, the two masters in charge of the boys, had gratefully accepted the offer of a late-night drink and had shown a disinclination to leave the sitting room for their rather spartan quarters in the gymnasium. And even when they had gone, there were still things to discuss.

"I'll go and see Matron or the Headmistress or whatever she calls herself tomorrow," John announced pouring himself out another modest drink. "Also I want to see for myself what the damage is before I meet the Governors."

"Yes, I suppose so," Rosamund agreed, twisting her own half full glass so that the light glinted on the facets of the cutting. "If it's really bad, will you let them stay on here?"

"It might be the simplest solution," John said thoughtfully. "For them, at any rate. It *is* the only place for miles around that can accommodate fifty children and the staff and still leave rooms available for classes."

"Classrooms," Rosamund repeated. "That would mean emptying the rooms of their furniture—is there room to store it?"

"Enough, I should think," John said consideringly. "Although if they're going to stay long, the boys won't be able to sleep in the gym. They'll want to put that to its proper use."

"Yes, of course," Rosamund agreed absently.

John glanced enquiringly at her.

"Tired?" he asked quite kindly.

"I am, rather," she admitted, and that was very true, but not so much physically, she could have added, as mentally. She felt as if she had lived a lifetime in a single day. So much had happened and it was all so—she groped for the right word—so *disjointed*. She felt as an actress might if she had to play one act from 'Romeo and Juliet' followed immediately by a second one from 'Othello' and the third—no, no play ever written could possibly contain an act even remotely resembling events since they had reached Lindacres!

It was all so completely unreal! And not the least fantastic aspect of it all was the way in which she and John had worked together to bring order out of chaos. How was it possible that two people, head over heels in love and on their wedding day, no less, could first meet with such bitter disillusion and then, all personal emotion put aside, could work together like—well, like two partners in a business enterprise? That it was an impersonal relationship, born of the emergency, she knew quite well, but they had trusted and relied on one another—

And that was the most incredible fact of all. John, who had made it so clear earlier in the day that he had lost all his faith in her, had asked her advice and accepted her decisions without question as they dealt with the problems of this extraordinary situation. Was it just force of necessity that had compelled him to turn to her or—was it something that went deeper than that though he didn't realise it?

She couldn't tell and she certainly couldn't ask. She had told John that she had married him because she loved him and that she would go on loving him. There was no more for her to say. The rest lay in John's hands.

The clock struck midnight and he stood up.

"I don't think there's anything more we can do to-night," he remarked. "You and Mrs. Brickwell have fixed up about food supplies for tomorrow. Some of their domestic staff will come over first thing to lend a hand—that seems to be the lot. No, there's one thing I forgot to tell you. The Press put in an appearance while you were coping with the food situation."

"Oh!" Rosamund exclaimed in dismay.

"Yes," John agreed grimly. "They thought they'd come to report on a simple human interest story—and stumbled on a scoop! We're news, Rosamund! Front page at that!"

"Yes, I suppose so," Rosamund agreed faintly. "What—what did you tell them?"

John shrugged his shoulders.

"Simply that, not wanting the fuss of a big wedding, we'd got married very quietly. I managed to choke them off seeing you, but of course, I had to co-operate to some degree, otherwise they'd have decided that there was a mystery about it and been on the trail like bloodhounds on a scent! Not that I think it was much use. I had to give them your name, of course, and one of them knew you. So, more than likely, they'll look up your aunt—and heaven knows what she'll tell them!"

"*I* know," Rosamund told him wearily. "She'll tell them that she knew all about it and thoroughly approved. She'll make it sound like the romance of the year—" she caught her breath in a little sob.

"Rosamund—!"

"Oh, but of course she will!" Rosamund declared recklessly. "Don't you see? You're rich. I'm your wife. She sells expensive clothes. She won't risk a word of criticism!

As a matter of fact, she said in her letter that she'd expect me to come to her for my clothes. It was to be the price of not letting you know that, as she believed, I'd known all along—"

Silence fell between them. A silence that seemed to intensify as the moments ticked past. A silence that neither of them could break.

It became unbearable. Suddenly Rosamund jumped to her feet.

"I—I think I'll turn in now," she said in a high-pitched, breathless voice. "I really am tired—"

"By all means."

John walked over to the cocktail cabinet and put his empty glass down with exaggerated care, his back towards her.

"I hope Mrs. Brickwell has fitted you up with everything you need?" he went on with studied politeness.

"Oh yes, thank you." Rosamund did her best to echo that impersonal tone.

John opened the door for her.

"Good night, Rosamund."

"Good night," she responded, her head in the air so that he wouldn't guess how near she was to tears.

The door was closed quietly but firmly behind her.

CHAPTER SEVEN

MRS. BRICKWELL had a sense of the fitness of things. No matter how drastic the emergency, from the very first she had put her foot down in one respect. While she had her strength, no one was going to be put in the principal suite of the house.

"It's not suitable—beautiful rooms like that!" she had declared adamantly.

And how right she had proved to be! Really, she felt, with Mr. John and his new wife turning up so unexpectedly, it really looked as if she had been *guided*!

So John and Rosamund were duly installed in the suite—two connecting bedrooms, two bathrooms and a small sitting-room which, within a very short time, was to become the hub of the house.

Rosamund was half awakened early on the morning after their arrival at Lindacres by the sound of a door shutting near at hand. For several moments she lay still, bewildered by her unfamiliar surroundings. Then memory flooded back and she buried her face in her pillow.

It couldn't be true! Two people as much in love as she and John had surely been couldn't become so terribly estranged within a few hours of being married! It didn't make sense.

And then, on top of that, all the crazy events that had followed! They had been pitchforked into a state of affairs that one would hardly expect to encounter once in a lifetime. And it had to happen on that particular day! And yet perhaps it had been just as well that it did. John and she had to forget their own differences in order to take a firm grip on a situation that was completely out of hand. To them had fallen the task not only of dealing with practical problems, but also with very personal ones, particularly where conflicting claims to authority had arisen.

By the end of the day, they had dealt with everything even if only on a temporary basis, and Rosamund for one had felt utterly exhausted as a result. Exhausted and oddly empty of all emotion. Too much had happened in too short a time. It was as if a careless photographer had taken several exposures on the same negative. The result was blurred—meaningless.

But now—she sat up in bed, hugging her knees—here was a new day to be faced. What would it bring? Could it bring anything except more confusion and more heartache? And if it did, could she find the courage and the wisdom to deal with it?

She had told John that she loved him and that she would go on loving him. That had been nothing less than the absolute truth—but how could she prove it to him?

She pondered deeply, unable to find a simple solution to such a complex problem. Then, from nowhere, it seemed, a quotation came into her mind.

> *"To thine own self be true,*
> *And it must follow, as the night the day,*
> *Thou canst not then be false to any man."*

"Yes, that's it!" she told herself, unconscious that she spoke aloud. "I've got to be absolutely honest. That means I've got to be *myself* as I really am, no pretence because it seems as if it might be expedient—that would be cheating John—and myself. And surely, what he must want to know for sure is that I *am* the girl he believed me to be when he asked me to marry him!" She sighed deeply. "But it won't always be easy—and it won't be quick—"

A light tap on the door interrupted her thoughts. John?

But in answer to her summons, Mrs. Brickwell came in carrying a small tray.

"Good morning, madam," she said briskly. "I've brought your tea myself because I thought it might be advisable if we discussed one or two things—"

"Good morning, Mrs. Brickwell," Rosamund said pleasantly though with a sinking heart. Problems so early! Still, better get it over. "By all means tell me what's wrong."

"Not exactly wrong, madam," Mrs. Brickwell explained rather diffidently as she handed over the tray. "It's—well, it's about clothes. I mean, seeing that you and Mr. John hadn't planned to stay here and consequently brought no luggage I thought perhaps you might prefer to wear something—a little different—"

"How very kind and thoughtful of you, Mrs. Brickwell," Rosamund said with very real gratitude. "And have you found something that will do?"

"It's been a bit difficult, madam," Mrs. Brickwell explained. "You see, you're rather tall and very slim—in fact," apologetically. "All I could find was a blue nylon button-through overall. It's a very nice one and quite new—"

"That will do splendidly," Rosamund told her serenely. "Of course, if we decide to stay on for a time, and I think Mr. John may feel that it's necessary, then I must see about getting my own clothes—" she stopped short.

But that meant going back to the canal—to the place where John and she had been so happy. How could she bear to do that? How *could* she! She swallowed the lump in her throat.

"Or else perhaps I could buy a few things more or less locally?"

"Well, you could," Mrs. Brickwell admitted doubtfully. "But if you don't mind me pointing it out, madam, I think you're going to be very busy today."

"I think so, too," Rosamund agreed. "There are bound to be a lot more decisions to be made. But—" she gave Mrs. Brickwell a quick, enquiring look—"I think you've got something particular in mind, haven't you, Mrs. Brickwell. What is it?"

"Well, actually, it's Cook," Mrs. Brickwell explained. "You see, as we understand it, the cook from the Orphanage is coming over here to work. And while that's only fair to Cook, seeing that she can hardly be expected to cope with all the extra work, you know what they say about two women working in one kitchen!"

"I do, indeed," Rosamund said feelingly. She considered for a moment. "Do you know anything about the Orphanage cook? I mean, is she younger than our cook?"

"Oh yes, madam, considerably, I'd say. And of course, only experienced in what you might call institution cooking—which is very different from the standard here!"

"I expect so," Rosamund agreed reflectively. "Well, perhaps Cook would like to discuss the matter with me? She may have a solution to the difficulty. Ask her to come and see me after breakfast. In the little sitting room here, please. There's less likelihood of us being disturbed. Will you ask her to do that?"

"Certainly, madam." There was an unmistakable note of respect in Mrs. Brickwell's voice. Really, young though she was and, so far as one could judge from what the newspapers said, not particularly *anybody,* Mr. John's wife certainly knew how to handle domestic problems! And she was to have further confirmation of this within a few moments. For, just as she was leaving the room, she turned with a vexed click of the tongue.

"I'm sorry, madam. I almost forgot to give you a message from Mr. John. He has gone over to the Orphanage to see just what the extent of the damage is and he said not to wait breakfast as he wasn't sure how long he'd be."

"I see," Rosamund said composedly. "Thank you, Mrs. Brickwell. But in future, if ever you have a message for me from Mr. John, will you please make a practice of delivering it at the first opportunity?"

"Yes, madam," said a subdued Mrs. Brickwell. "I'm sorry—"

Rosamund smiled her acceptance of the apology and Mrs. Brickwell went resolving that when she gave Cook the message, she would also tell her not to try anything on because the new Mrs. Lindsay wouldn't stand for any nonsense. Pleasant and sympathetic, yes, but a lady who knew her own mind and wasn't afraid to speak it. And quite right, too !

It was almost noon before John returned. Rosamund had spent much of the morning in the little sitting room to which she had taken quite a liking. It was obviously planned to be a woman's room, for the furniture, mostly really old, was elegant rather than sturdy. The armchairs and the seats of the smaller chairs were upholstered in soft green satin with a design in roses and satin bows on it. The curtains, though plain, toned with the green of the chairs and the polished floor had a few good rugs on it. There were two walnut occasional tables, a walnut-framed mirror and a workmanlike little desk. On this were two telephones, one presumably the house phone.

Rosamund had her breakfast there—a very simple one, but beautifully served. Newspapers had been brought up with the tray and she glanced at two with a growing feeling of distaste. Aunt Ruth had been interviewed and she had said much as Rosamund had expected she would—it didn't make reassuring reading. Then she had been visited, briefly, by Dr. Milward who had come to make sure that none of the children had suffered any harm, and for a longer period by Cook, a big, raw-boned Scotswoman who made the little room seem even smaller.

When John arrived, Rosamund was writing to Miss Alice.

"They told me you were here," he remarked casually.

"Yes. I thought it was a good idea to keep out of everybody's way as far possible until you had a chance to make any decisions. And I've found the room useful for interviewing people I really had to see—Dr. Milward and Cook. I hope you don't mind me taking possession of it like this?"

"Very sensible." John sat down in one of the armchairs, his long legs stretched out straight, his hands thrust into his trouser pockets. "It's essentially a woman's room, as you've probably realised. Bound to be. My mother planned and furnished it. She said she had to have one room where she didn't rattle about like the last pea in a pod. It rather vexed my father. You see—" there was a dry note in his voice—"he liked everything to be on a grandiose scale!"

"I see," Rosamund said, non-committally, as she thought.

He looked at her curiously.

"I gather you agree with my mother," he commented. "Don't you like the house?"

"I think that the grounds—what I've seen of them—are outstandingly beautiful," Rosamund told him. "But the house—"

"Yes?" He evidently meant to have a direct reply to his question.

"You referred to it as a soap-works," she reminded him. "I don't agree with you there. To me, it suggests a hotel. A very good hotel—but not by any stretch of the imagination a home." She deliberately changed the topic of conversation. "How did you get on at the Orphanage? Is it very badly damaged?"

"Just about gutted," John replied crisply. "And small wonder! The place should have been condemned as dangerous years ago, and to have had masses of children living there when the fire risk was so high was utterly infamous! How the devil it comes about that there were no casualties, I don't understand. Well, there's one consolation. The damage is so bad that they'll have to rebuild now, and a good job, too! But of course it will take time—"

"So you will let them stay on here?" It could have been a question or a statement. John took it as the former.

"Nothing else for it. I met Sir George Parks over there—he's one of the Governors—and he told me that one of the difficulties about rebuilding was the problem of where to put the children during that time. Well, I'm prepared to consider the possibility of them staying here for, say, a year. But I'm not willing simply to hand over, leaving them to their own devices—not after the chaos of last night. They'd wreck the place through sheer inefficiency. And though apparently neither of us like it, I see no reason why I should allow that. But it will mean that we have to stay here for a time until we're satisfied that it's properly organised. Will you mind?"

"No."

John accepted her brief reply without comment, and when he spoke again, it was of a different matter.

"You said you'd had visits from Milward and Cook. I suppose Milward's was simply a courtesy visit, but Cook—I imagine she was on the warpath! There's going to be trouble in the kitchen, mark my words!"

"I don't think so," Rosamund told him serenely.

John's brows lifted.

"You don't? You don't know Cook! Superb at her job, but a tartar if ever there was one!"

"Is she? I found her very co-operative."

John stared unbelievingly at her.

"Did you, indeed!" he ejaculated. "And just what form did her co-operation take?"

"She told me that there are two kitchens—the big one that was used when there was a big house-party, and a smaller one for when there wasn't."

"Yes, that's true," John acknowledged. "But—"

"And she suggested that they should use the big one while she had the smaller one," Rosamund explained.

"*She* suggested that? Oh, come, that's just not on! Why, even if she doesn't always use it, the big kitchen is the pride of her life! She'd never give it up without a terrific struggle. Now tell me, just what really happened!"

"Why not ask Cook?" Rosamund suggested coolly with a significance which was not lost on John. As clearly as if she had spoken the words, she was telling him that if he didn't believe her, he could easily check her statement. It was up to him.

John thrust his fingers through his hair in a familiar, boyish way that caught at Rosamund's heart. So many times in the past she had seen him make that gesture when he was puzzled or in any way put out. Then, it had usually been accompanied with a rueful grin—but he was not smiling now.

"I expressed myself badly." From the stiff way in which he spoke it was clear that he found even so inadequate an apology difficult to make. "But knowing Cook, I anticipated that you must have found her difficult to deal with. Consequently, I shall be interested to know what led up to her making the suggestion."

"Nothing very much," Rosamund said frankly. "I told her that we fully appreciated what a difficult situation it was and that we would be very glad if she could suggest a solution. So then she told me about there being two kitchens, which, of course, I didn't know before."

"I see—but are you absolutely sure you didn't get it wrong way round—that she intends to stick to the big kitchen?"

"Quite sure," Rosamund said confidently. "Because she did make one proviso—that she hoped she wouldn't be expected to cater for big dinner parties with only a small kitchen to work in but that she'd do her best if we wanted to entertain a few friends."

"To which, I suppose, you replied that if anybody could manage it, she could?" John suggested drily.

"Oh no," Rosamund answered composedly. "It's probably true, but I haven't known her long enough to know from personal experience, so it would have been rather insulting. As if I thought she was the sort of person who couldn't tell genuine appreciation from when someone was trying to curry favour with her."

"I see," John commented. "You seem to have taken her measure pretty accurately!"

Rosamund didn't answer. Did John mean that he thought she had acted with sincerity or did he think that she had simply been rather unpleasantly shrewd? She didn't know and she couldn't bring herself to ask.

After a moment or so John stood up.

"I'd better go and clean myself up for lunch," he remarked. "And I can do with it, seeing that I missed breakfast. Or is there anything else—?"

"Only you spoke of Dr. Milward's being a courtesy visit. Well, it was, for the most part. But he did tell me he's rather worried about Miss Fletcher."

"Oh?" John said without much interest. "What's wrong with her—other than that she's an infuriating old twitter-pate?"

"She's apparently had a grumbling appendix for some time and he's afraid it may be coming to a head. But she won't do anything about it—not even let him make a proper examination."

"Stupid old idiot," John said unsympathetically. "Why the deuce not? Can't Milward scare her into being sensible?"

"Apparently not."

"Well, where do you come in, anyhow?"

"Dr. Milward thinks there's some reason that she won't tell him why she's so scared, and he thought perhaps I might persuade her to tell me," Rosamund explained.

"Now look here, Rosamund, you can't take everybody's problems on your shoulders!" John protested. "If you do, you'll be regarded as Public Relations Officer to the whole shooting-match!"

"Well, why not?" Rosamund demanded, stung to sudden defiance. "Do you think I want to have time to sit and twiddle my thumbs and—think? Believe me, that's the last thing I want to do!"

Deliberately she turned her back on him and picked up her pen. John accepted the dismissal without comment. She heard him close the door behind him and she blinked back the tears she had been too proud to let him see.

"I'm desperately sorry, Rob," Miss Alice said heavily. "I've let you down badly."

"No, you haven't, my dear!"

They were sitting opposite one another at the table of the *Pride of London's* cabin, and he put out a hand to grip hers as it lay inert before her.

"There's nothing you could have done. I shouldn't have gone away, no matter how important it seemed that I should. Though, to be quite honest, I don't think I could have done anything either."

For several moments neither of them spoke. Then Dr. Rob picked up one of the newspapers that lay on the table and frowned at it.

"You know, Alice, there's something that puzzles me.

Neither you nor I like this marriage. But why? I mean, on the face of it, what is there to dislike? Other, I mean than that we feel rather hurt at having been left out. But that's unreasonable. After all, they had every right to make their own decision—"

"Oh, but it goes deeper than that, Rob," Miss Alice said quickly. "Much, much deeper."

"Yes, but why?" Dr. Rob asked impatiently. "You tell me that they're very much in love with one another. Then, from a worldly point of view, Rosamund has done very well for herself. In addition, Ruth must know that she's met her Waterloo now."

"Has she?"

Dr. Rob looked at her sharply.

"You don't agree? Why not?"

"Because I can't see Ruth missing an opportunity like this," Miss Alice explained. "Don't you see, Rob, that as the wife of a very wealthy man, Rosamund could be a very valuable client? No, Ruth will do everything in her power to prevent there being a breach."

"But can she do that?" Dr. Rob frowned. "I mean, from the very little Rosamund did tell you, and what we've been able to read between the lines, won't she seize the opportunity for making a clean break with her aunt?"

"If she can."

In her turn, Miss Alice picked up a newspaper and studied it.

"I don't like the sound of what Ruth told the reporters. About Rosamund not knowing how well off John is."

"You don't believe it? Why not? Simply because Ruth said it?"

"Partly," Miss Alice admitted. "But what I wondered was, true or false, why does she lay such emphasis on it? She does, you know. It's not just coincidence that every report features that aspect."

"H'm," Dr. Rob pondered. "Well, there's one reason you can dismiss out of hand. It wasn't because Ruth is a romantic at heart and believes in true love! There's nothing sentimental about Ruth!"

"Then there must have been another reason why she took such a definite line," Miss Alice insisted. "And there's only one I can think of that fits—I don't think it was because she believes it but because she's convinced that it's what Rosamund wants John to believe!"

"Do you mean to say that after all, you don't think Rosamund married for love?" Dr. Rob asked sharply. "That she married him for his money?"

"Of course I don't mean that," Miss Alice denied indignantly. "And you ought to be ashamed of yourself for even suggesting such a thing! Rosamund just isn't the mercenary type. I've no doubt about that! But I'm equally sure that John didn't tell her he's well off."

Dr. Rob scowled.

"That sounds rather unpleasant to me," he remarked distastefully. "Deceitful—underhanded—"

"Rubbish!" Miss Alice declared robustly. "If it were the other way round, if he'd pretended to be rich when he wasn't, then you'd have reason for criticism. But that isn't the way of it at all. You know, Rob, you and I are inclined to look at this purely from Rosamund's point of view. But how about John's? That young man is what is vulgarly described as a catch. And while I don't believe that Rosamund would have married him for his money, I'm afraid there are lots of girls who would. And then, how about friends? How could he ever be sure that they really cared for *him*? Pretty humiliating and disillusioning for a young man to believe that, without his money, nobody would be interested in him."

"I grant you that," Dr. Rob admitted grudgingly. "But even so "

"Wait a minute, Rob, let me finish. You and I come here for relaxation—to escape from the pressures of our normal lives. We live simply, well below the standard we could easily afford. Are we being deceitful because we don't go about trumpeting how much money we earn? Of course not! And nor was John. He came here for the same reasons that we do. Not perhaps exactly the same, but near enough. And it didn't occur to us to ask questions. Why should it?"

"All right, you've made your point," Dr. Rob admitted. "It wasn't our business. But not telling us and not telling the girl he wanted to marry are two very different things. Surely she had a right to know! What was he afraid of?"

"Himself, I think," Miss Alice said simply. "Just

imagine, Rob, how marvellous it must have seemed to him to know, absolutely for certain, that Rosamund really loved *him*! Oh, can't you see? Perhaps it was foolish, but I do feel that in the circumstances, it was natural. Besides—" she added reflectively, "just imagine how difficult it would have been for him to broach the subject! Rosamund is very sweet. She's also very sound. She's got her priorities right, and what's more, she's willing to fight for them. And unless John is an utter fool, he must surely realise that. So how could he, in effect, tell her that it didn't really matter she was quite happy to share love in a cottage with him because he's got lashings of money? Of course he couldn't!"

"He's told her since," Dr. Rob commented, picking up a single sheet of notepaper that lay among the newspapers and reading from it.

"Dear Miss Alice,
John and I decided that to avoid any fuss, we would get married very quietly at once. But we hadn't expected things to turn out quite the way they did.

"We had fully intended coming back to the Seven Stars after our wedding, but John took me to see Lindacres and as I expect you will have seen from the newspapers, we had no sooner arrived than we became involved in an emergency and simply had to stay to get things sorted out.

"To make everything more difficult, reporters came to Lindacres because of the children being there and when they heard of our marriage they made a big story of it.

"Will you forgive us for having caused you anxiety and for not having taken you into our confidence? If we could have told anyone of our plans it would have been you, but for family reasons, this just wasn't possible.

"I shall never be able to thank you enough for your kindness to me.

Yours affectionately
Rosamund Lindsay"

"Yes," Miss Alice agreed judicially, "he must have told her. Judging by the picture in the papers, Lindacres is the sort of place that only a very rich man could afford to run. I wonder if he told her spontaneously or whether—"

she paused and shook her head. "To my way of thinking, Rob, there's something missing in that letter!"

"Is there? It seems to me to cover everything."

"I don't agree. For one thing, she makes no mention of them coming back here sooner or later, as would surely be natural, particularly as there's quite a lot of their gear here."

"That's true." Dr. Rob glanced down at the letter again. "There's a suggestion of finality about the way she finishes off—as if it really is 'good-bye'."

"Exactly! And then there's this—the two of them, very much in love, have just got married. Wouldn't you have expected there to have been some reference to how happy they are?"

"I suppose you would," Dr. Rob agreed. "So what you're saying, Alice, is that you think something has gone wrong?"

"If I'm right in the conclusions I've drawn from the letter, then yes, I'm afraid that's what I do think!"

"H'm—of course, one can't help jumping to the conclusion that if that is so, then in some way this money question is at the bottom of it." Dr. Rob pondered. "Do you think the reporters let the cat out of the bag and Rosamund was hurt—no, that won't do. They were already at Lindacres before the Press turned up." Again he considered. "She speaks of wanting to avoid fuss. That could simply mean that they didn't want the publicity that they ran right into. On the other hand, she also refers to family reasons. Well, John, one gathers, isn't afflicted with relatives. But Rosamund—" he shook his head.

"Ruth?"

Dr. Rob nodded.

"I can't for the life of me see how she was involved at that stage," he confessed. "But I'm convinced that she was. There's something about this whole business that strongly suggests she had more than a finger in the pie!"

"But even if she did, does that matter now so long as Rosamund is happy?" Miss Alice demurred.

"But is she? Do you really think so? No," as Miss Alice shook her head. "And neither do I! But I grant you, I haven't, as things stand, the right to find out. So—" his face grew grim—"I shall do the only other thing possible—I shall go and see Ruth and get at least some of the truth out of her."

"But can you? I mean, until now, I thought you didn't feel that it would be any good to try direct methods of that sort. What's made you change your mind?"

"Partly it's the result of sheer desperation," Dr. Rob acknowledged. "There's still no result from my enquiries about Rosamund having been registered at birth as Dexter—nor, for that matter, as Hastings. But there is something that Ruth will find difficult to lie about— something that, like a fool, I've forgotten until very recently. Ruth is Rosamund's aunt. Rosamund's surname is—or rather, was—said to be Hastings. But since Celia and Ruth had no brother, that can't be true! And that Ruth will have to admit. It gives me something of an advantage, even if only a slight one."

"When will you go?"

"Tomorrow."

"Well, I wish you luck, Rob!" Miss Alice sighed as she began to fold up the newspapers.

"Meaning that you think I'll need it?" Dr. Rob suggested grimly. "So do I."

Within twenty-four hours of her arrival at Lindacres, Rosamund's problem about clothes had been solved in a totally unexpected and far from welcome way.

All her London clothes were delivered, beautifully packed and obviously sent at Ruth Hastings' orders, though no message had accompanied them.

Now, a fortnight later, as she stood in front of her open wardrobe, Rosamund surveyed the beautiful clothes hanging there with mixed feelings.

There was no doubt about it, she would have been in a quandary without them, particularly at this moment. John had invited Sir George Parks to dine with them so that they could finalise arrangements for the renting of Lindacres by the Orphanage authorities. It would be an informal affair, but none the less, she needed to dress the part of the mistress of Lindacres as she could not have done without these dresses to choose from.

But though John had made no comment when they had

arrived, Rosamund felt sure that he took it for granted the clothes had been sent at her request. The inference which he drew from that was only too clear—he assumed that she and her aunt were not only still on friendly terms, but also that they certainly had been in collusion right from the start. And, helplessly, Rosamund was beginning to feel that she could hardly blame him for his scepticism. Conclusive evidence, as it appeared, had piled up so against her—the interview which Aunt Ruth had given the Press had added considerably to it. And to counter it, all she had was her own bare word. What was more, the longer they remained in this strange state of armed neutrality, the more difficult it would become to make any real contact with one another.

Somehow, she was convinced, that barrier of silence between them must be broken down, but how, she had no idea, since she still felt that John and not herself must make the first move.

However, there was no time to brood on that now. She had thought she had left plenty of time to dress for dinner, but at the last moment Miss Fletcher had come to see her and had rambled on at great length with complaints about the sleeping arrangements. She was used to having a room of her own. She didn't think it suitable that she should have to share a dormitory with the children. She hadn't had a good night's sleep since coming to Lindacres—

Rosamund let her run on, not so much listening to the complaints, repeated over and over again, as making use of the opportunity to study Miss Fletcher. Very quickly she decided that Dr. Milward was right—there was something wrong with her visitor. Physically, she was a bad colour and far too thin. That, of course, might be due to the grumbling appendix. But there were other signs of trouble as well. The nervous twitch of her mouth, the restlessness of her hands and the way in which her eyes fell so quickly from one's own. She was in a state of considerable nervous tension. That might be apprehension at the possibility of an operation—but it might not.

Whichever it was, a glance at her watch told Rosamund that she had no time to try to find out now. She terminated the interview by standing up, leaving Miss Fletcher no choice but to do the same.

"Of course, Miss Fletcher, we must remember that in an emergency arrangements can't always be perfect," she pointed out. "And what final decisions will be made must, I think, depend largely on how long you are all going to be here. But that, as I'm sure you will appreciate, does not depend on me. However, Sir George Parks is dining with us tonight. I may have an opportunity of discussing your complaint with him—"

"Oh, please, don't do that!" Miss Fletcher said agitatedly, positively cringing. "The last thing I want to do is to make difficulties."

"I see," Rosamund said slowly and, indeed, she thought she did. Miss Fletcher, she was reasonably sure, was afraid of losing her job, and that fitted in with her refusal to go to hospital. "Well, thank you for letting me know how you feel, Miss Fletcher. And now, if you'll excuse me, I really am short of time—"

Miss Fletcher scuttled away and Rosamund went to her bedroom.

Twenty minutes later she joined John and Sir George showing no signs whatever of having hurried through her preparations.

She was wearing a gauzy silk dress of an unusual shade of green. It sparkled subtly with a hint of gold thread and the huge, bat-wing sleeves fluttered attractively with every movement of her arms. For the rest, it was very plain, moulded to her slim body with flattering emphasis. She had no time to do much about make-up or hair, though the sophistication of the dress would have warranted it. Her hair, which John was used to seeing loose, she had gathered into the nape of her neck, fastening it with a big Victorian tortoiseshell clip. It was a severe style, but it revealed the delicacy of her features to perfection. All in all, she looked charming, poised and essentially feminine. And she knew it—the sudden, startled look in John's eyes and the flattering appreciation in Sir George's left her in no possible doubt.

John made the introduction and as Rosamund offered her hand to their guest, she smiled disarmingly.

"I must apologise, Sir George, for not being here to

greet you," she said with the charming deference of a young woman to a considerably older man. "I was delayed by a slight domestic problem."

"Please don't apologise, Mrs. Lindsay," Sir George said warmly. "After all that you have already done to help us, you and your husband, I feel that it is an imposition to add to your burden by coming here to dine. But there is a lot to be decided and it is vital that an early decision should be made about the suitability of this house for any protracted period."

"Yes, indeed," Rosamund murmured. "A sherry, please, John," she turned her head to say as he walked over to the the cocktail cabinet. She turned back to Sir George who was eagerly waiting to resume their conversation.

"You spoke of a domestic problem, Mrs. Lindsay. I hope it really was a slight one—and that none of our people caused it?"

Rosamund smiled reassuringly.

"It really was just a trifle, Sir George, and as for your people—they're being most co-operative, I do assure you!" And if that was stretching the truth a little where Miss Fletcher was concerned, she had no intention of telling tales out of school. "Of course there are bound to be some adjustments to be made, but I'm sure that won't take long!"

"If that is so, then I'm quite sure, from what I have heard, that it will, in no small part, be due to your charming self!"

The compliment was rather too fulsome for Rosamund's taste, and as John handed her the glass of sherry, she saw from his expression that he hadn't liked it either.

She made up her mind that as far as possible, for the rest of the evening she would keep in the background or even, once dinner was over, that she would leave the two men to discuss the situation on their own. But this proved to be impossible. Sir George laid such stress on the value of a woman's point of view that she had no choice but to stay, and since he referred to her constantly, to give her opinions.

Fortunately, in the majority of cases, they happened to be the same as John's. None the less, as the evening wore on, she took matters into her own hands, explaining that she had several letters to write which must catch the early post in the morning—would Sir George excuse her?

A few more compliments—thanks for the perfect dinner and the valuable help she had given—an apology for having detained her so long—and she was free. But once the door had closed behind her, Rosamund hesitated. There were some letters she had to write, but they weren't really as important as all that—an overpowering desire to escape from the house, if only briefly, took possession of her and she surrendered to it before she had time for second thoughts.

Letting herself out by way of a side door, she walked swiftly to the open swimming pool. By day she had felt that its garish modernity was in doubtful taste, but now, in the gentle light of the moon, it was transformed. Dim purple shadows softened the angular lines of the low buildings which surrounded that pool and the still, dark water was spangled with stars.

Rosamund found a chaise-longue and with a little sigh of relief relaxed at full length on it. She lay perfectly still, gazing straight up at the heavens, and for a while she lost herself in the remote beauty, conscious only of a sense of being a part, however small, of it all.

Then, abruptly, the spell was broken. She swung her feet to the ground at the sound of approaching footsteps. It was John.

"Well," he drawled, "our visitor has gone at last! He evidently didn't feel it was worth staying once you had withdrawn your charming presence!"

Rosamund didn't answer. John was not only very angry, he was trying to goad her to a hot retort.

"And small wonder, of course," he went on ironically. "Since you were out to charm, weren't you? Both by your manner and your appearance! Enough to make any man lose his head! You know—" he regarded her critically, his head on one side—"you're an extremely beautiful woman, Rosamund. Far more beautiful than I had realised. But then, of course, I've never seen you in your fine feathers before, have I? You pay for dressing, my dear!"

Rosamund stood up. Her hands were clenched to her sides. She was almost at breaking point, yet somehow she must maintain her self-control. Otherwise there would be a complete breach between them.

"I'm tired," she said quietly. "And I shall need to get up early tomorrow—"

She turned to leave him, but his hand shot out, swinging her round to face him.

"Wait!" he commanded menacingly. "I've something more to say!" He surveyed her from head to foot with hot, possessive eyes. "Yes, quite lovely enough to make a man lose his head! Rosamund—" his hands were gripping her shoulders now with painful force—"we can't go on like this! Do you understand?"

Rosamund stood very still, neither responding to his grasp nor shrinking from it.

"Then what do you suggest we should do?" she asked almost inaudibly.

"Do?" John repeated harshly. "Well, for one thing, I suggest that you should remember something you seem to have forgotten—that you *are* my wife!"

CHAPTER EIGHT

DESPERATELY Rosamund tried to free herself, but there was no escape from the merciless arms that crushed her as John's lips sought hers in a kiss that held neither tenderness nor love. A kiss that made something in her shrivel and die.

This was not the John she had fallen in love with. This was a man who believed that everybody had their price and that money could buy anything, everything. And there was no appeal from that conviction. It was an ingrained part of his nature and the man she had believed him to be had never existed except in her own silly dreams.

Then, so suddenly that she stumbled, she was free. For a moment John stood rigid, staring blindly at her white, quivering face. Then his lips parted.

"I wish to heaven we'd not got married!" he told her

with a vehemence so intense that it had the quality of a physical blow.

He turned sharply away, leaving Rosamund to a silence from which all peace and tranquillity had been wrenched. In its place was the silence of utter despair.

At first, when John's footsteps had died away, she sat motionless on the chaise-longue, too numbed to think coherently. Then, vaguely aware that she was shivering violently, she made her way slowly back to the house and gained the sanctuary of her own room. For a while she listened, but heard no sound to tell her if John was in his room or whether, indeed, he had returned to the house at all.

Mechanically she undressed and got into bed to lie wide-eyed and rigid, unable to sleep, unable to feel—

Then, slowly, agonisingly, feeling returned.

John had said he wished they'd not got married. The words hammered relentlessly in her brain. And then she realised that she was speaking aloud, just as if he was there and she was answering him :

"And so do I!"

It was true! If they had never met, if, in her blind adoration of John, she had never known such happiness, then she would never have experienced the bitter disillusion that was hers now.

She lashed herself with bitter scorn. What a fool she had been—what a naïve, credulous little fool with her schoolgirl hero-worship and her belief that love conquered everything! She had been so sure that John was everything that was fine and true and all the time—she closed her eyes as if to shut out the memory, but it was useless. She knew John now as he really was and with that came understanding. There was only one thing for her to do. She must leave him—for good. What else was there to do when their marriage was such a mockery? All her dreams were shattered—and it was John who had destroyed them.

Until now she had found excuses for his lack of faith in her. The evidence had looked black against her. And quite likely, before they had met, there had been people to whom his money had meant more than his friendship. Because of that, she had made up her mind that, however difficult it might be, he should always find a loyalty and a love in her which would restore his faith in himself and his fellow beings. Now she knew that to have imagined such a thing to be possible was just one more foolish dream.

But there would be no more dreams. On that she was determined. From now on, she would accept only reality, however unpleasant it might be. Dreams were part of the past on which she would shut the door, never to open it again.

Not that she could ever again be the heart-happy girl of those few weeks which had followed the day when she had freed herself from the bondage which her aunt had imposed on her. She could put John out of her life in the sense that she would never see him again, but always his shadow would darken the future. Never again would she trust or believe in any human being alive! John had imbued her with his own lack of faith and always she would doubt her own judgement. She would even discredit her own motives—

She slept at last as dawn was filtering through the curtains to wake when her morning tea was brought in. And her first thought was simply a repetition of her decision of the night before :

"*I will leave Lindacres today!*"

And nothing should be allowed to stand in her way.

Then she saw that propped up against the teacup was a letter addressed to her in John's handwriting.

Her face hardened as she picked it up and held it, unopened, in her hand. Since nothing John could say would make her change her mind, what was the point in reading it? Then, with a shrug, she slit it open. It would make no difference, but she might as well know what he had to say—

Her eyes widened as she read. Without preamble, John had written :

"*After my discussion with Sir George last night, it is necessary for me to go to London to consult my solicitor on various points that emerged.*

"*I expect to be away about a week and I shall be grateful if you will take over in my absence on the clear*

understanding that you have entire authority to make whatever decisions you may feel are necessary.
John."

Her hand shook as she laid the letter down on the quilt. Her first reaction was one of resentment. After what had happened last night, after what he had said, what right had he to take her compliance for granted like this? Even his use of the word "grateful" didn't mollify her. It was nothing more than a form of words carefully chosen to mask the fact that in reality he was giving an order. Sheer expediency, that was all.

She was quite sure of that. John saw everything from one point of view only—his own. To the feelings of others he was completely insensible unless he had to take them into consideration in order to get what he wanted. From such a man one could expect neither compassion nor kindliness. And certainly not love as she had dreamed it could be. Well, one thing was very sure. Never again would he be able to hoodwink her in that way and never, never again would she allow herself to dream! It made one too painfully vulnerable.

As for John's request—no, she would not accede to it. If she were truly his wife—even if she had been a paid employee—she would have done her best to stand in for him. But she was neither. She owed John no duty whatever. And so she would carry out her plan to leave Lindacres today—for good.

Abruptly the house phone bell rang in the sitting room. Rosamund tried to ignore it, but it kept on persistently and at last, simply to silence it, she slid out of bed and answered it.

An agitated male voice answered her.

"Tim Ferris speaking, Mrs. Lindsay. I'm terribly sorry to bother you, but there's a flap on and we don't—"

"Mr. Ferris, please understand that I'm not responsible for your problems," Rosamund interrupted firmly. "You really must deal with them yourself—"

"This isn't quite like that, Mrs. Lindsay," Tim interrupted in his turn. "Miss Fletcher has been taken ill—very ill, we think, and she absolutely refuses to allow us to send for the doctor!"

It was exasperating, but knowing as much as she did about Miss Fletcher's health, it was impossible to stand by and do nothing.

"If she's really ill, of course the doctor must see her, whether she's agreeable or not," Rosamund answered crisply. "I'll get through to him myself. But first tell me what's wrong."

Obviously thankful to have her co-operation, Tim gave the necessary information and Rosamund grimaced sympathetically at his vivid description. It certainly sounded as if Miss Fletcher was very ill indeed.

"I see. Very well, I'll get on to Dr. Milward at once," she promised. "In the meantime, try to keep her as quiet as possible and don't on any account give her any stimulants!"

"Right!" Tim promised, and rang off.

Dr. Milward answered the telephone himself and swore fluently at the news.

"Sorry, Mrs. Lindsay, but my feelings got the better of me! This is just what I've been warning the silly old girl could happen. I'll be right over."

For a moment or two Rosamund hesitated. Surely, in summoning the doctor she had done all that could be expected of her. It was for him to issue the orders now.

And yet how could she leave it at that? To be old and ill and frightened—and, perhaps even worse, to be one of those unfortunates who don't inspire affection—it didn't bear thinking of.

Hurriedly she put on her dressing gown and slippers and ran downstairs to be met in the hall by Tim.

"He's on his way," she said briefly in reply to his enquiring look. "Where's Miss Fletcher?"

"In the staff sitting room—we got her there out of the way of the kids—" Tim explained, but found that he was talking to Rosamund's retreating back.

She walked swiftly into the pleasant room that had been set aside for the use of the Orphanage staff's use.

Only two people were there, Miss Fletcher and Mrs. Brickwell.

As Rosamund came in, Mrs. Brickwell caught her eye and shook her head with gloomy foreboding. Miss Fletcher, she was quite sure, was not going to recover.

Miss Fletcher wasn't even aware that Rosamund was there. She was sitting crouched in an armchair, her head lolling against one of its wings. Her eyes were closed, but little moans fluttered feebly through her livid lips. Her thin hands were clutching with claw-like tenacity to the arms of the chair. There was no doubt about it, Miss Fletcher was a very sick woman.

Rosamund dropped on her knees beside her and took one of those frightened hands in her own warm grasp.

"Miss Fletcher!" She spoke quietly but very clearly. "I want you to try to understand what I'm going to say. There's nothing for you to worry about. You must believe that. Dr. Milward is on his way here and he'll know what to do to help you——"

The closed eyes opened momentarily and there was stark fear in them.

"Not—operation," Miss Fletcher moaned. "Only—only indigestion!"

"We'll let Dr. Milward decide that," Rosamund said with gentle firmness. "He'll know best. And I don't think that the idea of an operation is what's really worrying you, is it? It's afterwards that frightens you, isn't it?"

The only answer was two tears that forced themselves out from under the closed lids and trickled unheeded down Miss Fletcher's parchment-like cheeks.

"Yes, I thought so! But there's no need for you to be afraid of that." Rosamund tightened her grasp and raised her voice a little. "Because you're not going to lose your job! Or, if you decide you don't want to go on working, then there'll be enough money found for you to live in comfort. You must believe that, Miss Fletcher, because it's true! I promise you it's true!"

For a moment there was no response and Rosamund was afraid that Miss Fletcher was too near unconsciousness to have understood her. Then she opened her eyes again and the burning gratitude in them told Rosamund that she had guessed correctly.

"That's all right, then!" Rosamund said, and then, looking over her shoulder, she added thankfully: "And now here's Dr. Milward!"

She stood up, still holding Miss Fletcher's hand in hers. Indeed, she could not have released herself without using considerable force, which she was reluctant to do. She glanced enquiringly at Dr. Milward, who nodded approvingly.

"Stay just like that, if you don't mind, Mrs. Lindsay," he said quietly. "Now, Miss Fletcher—"

He bent over his patient and made a brief examination, asked her a few questions to which a simple "yes" or "no" was sufficient answer. Then he stood erect.

"No doubt about it," he said under his breath to Rosamund. "Absolutely typical! Now, Miss Fletcher, I'm going to take you along to the hospital and we'll put this trouble of yours right before you can say Jack Robinson! But first of all, I'm going to give you a little jab that will ease the pain for you. Will you roll back her sleeve, please, Mrs. Lindsay?"

Rosamund did so as Dr. Milward prepared the syringe. The injection was given and after a moment or so the doctor gave a satisfied grunt.

"That'll hold her for a bit," he said softly as they looked down at the unconscious woman. "Poor old soul, she's been an absolute idiot, but you can't help feeling sorry for her."

"No, you can't," Rosamund agreed. "Dr. Milward, will she be able to stand the operation?"

"She's got to," he replied grimly. "It's that or—" he left the sentence unfinished, but Rosamund had no difficulty in finishing it for herself. "As a matter of fact, physically, she's in reasonably good shape. Her heart's above average for her age. It's her mental condition that worries me. I don't mean she's off her head or anything like that, but she's the sort that can scare herself to death when she ought to recover."

"She won't," Rosamund assured him positively.

Dr. Milward looked at her with considerable interest.

"You sound very sure of that," he remarked. "May I ask why?"

Briefly Rosamund told him of her promise and its effect and he nodded understandingly.

"I see. Yes, of course. I should have known that for myself. Well, that gives her an excellent chance. Now, if I may use the telephone—I alerted the hospital before I left home, but I must confirm that she is coming in. They promised to hold an ambulance for half an hour unless there was any other emergency call. Stay with her till I come back, will you, Mrs. Lindsay? I won't be long."

He was back in very short time looking considerably relieved.

"Everything laid on," he said with satisfaction. "Twenty minutes at the outside. I'll stay with her if you want to—" he stopped tactfully, but Rosamund flushed as she remembered that she was still in her dressing gown.

"My goodness, yes!" she exclaimed ruefully. Her hand went up to her hair. "I must look an absolute mess! I'd only been awake a few minutes when they called me down."

Dr. Milward grinned in a friendly way.

"You look, if you don't mind me saying so, about sixteen in that rig," he told her. "And yet—" he put a hand on her shoulder and turned her to face the light—"you also look very strained and tense. Anything wrong, Mrs. Lindsay?"

"Well, of course there is," Rosamund said quickly, pointing to Miss Fletcher. "Isn't an upset like this enough—" Her voice trailed away as she saw him shake his head.

"No, I don't think so—you're too sensible to let a thing like this get you down. Besides, whatever's troubling you is of longer standing than just the last half hour or so."

Rosamund shrugged her shoulders.

"Then in all probability it's just that you've not seen me without make-up before," she suggested. "All women look hags when they are only wearing their natural faces, you know!"

"But you hardly use any make-up," Dr. Milward persisted. "I remember noticing that the first time I saw you. No, all right, Mrs. Lindsay—" as he felt her shoulder move restlessly under his hand, "I'm not going to probe. All I'm going to say is that young though you are, unrelieved tension could work havoc with you as it has with Miss Fletcher, even if not in the same way. No, there's one other thing. If there's any way in which I can help, let me know. I've got the habit of keeping any confidences that are given to me!"

"I'm sure you have," Rosamund said gratefully. "But truly, there's nothing—"

It had been on the tip of her tongue to say *"nothing that you or anybody else can do,"* but she left the sentence incomplete. Fortunately Dr. Milward didn't seem to realise that, and she made her escape.

Ten minutes later, rather breathless, she was downstairs again in time to see the still unconscious Miss Fletcher off in the ambulance. Dr. Milward went with her saying that he'd got someone to run him back to Lindacres later so that he could collect his car.

Rosamund went slowly back into the house and was met in the hall by Mrs. Brickwell.

"Young Mr. Ferris asked me to give you a message, madam," she announced. "He asked me to say that two of the non-resident mistresses are coming in half an hour earlier than usual to ease matters."

"Oh, good!" Rosamund said fervently. Evidently Tim had taken her earlier warning to heart and was settling problems on his own.

"Also, madam—" there was a note of conscious virtue in Mrs. Brickwell's voice—"I have personally been giving assistance supervising the children at breakfast—"

"Splendid, Mrs. Brickwell!" Rosamund spoke with all the enthusiasm of which she was capable. "I don't know what we'd do without you!"

She went upstairs, free at last to consider her own affairs. But no, she wasn't! She'd made a promise to Miss Fletcher and it was a promise that she must see would be substantiated. She considered for a moment and then went to the sitting room. She looked up Sir George Parks' number and with a little grimace of distaste, got through to him.

"Mrs. Lindsay speaking, Sir George," she began briskly, but was immediately interrupted.

"How delightful to be rung up so early in the morning by such a charming neighbour! And what can I do for Mrs. Lindsay this bright and smiling morning?" he asked with that same overdone flattery which had annoyed her so the previous evening.

She wished she could slam down the telephone in protest, but she mustn't offend him if it could be helped because she knew that in him lay the best chance of keeping her promise to Miss Fletcher. None the less—

"For me, personally, nothing," she told him. "But for Miss Fletcher, quite a lot, I hope!"

"Miss Fletcher? Who's she?" Sir George asked blandly. "I don't know anyone—oh, you mean Miss Fletcher at the Orphanage! Well, what's the matter with her?"

Briefly Rosamund explained and heard Sir George click his tongue with impatience.

"How extremely troublesome of her! Really, to choose a time like this—"

"That's just the point, Sir George," Rosamund said crisply. Really, the man was impossible! "This trouble has been looming for some time, as Dr. Milward will confirm. But Miss Fletcher has been afraid to do anything about it in case her absence meant that she lost her job."

"Well, of course, we have been considering the advisability of replacing Miss Fletcher with someone younger and more able," Sir George admitted. "We have, however, as you may not be aware, already stretched a point in keeping her on several years beyond normal retiring age."

"But that's just it, Sir George," Rosamund said earnestly. "Miss Fletcher felt that she *must* stay on if she possibly could because otherwise, she'd starve!"

"Oh come, Mrs. Lindsay!" Sir George was taken aback by her bluntness and also put out by it. "I really can't believe it's as bad as all that!"

"I'm afraid it's more than likely to be," Rosamund insisted. "You see, so far as I've been able to discover, she has no relative with whom she could live. So even the most modest rent would be a terrible strain on her resources. It would mean going short of food and warmth—"

"Now really, Mrs. Lindsay, don't you think you're exaggerating?" Sir George suggested, very much on the defensive. "I think your kind heart is running away with you. After all, other people manage."

"Yes, but usually one finds that they have other resources—relatives who help, or perhaps a little nest egg. Or even a pension from their employers. Of course, if Miss Fletcher knew that she would be getting a pension from you, it would make all the difference in the world—" she paused hopefully.

"I'm afraid there's nothing like that, Mrs. Lindsay," Sir George said stiffly. "I don't say we wouldn't like there to be, but our funds are limited and overheads are increasing all the time—"

"Oh dear!" Rosamund said regretfully. "I had so hoped that *you* would be able to help!"

Sir George didn't answer immediately and when he did speak again it was in a far more conciliatory way.

"Now, you mustn't misunderstand me, Mrs. Lindsay," he began ingratiatingly. "I'm not a hard man, believe me! But my fellow Governors and I have the responsibility of handling money that isn't our own. Consequently, we have to be realistic. And that, as I'm sure you will see, means putting the needs of the children first."

He paused as if he expected her to agree with him, and Rosamund realised that he had, rather cleverly, taken the wind out of her sails since one could hardly argue that the children shouldn't be put first. At a loss how to answer, she said nothing at all, realising only too well that she had been over-optimistic in making that promise to Miss Fletcher, at least as far as Sir George was concerned. And, surprisingly, her silence had far more effect than any answer could have had, for Sir George ploughed on with, surely, a growing note of anxiety in his voice :

"However, appreciating, as I do—as we all do—all that you and your husband have done to help us in our recent dilemma, I should not like you to feel that we are not grateful! And since you make a personal matter of Miss Fletcher's case, I'll do all I can. Mind, I'm not making any promises at this juncture, but I will go so far as to say that if, after thorough investigation, your anxiety on her account is felt to be justified, then we will see if anything can be done ! Now, does that satisfy you, Mrs. Lindsay?"

"Yes, indeed," Rosamund said earnestly. "It's most reassuring because I'm quite sure that you wouldn't go as far as that unless you, too, intended to make a personal matter of it—and if that's so, then I'm quite sure something will come of it! For you must, I'm convinced, have a great deal of influence where the other Governors are concerned !"

It was the sort of compliment that Sir George himself might have paid, and Rosamund hadn't found it pleasant to use such tactics, but certainly they were successful. Sir George positively purred!

"Well, dear lady, I mustn't boast, but you may be right, and I will certainly exert it to the utmost in view of your confidence in me. One does like to live up to the expectations of one's friends—I hope I may call you that?"

"Of course," Rosamund murmured.

"Delightful! And fellow conspirators as well, of course. This shall be our little secret—we will form a Miss Fletcher Benevolent Appeal, shall we?" Sir George paused expectantly.

"What an amusing idea!" Rosamund said lightly. "I *knew* I could rely on you, Sir George!"

"I will let you know how matters progress," he promised expectantly.

"I shall be most interested to hear," Rosamund said cordially. "But of course, the really important thing is to let Miss Fletcher know as soon as possible if it's good news. It would, I'm sure, facilitate her recovery from her operation."

"Yes, of course," Sir George agreed without much interest. "I will take immediate steps—"

"Thank you *so* much!" Rosamund said earnestly. "Then I won't waste any more of your time, Sir George. Good-bye!" and rang off before he had time to say more.

For a moment or two she sat still at the desk, her elbows on its polished surface, her face buried in her hands.

She was reasonably sure that Miss Fletcher's future was now assured—Sir George would see to that. For one thing, his change in manner could only mean that it had suddenly occurred to him how dependent he and his fellow Governors were on the good will of John and, in hardly a lesser degree, herself. Indeed he had almost said as much. And then appealing to him in the way she had done had pandered to his vanity. He would just hate to admit that he hadn't got the influence necessary to sway the Board!

She gave an impatient little sigh. Was John right! Had everybody got their price? Was expediency always the controlling factor? It certainly seemed like it now—

adays, so why not run with the herd? Why put oneself at a disadvantage by believing in such old-fashioned things as disinterested kindness and generosity? It simply didn't pay! Much more sensible and far less painful to accept that as fact and harden one's own heart.

Her thoughts were interrupted by the arrival of a maid with her breakfast tray.

"Cook asked me to say that she's that sorry it's so late, madam, but somehow, with all the upset, the kitchen got sort of out of routine—" she apologised.

"It's all right," Rosamund said mechanically. "I'm only just ready for it. Thank you, Rose."

There were, she saw, two letters lying on the tray, but she left them unopened until she had poured out her coffee and drunk half of it. Then, leaving the food untasted, she turned her attention to the letters. The first she opened was from her bank manager, acknowledging her request that her account should now be in her married name. The second—she flinched as she saw the familiar handwriting—was from her aunt. It was very much to the point.

"It may come as a surprise to you to know that financially, I'm in very low water. Why? The usual reasons—ever-increasing overheads and less money being spent on luxuries.

"None the less, I'm confident that I can make out if I can keep going for another year. Unfortunately, I can't find anyone to agree with me—and who also has the capital to back me.

"So, naturally, I turn to you! You are now the wife of a very rich man to whom the ten thousand pounds I want is a mere trifle. In all probability, he has by now settled a pleasant amount on you, but whether he has or not, I want ten thousand and I mean to have it by fair means or foul.

"Understand, Rosamund, I mean that, and you'll be a fool to turn me down.

Ruth Hastings."

Rosamund didn't hesitate. Of course she couldn't do as her aunt wished, threats or no threats. She pushed the breakfast tray to one side and wrote a brief reply.

"What you ask is out of the question. Please understand that this is final.

Rosamund Lindsay."

She put the letter into an envelope, sealed and addressed it and then hesitated uncertainly with it balanced on the palm of her hand. It wasn't that she was afraid of her aunt's threats—she had already done so much harm that it was difficult to see what more she could do. But it was clear that she intended to make an issue of it, and that being so, it was doubtful if she would accept such a curt dismissal of her request.

There was, in fact, only one way in which to convince her—by explaining just why it was out of the question. And that Rosamund shrank from doing in writing, unreasonable though that was. Her determination to leave John was an admission that her marriage was in ruins and that it was beyond her ability to rebuild it, even if she wanted to. And yet—there was such a finality about the written word—

"I'll go and see her," she decided. "Tell her that I can't help her, let her make all the threats she likes and then explain why. It won't be easy, but it will put an end to it once and for all."

Having made up her mind, Rosamund wasted no time. She consulted a time-table, arranged to be taken by car to the nearest station and that done, changed into clothes more suitable for London. Finally she rang through to Mrs. Brickwell, explaining that she had to go to Town on business but she would be back in time for dinner.

"I think that's all—" she thought as she replaced the house phone. "Gloves, handbag, money—yes, that's everything." Then she caught sight of the letter she had written still lying on the desk. "I'll take it with me," she decided. "In case I can't get hold of Aunt Ruth."

It was as well she did take it, for her aunt was at neither the flat nor at the Salon. She had, it appeared, flown to Paris the previous evening and was not expected back until the following morning.

Rosamund left her letter at the flat with instructions to the hall porter to see that it was delivered immediately Miss Hastings returned. Then, with nothing left to do, she left the block of flats and wandered aimlessly along the busy, noisy street.

How incredible, she thought idly, that at one time not so very long ago this had been part of the familiar background of her life that she had accepted without question.

"But never again!" she decided. "Whatever happens, I'll never live in London again—never! It's intolerable."

The thought brought to her mind the need to decide just what she was going to do. In no circumstances, once she had left him, would she accept any money from John. Anything else was out of the question. She had enough money of her own saved which would tide her over for some time, but ultimately she must find work. Work as different as possible from that which she had previously done—it might not be easy—

Her thoughts were interrupted by the realisation that someone was obstructing her way. Automatically she stepped to one side, but came to a halt at the sound of a familiar voice.

"Rosamund, my dear, how very nice to have met you!" said Dr. Rob.

With a little gasp, Rosamund looked up into the pleasant, smiling face. There was no reproach there, no suggestion that he regarded anything that had happened as being in the least out of the ordinary. Reassured, Rosamund pulled herself together.

"How amazing that we should have happened to meet," she said lightly, "for I'm only up in Town for a few hours."

"Then perhaps we may regard the coincidence as a special dispensation of Providence," Dr. Rob suggested just as lightly, "and make the most of it! Have you lunched yet?"

"No, I haven't," Rosamund admitted reluctantly, realising what was coming and how she could possibly excuse herself. "But—"

"No?" Dr. Rob interrupted gaily. "Then perhaps my luck is in! Will you indulge an old fogey who doesn't often have the opportunity of entertaining a pretty girl by having it with me?"

It was impossible to refuse, for, without waiting for her

141

to reply, Dr. Rob had slipped his arm through hers and had hailed a passing taxi.

He took her to his club for lunch—a solid Victorian building which had a reassuring air of permanency about it. It was also very quiet and peaceful, and as he led Rosamund through the entry hall to the restaurant, he had the satisfaction of seeing that she relaxed a little—but only a little. Clearly, there was something very far wrong and he was determined to do his best to find out what it was—but not immediately. He must lead up to it gradually—gain her confidence.

"Now," he said cheerfully as they sat down at a table, "I don't know how you feel about it, but as far as I'm concerned, a light meal is preferable this weather. Does that suit you?"

"Yes, please," Rosamund said, pulling off her gloves. "As a matter of fact, I had rather a late breakfast."

"Oh? Did you sleep in?" Dr. Rob asked casually.

"No, nothing like that. Just there was an upset. One of the Orphanage staff had to be rushed off to hospital for an emergency operation," Rosamund explained, thinking with surprise how long ago all that seemed. "She'd had a grumbling appendix for some time and it came to a head suddenly."

"I see. But, Rosamund, how did you get involved in that? I mean, surely some other member of the staff could have dealt with the situation?"

"I expect they would have done if they'd been at the Orphanage," Rosamund said quickly. "But they haven't been very long at Lindacres, you know. And it takes time to get settled—"

"Also—" he looked at her thoughtfully, "I have an idea that you're the sort of person to whom other people turn in an emergency," he suggested quizzically. "Partly because you keep your head—and partly because they know that they can rely on your kind heart coming to the rescue?"

At that moment the waiter brought the iced melon Dr. Rob had ordered and she was able to avoid replying immediately, and to her relief, when Dr. Rob next spoke, it was on some entirely different and trivial subject.

For the rest of the meal he very skilfully maintained an

almost one-sided conversation about nothing in particular until, over their coffee, he said suddenly :

"I don't know if you're aware of it, but Miss Alice is in town at present. Would you like me to take you to see her?"

"Oh!" Rosamund shrank back a little and her coffee cup clattered slightly as she set it down in its saucer. "I—I'm not sure that Miss Alice would want to see me. You see I—it must seem to her that after all her kindness I treated her rather shabbily—though, honestly, I couldn't help it, Dr. Rob!"

Her eyes—so like another pair of eyes that he remembered—pleaded with him to leave it at that, and almost he was tempted to do so. The child was so near to breaking point that even the slightest extra pressure might be the last straw. And yet—he drew a deep breath.

"Rosamund, my child—" he spoke very gently and laid his hand momentarily over hers, "I'm not a doctor for nothing, you know! I can see, only too well, that you're in trouble. Won't you tell me what it is? I might be able to help."

"No, nobody can do that," Rosamund told him dully. "I—I can't talk about it. And anyway, it isn't fair to burden someone who is—"

"Who is practically a stranger?" he suggested, finishing her uncompleted sentence for her.

"That sounds ungracious when you're so kind," Rosamund admitted. "But yes, something like that."

"I see." Dr. Rob nodded, his fingers tapping a little tattoo on the tablecloth. "Well, if that's how it is, I'll do no more than ask you one question which, of course, you don't have to answer if you don't want to—"

He paused. Rosamund had stiffened defensively and her eyes were full of apprehension. But he had gone too far to draw back now.

"It's quite a simple question," he assured her. "Just this—will you tell me what your mother's name was?"

"Oh!" Rosamund almost laughed with relief. She had expected something very different from this! "Celia. Celia Elizabeth Hastings. But—but why do you want to know?"

For answer, Dr. Rob took his wallet from his pocket

and extracted a folded paper from it which he handed to her in silence.

Wonderingly, Rosamund unfolded it and saw that it was a marriage certificate. She read it once—and a second time—with a growing sense of amazement.

"But—but—" she stammered, her eyes still on the certificate.

"Yes," Dr. Rob said deliberately. "The certificate of the marriage of Celia Elizabeth Hastings and Robert Irwin Dexter. *My* marriage certificate—and your mother's. Now do you understand why your happiness means so much to me—*daughter*?"

CHAPTER NINE

ROSAMUND sat beside Dr Rob, her hand held comfortably in his. When they had left his club, he had brought her to his Harley Street flat and now, though she was still dazed at the discovery that she had a father, she was beginning to believe that it was true.

But there was much that they had to explain to one another. Dr. Rob told his story first, and he did not spare himself.

"Looking back, I realise what a thoroughly objectionable young man I was," he said wryly. "Cocksure of my own abilities, ambitious and singularly unappreciative of any other point of view than my own!"

Rosamund caught her breath at the description and Dr. Rob paused to look at her enquiringly, but she shook her head.

"No—nothing. Please go on."

"Well, to sum up in one word, I was arrogant beyond belief. I was quite sure that I could solve all the world's problems with one hand tied behind my back. And it was when I was at the callow stage of my development that I met your mother." He stared straight ahead as if he was gazing into the past and his voice softened as he went on: "She was quite lovely—like a fragile flower." He paused momentarily and then went on slowly as if he was choosing his words with great care. "And, like a flower, she needed support to withstand the storms of life. That she had always had from her sister Ruth. It's odd," he remarked parenthetically, "how often you find those two strains in the same family—the dominant type and the dependent. And, to be honest, I don't know what Celia would have done without Ruth. And so it worked out quite well for a time. But Ruth's ambition matched my own. She was beginning to make her name as a designer and she meant to miss no opportunities. Admittedly, she drove herself to incredible lengths—but she also drove Celia, who was her leading model, to a point beyond endurance."

"I know!" Rosamund said quickly. "She did the same to me. It makes you feel like a bird beating its wings against the bars of a cage that's too small anyhow!"

"Exactly," Dr. Rob agreed. "But you, my dear, had the strength to get out of the cage by your own efforts. My poor little Celia hadn't. And that was where I, in my arrogance, took command! I insisted that we should get married at once. Then I would have the right to defend her from Ruth's demands. At first, Celia wouldn't agree. She was by no means sure that I was right in thinking that Ruth would accept the fact that she no longer had exclusive claims on her devotion and would consequently be less demanding. But I over-persuaded her and we were married. And immediately it was clear that Celia had been right and I completely wrong. As soon as she heard what we'd done, Ruth sacked her!"

"Oh no!" Rosamund exclaimed incredulously. "Surely even she—her own sister—"

"That made no difference," Dr. Rob said grimly. "It may even have made matters worse in Ruth's eyes. So there we were, entirely dependent on what I earned—which wasn't very much—with Ruth taking care that Celia didn't get another job. As a result, we had to live in near squalor with little or no prospect of any improvement in the near future. I worked as hard as I knew how to, but that meant I was away for very long hours and Celia, poor child, was lonely and bored, particularly as there was no money to spend on entertainment of any sort. Inevitably, we both became disillusioned and being young, we each blamed the other for things having gone wrong."

He sighed and Rosamund gave his hand a sympathetic little squeeze which seemed to encourage him to go on.

"Just what would have happened if we'd been left to ourselves, I've often wondered. But of course, we weren't. Ruth hadn't finished with us yet—and she held the trump cards. She came to see Celia when I wasn't there and offered her work for a few days in an emergency. That, of course, was just the beginning. Every now and again, Ruth would offer her work and she would accept it. Then, out of the blue, I had the offer of a post in America. It was a wonderful chance for a young man, one which could make all the difference to my future career. I went home, very cock-a-hoop, and told Celia that all our troubles were over, we were leaving for America in a month's time. To my astonishment, she told me bluntly that I could go if I liked, but she wasn't coming with me. I'd let her down once and for all she knew I might do the same again. We quarrelled half the night—and then she admitted that Ruth had already offered her her old job. I knew it was hopeless then. A month later I left for America—alone. Celia and I never saw each other again. I wrote several times and I sent money to her, but I never had a reply. Yes, my dear?" as Rosamund made a convulsive little movement.

"Aunt Ruth told me that my mother wrote several times to you to tell you of my birth," Rosamund told him shakily.

"Letters which, I've no doubt, Ruth undertook to post," Dr. Rob suggested grimly, and when Rosamund nodded : "And never did, of course, though I've no proof of that—" he looked at her questioningly.

"You don't need to prove it, not to me," Rosamund said firmly. "Not only because I know Aunt Ruth, but because—I believe it because you say so !"

"Bless you for that, child !" Dr. Rob said, deeply moved. "It's the most wonderful thing you could possibly tell me !" He was silent for a while. Then, with an effort, he went on : "I had one letter—from Ruth, nearly a year later. It simply said that your mother had died of influenza and enclosed the certificate. Still nothing about you. And that, I concluded, was the end of a sad little story—until, by chance, you suddenly turned up at Yeoman's Reach. It *was* by chance, wasn't it?" he paused to ask.

"Yes, just chance," Rosamund confirmed gravely. "But *I* can't prove that!"

"You don't have to, my dear. Not to me! Well, Alice, bless her, realised how like your mother you are, even to the colour of your eyes. She sent for me and we put two and two together with the result that we concluded that you might well be my daughter, particularly as you gave your name as Hastings. That, and other odds and ends you let out—like never having been out of the country, which could mean that you'd never seen your birth certificate as you'd have had to do if you applied for a passport." He looked at her enquiringly.

"No, I've never seen it," she confirmed.

"Didn't it occur to you to wonder how it came about that your surname was the same as your mother's maiden name?" Dr. Rob asked. "Or did Ruth tell you that you were illegitimate?"

"She didn't tell me so, but when I grew up I assumed that was the case, particularly as she never spoke of my father. And though by the time I—I married John, she told me that I was legitimate, it didn't occur to me that the fact held any significance as regards my surname. I've become so accustomed to accept it as being Hastings, you see."

Dr. Rob drew a deep breath.

"Ruth is, in many ways, an extremely clever woman," he commented grimly. "Particularly when it comes to getting her own way. Sometimes I find myself wondering if, perhaps, she even convinces herself that she's telling the truth! Well, that's my story, my dear. Now tell me yours."

Rosamund didn't reply, and after a moment Dr. Rob put his arm round her shoulders and gave her an encouraging hug. At first there was no response. Then suddenly Rosamund turned and buried her face on his shoulder.

"There isn't really much to tell," she said in a muffled voice.

"Well, tell me what little there is," Dr. Rob coaxed. "Perhaps two heads will be better than one."

"There's nothing anybody can do," Rosamund said

dully. "It's too late! You see, John thinks I married him for his money and—"

"What!" Dr. Rob almost shouted. "The damned young fool!"

"No, he's not really," Rosamund denied tonelessly. "I don't see how he can believe anything else—there's so much evidence—"

Dr. Rob scowled portentously.

"Is Ruth mixed up in this?" he demanded. "She is? Then, my dear, I want you to tell me the whole story, please. I've a feeling that this time she may have over-reached herself! So tell me, Rosamund."

So, haltingly and occasionally interrupted by a pertinent question from Dr. Rob, Rosamund told him all that had happened—or almost all. She couldn't bring herself to tell him of that humiliating kiss—

At last it was finished and Rosamund stole a timid glance at him as he sat pondering and frowning.

"H'm, it doesn't help us much, does it? I'd hoped you'd be telling me something that would at least help to give us the whip hand over Ruth, but it seems that her luck still holds. We're just where we were—"

"Not quite," Rosamund suggested softly. "We've found each other—"

"So we have," Dr. Rob agreed, his expression softening momentarily. "And of course, that's something Ruth doesn't know—though I'm pretty certain she suspected we had much earlier—as we might well have done if I hadn't felt it advisable to make absolutely sure that you are my daughter before I spoke of it to you, and if I hadn't gone to America—America seems to be my jinx, doesn't it? That's the second time I've played into Ruth's hands by going there."

"What I don't understand is how Aunt Ruth found out where I was," Rosamund remarked. "I literally hadn't told a soul where I was going—how could I, I didn't know myself!"

"Well, one can only guess at that," Dr. Rob admitted. "But it seems to me more than likely that it was just one more case of Ruth's luck holding. You see, it probably never occurred to her that you'd have the courage to go off into the blue as you did with no haven in sight. And so it wouldn't be surprising if she assumed that you'd found out I was your father and had come to me. If she had *me* watched and followed, she could easily find out where my week-end retreat was and the rest followed. By incredible chance, her guess turned out to be right though her reasoning had been wrong." He paused, frowning. "Do you remember if you said anything that would tell her that though we had almost certainly met, you knew nothing of our relationship?"

"I'm not too sure—" Rosamund hesitated, trying to remember. "Yes, I did, I asked her if I was illegitimate. that was when she told me that you'd—you'd—"

"Deserted your mother?" Dr. Rob finished grimly. "Yes, of course, that told her that I'd said nothing so far—fool that I was!"

"Please don't blame yourself," Rosamund begged gently. "How could you have known?"

"I ought to have learned that where Ruth is concerned, one shouldn't take chances, however well intentioned," Dr. Rob replied morosely.

They sat in silence for several moments. Then, suddenly, Dr. Rob asked a question.

"Rosamund, why did you come up to Town today? You said that John was already up here. Was it to meet him?"

"Oh *no*!" Rosamund said quickly. "I came to see Aunt Ruth—"

"To see Ruth!" he stared at her in amazement. "But my dear child, why on earth—?"

"Because I had a letter from her this morning—" Rosamund began.

"A letter? You didn't tell me that!" Dr. Rob ejaculated. "What did she say? Have you got it with you?"

"No, I left it at Lindacres," Rosamund explained. "But I can tell you just what she said—" And as nearly as she could, she repeated the contents of the letter while Dr. Rob listened spellbound.

"And what did you tell her?" he asked with a softness which somehow made the question all the more urgent.

"I didn't see her. She's in Paris. so I left the letter I'd written before I decided that I would probably make more impression on her if I told her face to face—"

"And just what did you say in that letter?" Dr. Rob asked without raising his voice.

"I told her in so many words that it was out of the question to do as she asked."

Dr. Rob brought his hand down with a resounding thwack on the arm of the settee.

"That's it!" he exclaimed triumphantly. "That's what we wanted! Now we've got her! My dear, don't you see? If Ruth is desperate for money, she'll do anything to get it—even to the point of telling the truth!"

"But you don't understand," Rosamund said desperately. "I *meant* it. I haven't got the money to give her and I can't—I *won't* ask John for it! How can I when—" she bit her lip, unable to complete her sentence.

"I'm not suggesting that John should come into this at all," Dr. Rob said bluntly. He didn't add that, in the circumstances, he couldn't see John paying up even if he was approached. No need to hurt the child still further. "This is *my* job! If she gets any money at all, it will be mine! Is that clear?"

"Yes, but why should you—"

"Oh, for a variety of reasons. To begin with, I want to get things straightened out for you. That's the best reason of all. Then to clear myself beyond all doubt in your eyes of the neglect of which Ruth accused me. And finally—" his lips twisted in an unmirthful grin, "I must admit that it would give me tremendous satisfaction to get the better of Ruth at last! Yes, it's my job all right! But it wants thinking out carefully. There mustn't be any mistakes—"

His voice trailed away to silence. Rosamund leaned back and closed her eyes. It was wonderful to have discovered that Dr. Rob was her father. Perhaps even more wonderful to know that he hadn't callously ignored her very existence all these years. But in other ways, nothing was altered, nor would it be. It wouldn't make any difference to the way John felt, or the way she did. Whatever Dr. Rob—she couldn't get used to calling him "Father" yet—might say about getting things straightened out for her, there was no future for John and her. It was too late for that.

She was roused from her apathy by Dr. Rob saying with satisfaction:

"Yes, I think I've got it. When did you say Ruth was expected back?"

"Tomorrow morning."

"So she'll have your letter then. You, of course, will have one from her the following morning—"

"Will I?" Rosamund asked doubtfully. "You don't think that, seeing I've said I won't help her, she'll just carry out her threat—whatever it is?"

"Oh no," Dr. Rob said positively. "Not if she wants money so badly. And if she once broadcasts whatever it is she's so sure you don't want known, then she's lost her hold over you and she could whistle for all the money you might have paid her to keep quiet."

"I see. But—" Rosamund shook her head—"I simply can't think what there can be that she feels she can use to blackmail me like this. Because it is blackmail, isn't it?"

"It's blackmail, all right," Dr. Rob said sternly. "And of course, she may be bluffing and really there's nothing at all. But somehow, I don't think that's so. Don't misunderstand me, Rosamund. It isn't that I imagine for a moment that you've done something you shouldn't have, but Ruth is no fool. *She* thinks she's got something. So we must find out what it is—in other words wait for her next letter. Until that comes, I shall stay out of it. But once it does come, you must let me know *at once*. Then I'll go and see her. Is that clear?"

"Yes, quite clear," Rosamund said with a little shiver. "Father, is it true, do you think? Will people do anything for money?"

"A great many will, no doubt. But certainly not everybody. *You* know that because you're one of those who won't."

"Sometimes I've wondered if that's true," she told him despondently. "Perhaps I've got my breaking point like other people—" She looked at her watch and gave a little exclamation. "As late as that! I'll have to go now if I'm to be back in time for dinner."

"Stay and have it with me," Dr. Rob suggested, but Rosamund shook her head.

"I'd like to, but I think it would be better if I go back at the time I said I would—in time for dinner. You see, I said I was coming to Town on business, but if I'm late, it would look as if it was something more than that, and I just don't feel I can stand any more complications," she finished wearily.

Dr. Rob didn't argue.

"Right, my dear, if that's how you feel," he said, standing up. "There's just one other thing, though."

He went over to a small bureau, unlocked a drawer and took out a key which he handed to Rosamund.

"The key of this flat," he explained. "I want you to feel absolutely free to use it if ever and whenever you wish—and whether I'm here or not. Promise?"

Rosamund gave her promise and took the key. A few minutes later, she and Dr. Rob took a taxi to the station and he saw her off.

She reached Lindacres to find, to her relief, that nothing untoward had happened in her absence. Indeed, there was good news. Dr. Milward had phoned through to say that Miss Fletcher had stood the operation very well and that so far everything was going satisfactorily.

From John there was no message at all.

Just as Dr. Rob had predicted, on the next morning but one, a letter came from Ruth Hastings, even more malicious and to the point than the first one had been.

"You little fool, do you think I don't mean what I say, or that I'd blackmail you—oh yes, I know what it is!—if I hadn't got very good cause to know in just how strong a position I am to make you do what I want?

"Why? I'll tell you, my dear!

"I gather you've always assumed that your surname is the same as your mother's maiden name because you are illegitimate. Well, that's not so. Your parents were married, but I let you be known as Hastings simply because it suited me. But legally it isn't your name and never was.

"Consequently, when you got married, you made a false declaration and as a result, your marriage was not a legal one. A pity, isn't it, after all the trouble you took to hook a wealthy man!

"Well, you know best, no doubt, whether or not he'd like to be free of you—my own belief is that he would.

You see, I happened to see him dining at a London restaurant a few evenings ago, and believe me, the way he looked, it was very easy to see that your dear John is far from being a happy bridegroom. What have you done to disillusion him so soon, I wonder?

"*Still, disillusioned or not, it's up to you to get the money out of him. Do that and I'll hold my tongue. Refuse—and I will most certainly let your dear husband know that he's nothing of the sort! And then where will you be? Out in the cold, my dear, with all your efforts wasted!*

"*Wouldn't that be a pity?*

    Ruth Hastings."

Rosamund let the letter fall on to the desk and sat staring blindly at it.

So this was what her aunt was so sure gave her the whip hand! Well, since she measured everyone by her own standards, that was no doubt natural enough. It would simply never occur to her that, in fact, by her own action she had destroyed any possible chance she might have had of obtaining the help she wanted.

For, shorn of its malice and cynicism, which was really of no importance, one fact stood out. Here, beyond all argument, was the way of escape from an intolerable state of affairs. She and John were not legally married. That lovely service—all the vows they had taken—meant nothing at all. They never had. How very fitting that seemed, Rosamund thought bitterly, in view of all that had happened since.

But it was pointless to dwell on that. Married or not, John's future and hers lay apart. They both knew it. All that had changed was that now, presumably, it wouldn't take so long to make the break. Indeed, she must take the first steps in making it at once.

She pushed her hair back from her face, unconscious of the nervous tenseness which prompted the action for it seemed to her that she was entirely cool and collected.

First of all, she must ring through to her father.

Dr. Rob himself answered her so promptly as to suggest that he had been waiting for her call.

"I've had another letter—" she began, and came to a

full stop. Her mouth felt constricted and dry. Somehow it seemed impossible to put it into words—

"Yes, my dear?" Dr. Rob encouraged.

Rosamund swallowed convulsively.

"She says—that John and I aren't really married," she said baldly.

"Not married! But, Rosamund, surely—" Clearly Dr. Rob was taken aback.

Rosamund laughed mirthlessly.

"Oh yes, we thought we were! But, you see, apparently, if you get married in a name that isn't your own, it isn't legal. And of course, that's what I did."

"But without realising—"

"I don't suppose that makes any difference."

"Perhaps not. All the same, I'm not too sure—look, Rosamund, this will have to be gone into properly. We can't just take Ruth's word for it, you know!"

Rosamund's heart gave a convulsive leap. Everything had seemed so settled—so simple. Now it seemed that there might be a doubt—

"But so long as we don't know for sure, you can't stay on at Lindacres, Rosamund," Dr. Rob went on firmly. "You appreciate that?"

"Yes," she agreed faintly. Odd that she had been so determined to leave Lindacres, and yet now that there was no alternative, she should feel almost reluctant—

"Of course, you'll have to let John know at once," Dr. Rob continued. "By letter I think would be best."

"Very well," Rosamund promised. "But I shall have to leave it here for him. I—I don't know where he's staying in town."

"No?" Dr. Rob spoke calmly as if there was nothing unusual in a husband leaving his wife in ignorance of his whereabouts in this way. "Well, the delay can't be helped, in that case. But make very sure, Rosamund, that he will have it as soon as he returns. And also, it's essential that you should tell him where you are."

"Is it?" Rosamund said doubtfully. "Very well, if you say so. But there's one thing you must know before I come to you, Father—"

"Yes, my dear?"

"If it's true—if we're not married—then nothing will

persuade me to get married to him. And if we *are* married, then there will have to be a divorce."

"My dear, it's early days to talk of divorce," Dr. Rob said gently. "You've hardly given yourselves time to get to know one another—"

"I know it must seem like that to you," Rosamund admitted wearily. "But really, the trouble is that we didn't give ourselves time *before* we were married. Afterwards, it was too late."

"Well, we'll have to find out the truth about the legality of your marriage before we think of the next step," Dr. Rob pointed out. "Now, when can I expect you? Today?"

"Yes, if you don't mind," Rosamund said eagerly. The last thing she wanted was to meet John face to face. "Some time this afternoon?"

"Excellent! Oh, bring both of your aunt's letters, will you? I shall go and see her this evening and with those for evidence, she can hardly deny what she's been up to! That reminds me, did she tell you your real name?"

"No—she just said it wasn't Hastings."

"Just like her," Dr. Rob commented. "Still holding on to what she thinks is a trump, even if a small one! Well, never mind, she'll soon know now how little value it is to her. I must go now, my dear, I've a patient due in a few minutes. I'll see you this afternoon, then. Good-bye, Rosamund."

"Good-bye," Rosamund repeated mechanically, and rang off.

She sat very still for several minutes. Now she had the most difficult task of all to do—write her letter to John. She made several false starts before, at last, she scribbled away desperately and put the letter into an envelope without reading it through. It would have to do because, after all, what was there to do but simply make a bald statement of the facts?

It was late when Dr. Rob returned to the flat. He looked tired and troubled as if he carried a heavy burden on his shoulders. Rosamund jumped to the obvious conclusion.

"She wouldn't—?"

Dr. Rob sat down wearily in an armchair and leaned his head on one hand.

"Oh, she admitted everything—in writing," he said heavily.

"Then—?" Rosamund asked uncertainly.

Dr. Rob didn't answer immediately. Then he said slowly :

"I never thought I'd say this, Rosamund, but I've come away with a feeling of admiration for Ruth! Oh, not for what she's done—she's knowingly and without mercy sacrificed us all—first Celia and myself and then you and John—simply to suit herself. That is unforgivable. But none the less, she has very real courage which I, as a doctor, could not fail to recognise—and admire."

He paused and Rosamund waited in silence, puzzled at the turn events had taken.

"She has a very serious heart condition," he went on gravely. "So serious that the end may come at any time—"

"Oh no !" Rosamund exclaimed compassionately.

Dr. Rob looked at her curiously.

"So you can find it in your heart to pity her," he said gently. "I'm glad of that, Rosamund. Even though I know it makes you desperately vulnerable, I wouldn't have you hard-hearted !"

Rosamund shook her head. She hardly knew just what she did feel towards the woman who had contributed in such a large degree to the wrecking of her happiness, but she could at least recognise Ruth for what she was—a woman who, nearing the end of her life, stood utterly alone because she had never been able to command affection.

"Does she know?" she asked.

"Oh yes, she knows—she also knows that with care and rest she could hope to prolong her life for some time—though no one could say for how long. But she laughed—with quite genuine amusement—when I suggested that it would be wiser for her to retire. No, she intends to go out fighting and, for the life of me, Rosamund, I can't help but admire her courage !"

"Yes, I think I feel the same," Rosamund confessed thoughtfully. "All the same, it doesn't surprise me. When you come to think of it, she's never been afraid to take risks all her life!"

"True enough," Dr. Rob agreed. "Well, there it is. It's no excuse for her having tried to blackmail you, but if one *can* look at it through her eyes, she is genuinely desperate for money. She's in very low water—there's no doubt about that. She showed me her accountant's statement. There's also no doubt about it that, given a little time and sufficient money to tide her over, she'll get the Salon on its feet again. She convinced me of that—and I wasn't in a mood to be convinced, I need hardly say! She believes she can do it in a year and she intends to defy all the probabilities in an effort to do just that! Personally, I wouldn't say but what she may pull it off—from the point of view of her health, I mean," he added reflectively. "I've seen far too many people die when logically they should have survived and many, too, who have pulled through when there appeared to be no hope for them. It's a question of having guts—and something to live for. She has. It may not seem a very worth-while something to us, but to her that salon means everything."

"Yes, it does," Rosamund agreed. "Really, I suppose, that explains everything—" She pondered for a moment. "You know, Father, I feel I ought to offer to go back to her—"

"She wouldn't have you," Dr. Rob said bluntly. He had been afraid of a reaction of this sort from Rosamund and he was thankful that he could truthfully go on: "She made that quite clear. In fact, she sent you a message to the effect that she wanted neither help nor pity from you or anybody else. She said that she had always stood on her own feet and she preferred to do so now! No, my dear, there's nothing to be done beyond—" he stopped short.

"Beyond what you've already done," Rosamund said softly. "Because you've given her the money she wants, haven't you?"

"Yes, I have," Dr. Rob admitted. "Although, to my own surprise, I regard it less as being in payment for *this*—" he took several folded sheets of paper from his pocket, "than in the hope that she will live long enough to achieve her ambition. Strange, isn't it?"

"Not very. You say you're glad I'm not hardhearted, Father. Well, if I'm not, I think I owe that to something you've passed on to me!"

"Do you?" Dr. Rob looked at her, smiling rather wryly. "I don't know, my dear. Nor do I know, if it's true, whether or not you should thank me for it. As I said, it makes one extremely vulnerable."

Rosamund didn't reply and after a moment Dr. Rob stood up and handed the folded sheets to her.

"It doesn't make very pleasant reading, but none the less, I think you should read it. It may well prove helpful to you in sorting out your own problems. Then tomorrow I'll let my solicitor have it to deal with." He hesitated momentarily. "As a matter of fact, Rosamund, I have already had a word with him on the telephone, and he told me that since you were married in the name by which you had been known all these years he is of the firm opinion that your marriage is legal."

"I—see," Rosamund said dully.

"Well—" Dr. Rob, understanding her need to be alone to face her problem, yawned and stretched his arms, "I think I'll turn in now. This has been quite a day, and I've got a busy one tomorrow. Everything satisfactory in your room?"

"Yes, thank you," Rosamund assured him.

"Splendid! Goodnight then, my dear." He hesitated and then, almost shyly, went on: "I'm glad that—at last—my roof is giving you shelter, Rosamund."

He bent to kiss her, gave her shoulder a gentle pat or two and left her.

Rosamund stood looking down at the sheets of paper she held. Then, without unfolding them, she laid them down on a table. After all, what was the good of reading what Aunt Ruth had said? Nothing anyone said or wrote could help, as her father had put it, sort out her problems. It was too late for that.

Three days later John came to the Harley Street flat. Rosamund answered his ring and when she opened the door and saw who it was, she fell back a pace or two.

"I—I asked you not to come here," she reminded him breathlessly.

"I know you did," he admitted. "But I felt it was necessary for us to meet. However, if you're alone, perhaps you'd prefer that I should come back some other time?"

He stood still, waiting for her reply. Rosamund, feeling that his consideration had put her at a disadvantage, gave him a quick, uncertain look.

How serious he seemed to be. How absolutely lacking his expression was of all emotion—as if he was keeping a very tight hold on himself. Well, she would show him that she could match his self-control—

"Since you're here, you may as well come in," she said with deliberate indifference, and led the way to the sitting room. "Do sit down," she added as impersonally as if they had just met for the first time.

But John preferred to stand—not very near to her, but so that he had a full view of her face. For an appreciable time, neither of them spoke. Then John said quietly:

"First of all, may we deal with the question of your maiden name since, as you will appreciate, it's something that must be cleared up as quickly as possible." And when Rosamund nodded, he went on: "Will you tell me a little more about it all? How you came to be called Hastings when your real name was—what was it, Rosamund? You didn't tell me that."

"Dexter," she told him reluctantly.

"Dexter!" John exclaimed. "do you mean that Dr. Rob—?"

"He's my father," Rosamund explained matter-of-factly. "And though I don't expect *you* to believe it, until this week, I had no idea that was so, any more than he had known, all these years, that he had a daughter."

"I see." John made no attempt to rise to the unmistakable taunt at his probable incredulity. "Will you tell me how that came about? Please understand, I'm not just asking out of curiosity, but because I *must* know since I'm as deeply involved in the matter as you are."

It was true, of course, so as briefly and clearly as possible, Rosamund told him the whole story. John listened in silence, but when it was finished, he drew a deep breath.

"And you say that your aunt had made a written statement of her share in it all?"

"Yes."

"Good! That's likely to be very helpful. I'll let my solicitor know and he'll tell us what the next step must be. He will, of course, need to see the statement."

"I suppose so."

Silence fell between them. Then, as if it took considerable effort to ask the question, John said:

"Rosamund, have you—or has Dr. Rob—made any enquiries about the legality of our marriage?"

Rosamund nodded and then, her head still bent, stared at the ring which John had put on her finger.

"In that case," he went on deliberately, "you know that beyond doubt—we are husband and wife?"

"Yes, I know that," Rosamund admitted in a voice completely devoid of emotion. "A pity, isn't it?"

CHAPTER TEN

"IS it?"

Rosamund looked up, startled. She had said that it was a pity that their marriage had been legal and John was questioning the statement.

"But of course it is." Deliberately she kept her voice steady, unemotional. "Since we both feel it was a mistake."

"Not as far as I'm concerned," John stated unequivocally.

Rosamund stared at him in amazement.

"But you said—"

"That I wished to heaven we hadn't got married," John nodded. "Yes, and I meant it! For the first time, you see, I realised—" he paused. "Look, Rosamund, though I admit that you've every justification for sending me packing, will you let me tell you all that led up to that—incident?"

"If you like," she shrugged indifferently.

"Thank you," he acknowledged gravely. "I'll cut it as short as I can, but I need to go back a bit—to a time before you and I met. My father was an extremely rich man and a very generous one. Too generous, perhaps, as far as I was concerned. There simply wasn't any need or incentive for me to work, so, as most young men in that situation would probably do, I devoted all my energies to having a good time. Then my father died and instead of having an allowance, however generous, I was a rich man in my own right."

"*'One of the most eligible bachelors of the day*'," Rosamund murmured.

"Just that," John agreed. "At first, though it may seem improbable to you, I didn't appreciate what that meant. And then something happened which drove the fact home beyond all doubt. There was a girl—I fell in love with her and I believed she cared for me. I was on the point of asking her to marry me when—I overheard a conversation between her and my best friend." He paused and then went on grimly : "I heard Viola admit that she loved him, but it was out of the question for them to think of getting married since he was a poor man without prospects and she—she was very frank about it—hankered for the fleshpots. So, she told him coolly, she intended marrying me because I could give her everything that she wanted. He took it badly—tried to persuade her to change her mind. When he found that was impossible, he told her that this was the end and that he hoped he never saw her again. And then she laughed and told him that there was no need for melodrama. It wasn't as if she loved me—he had no need to be jealous. They'd have to be very careful, of course, but—she didn't finish the sentence, but there was no mistaking her meaning. Though she would be married to me, they would be lovers. He turned the idea down flat—but she was very lovely and he was deeply in love, so—" John shrugged his shoulders. "Perhaps I ought to have told them then and there that I'd overheard them. But I didn't. I was too sick at heart. I simply went away and left them to draw their own conclusions." He drew a deep breath. "And while I'm not asking you to regard this as being an excuse for—all that has happened between you and me, I think perhaps you'll agree that I had some reason for becoming a misanthrope where money was concerned."

He looked at Rosamund enquiringly as if doubtful of her probable reactions.

"*Every* reason," Rosamund declared with a vehemence that surprised her.

"Thank you, that's generous of you," John said quietly. "Inevitably, of course, I lost faith in myself. I'd always realised that some of my circle were opportunists who regarded friendship—or what passed as that—as a means of feathering their own nests. But they didn't really matter. Those two did. I'd thought that they both, in different ways, really cared for me. I'd have sworn it! At first, I was too stunned to think very coherently. Then I began to ask myself what I'd ever done to merit love or loyalty, and the answer to that was—nothing! I'd played my way through life on the money my father had earned. I'd never made the least effort of my own—except for an odd bit of writing now and again and that only in a dilettante sort of way, although I had had the idea for a play in my mind for some time. Now I decided that I'd really get down to it. I'd go away, live on the money my mother had left me and see if I could make anything of myself. I hunted for somewhere quiet where I wasn't known and found the *Seven Stars*. It seemed ideal—then you turned up—"

Until now, Rosamund had listened in silence, sitting very still. Now she moved restlessly.

"John, please, is it any good going on? It can't get us anywhere, you know. I mean, you've filled in the details, but I'd guessed that it must be something like that when I read the caption under your picture. That was why I—" she checked herself hastily, but not before it was clear what she had been going to say.

"Why you said nothing to me about your discovery?"

"Yes," Rosamund admitted slowly. "I think, without actually putting it in words to myself, I knew then that it wasn't really *me* you'd fallen in love with. It was just that *I* was in love with *you* and not with your money."

"You're quite right." He spoke dispassionately, almost coldly, but he walked over to the window and stood with his back to her before he continued deliberately :

"There's nothing I can say which can justify me in my own eyes for what I did. Don't think I didn't find you attractive—I did. But your chief attraction to me was the fact that your love was disinterested. That boosted my ego tremendously. I felt that, after all, I did amount to something!"

"Don't!" Rosamund begged, flinching at the bitterness in his voice.

"Why not? I've got beyond the point where I'm willing to sail under false colours, even to get what I want. Besides, you've a right to know and to condemn me for that and for my refusal to believe you told me the truth."

"But I don't condemn you for that—I never did," Rosamund protested. "After all, it was only my bare word—"

"That should have been enough," John insisted sternly. "Even the little I knew of you should have told me that!" He paused. "Then—Lindacres. And in a breath, it seemed, you became a different person. Not the sweet, unworldly, trusting girl I thought I'd married. Nor the calculating gold-digger I afterwards believed you to be, but a loyal companion who stood by me in an emergency and to whom everybody turned for help, confident that you'd play fair and make the right decisions. Oh yes, that's true," as Rosamund made a little gesture of dissent. "Mrs. Brickwell, Cook, Miss Fletcher—they all looked to you for leadership because they knew they could trust you to be both practical and kind. And the same goes for Dr. Milward and young Ferris and Weeks. Even Sir George—" He paused and then repeated slowly: "Sir George. I suppose you didn't realise, Rosamund, that I was absolutely eaten up with jealousy that evening he dined with us?"

"But why? I didn't like his sort of compliments any more than you did."

"I wasn't in any mood to appreciate that," John confessed wryly. "You see, short though the time has been, it's been long enough for me to realise what a blind fool I was ever to have thought that money came into it. Over and over again you proved yourself to be loyal and sincere and—altogether desirable. Is it any wonder that *this* time, I fell in love with you—*you*, not just as a salve to my injured vanity, as a real person."

163

"No, John, no!" Rosamund's hands flew up as if to defend herself from an actual blow.

"It's true. Quite true," he said doggedly. "Though I've no way of proving it. Particularly seeing that—it's the fact that I tried to snatch what should only have been mine if it came as a gift from you that you can't forget or forgive, isn't it?"

She nodded silently, her lips pressed close together.

"Yes, of course it is. Before—all this trouble, your kisses had been so sweet, so generous that I knew mine were welcome to you. And so, when I felt you shrink away from me, I knew what I'd done—and I loathed myself. That was why I said we shouldn't have got married. In every possible way I'd betrayed your trust in me and, as a result, I'd lost you! If only I'd waited a little instead of rushing you into getting married so soon, I might have learned—"

Rosamund didn't reply. Everything he had said was true—there was nothing more for either of them to add. But John seemed to think differently.

"I told you that I had come to Town to see my solicitor about the Orphanage and Lindacres. That was perfectly true, but all that was settled in one comparatively short interview. For the rest of the time I was trying desperately to discover some way in which to repair the damage I'd done. I came back to Lindacres to beg you to give me a chance to do that, though I'd no right to expect that you would. When I got there, I found your letter waiting for me and I knew that my task would be doubly hard since you so clearly wanted to have nothing more to do with me." He paused as if expecting a reply, but when it didn't come, he went on haltingly: "So it comes to this—we are married. But you need never again be afraid that I'll try to snatch at the shadow. I want the substance of love, Rosamund. And I want you to have it as well. But I can only *tell* you that. Only time can prove to you that it's true. So that's what I'm asking you to do, give me time—will you do that? Because more than anything else in the world, I want you for my wife. So don't put me out of your life, for if you do—" He left the sentence unfinished, but the torment in his eyes completed it for him.

But Rosamund hardened her heart. John had hurt her too badly for her to be willing ever to trust him again. Why, he himself had said that he had no right to ask it of her.

She heard him speak again, very quietly yet with an emphasis which was convincing.

"If ever you come to me, it will have to be of your own free will, Rosamund!"

"Then it will be never!" Rosamund declared passionately.

"That may well be," John acknowledged gravely. "But those are my terms. I don't want you on any others!"

And without waiting for her reply, he turned and walked quickly out of the room. A moment later she heard the outer door close.

During the next two weeks Rosamund saw John twice—both times briefly at the solicitor's office and with Dr. Rob present as well. There were statements to be made and sworn and documents to be signed, but on each occasion, once the business was concluded and they reached the street, John had said a brief good-bye and had left them.

Both times Rosamund was left with a feeling of anticlimax. Despite John's insistence that she had no need to fear him, she *was* afraid. Afraid that despite all the dictates of common sense, he would somehow persuade her to surrender to him. How or why that was to come about, she did not stop to think. Simply, she had made up her mind that she would not retreat a single inch from the stand she had taken. The past was over and done with. The door to it was firmly shut and that was how it was going to remain.

So she told herself on each occasion when she set out with her father to meet John and deliberately braced herself to resist even the slightest move on his part towards reconciliation.

But he had not made any such attempt. His manner had been impersonal, businesslike and courteous—nothing more. There was nothing for her to resist, which made her feel rather foolish, though not entirely reassured. John *might* have accepted her refusal to give him the chance he asked for as definite and final—or he might be deliberately putting her off her guard. But it really didn't matter which, she told herself firmly. Meeting John for the purpose of straightening out the tangle of her having been married in the wrong name was one thing. It was unavoidable. But to meet him on a social footing was a very different matter and a state of affairs which she could and would see never happened. So that, very definitely, was that. And John would have to realise it.

All the same, she wished she hadn't got so much time on her hands. For so many years she had been accustomed to working hard and though the time had come when she had desperately needed a holiday, the desire for relaxation had gone. What she wanted more than anything else was for time to pass as quickly as possible, and to work hard was, she was sure, the only way to bring that about.

She explained this to Dr. Rob, but though he agreed that she was right in principle, he was far from encouraging when it came to the questions of her putting precept into practice. In fact, he asked her point blank not to do so, and it was a request which, coming from him, she hadn't the heart to refuse.

He had been so good to her, but more than that, she was very much aware of the warmth of his feeling for her and the deep satisfaction which it gave him to look after the daughter he had only so recently known existed. Satisfaction—and something more. Peace of mind. Rosamund knew that he blamed himself to a large degree for the estrangement from her mother, and in caring for her, he felt he was making a belated atonement.

So she agreed to wait for a time before looking for work and turned her hand to whatever she could to occupy her mind. And here Dr. Rob helped. He introduced her to the big London teaching hospital at which he was a consultant and Rosamund quickly found herself involved in a variety of ways. She helped with the shop on wheels which did the rounds of all the wards, and with the hospital library as well. She wrote letters for patients who for one reason or another couldn't do it for themselves, and she did her best to amuse children bored by enforced inactivity. It was satisfying work, but it was too piecemeal to be entirely absorbing. However, it did suggest the possibility of training for some full-time hospital work, and she wondered if that was the reason why Dr. Rob had got her interested in it. If it was, he made no mention of the idea, evidently feeling that the decision must be entirely hers.

Nor was that the only evidence of his tact and understanding. Knowing just how much his weekends on the *Rosebud* meant to him, she had dreaded the possibility that he might take it for granted she would go with him on these trips. But that would have been something she would have had to refuse him. That brief interval of happiness when she had lived in a fool's paradise was too bitter a memory for her to want to recall it. However, the question didn't arise, for Dr. Rob suggested that, since she had seen so little even of her own country, they might do some exploring together. Thankfully, Rosamund agreed, and the first weekend they spent at a centuries-old hotel in Suffolk, which was almost as unknown to Dr. Rob as to her. She liked the tranquil, unspoilt countryside, and if the two of them didn't talk very much, they were none the less conscious of a sense of companionship.

The second weekend they spent at the home of some old friends of Dr. Rob's in the heart of Sussex, and though Rosamund didn't enjoy that so much, she admitted to herself that it was a good thing to meet people. It compelled one to forget one's own troubles.

Miss Alice felt old and tired and dispirited. Everything had gone wrong and so far as she could see there was nothing that could be done to put matters right. And such a short time ago everything had looked so promising. She knew, none better, just how much Rob regretted his share in the failure of his marriage. Then, at last, it had looked as if he was going to get some happiness out of it. She'd rejoiced wholeheartedly with him over Rosamund's unexpected arrival in his life, not least of all because she had been able to help there. But now much of his joy in the discovery that he had a daughter had been ruined by other people—by Rosamund herself, by John and, of course, by Ruth. She knew the whole story from Rob's letters and because it was his happiness which mattered most to her, she felt cross and impatient with the people who had stood in the way of its fulfilment.

"Bother them and their complexes and inhibitions," she muttered irritably. "Why should any of them expect that life should be arranged just to suit them? If they were less concerned with getting what they want out of it and thought more—my poor old Rob!"

In this brooding state of mind, even painting brought no solace. She found difficulty in concentrating and she was thoroughly dissatisfied with her watercolours of the canal scenes which had once provided such satisfying material.

"No life in 'em," she said disgustedly, and tore them up into fragments. "Might as well give up and go back to Town—"

But she stayed on, lonely and disconsolate and yet oddly reluctant to leave the *Pride of London*.

"Almost as if I felt that somehow or other I'll be able to help, just staying here," she mused wonderingly. "though for the life of me, I don't see how that can make sense! Oh well, I'd better make a cup of tea, I suppose!"

Drinking her tea, she made up her mind that she would stay just two more days. If nothing happened by then, she would admit defeat—

The very next day John turned up. Miss Alice, sitting idly on deck in the sunshine, saw him come through the gate in the hedge and caught her breath. Had she been right? Was there a purpose behind her decision to stay on here? It made one wonder—

As he reached the gangplank of the *Seven Stars* he saw her, hesitated and then walked slowly towards her.

"Good afternoon, Miss Alice."

She looked at him with unfriendly eyes.

"And what are you doing here?" she demanded.

"My tenure of the *Seven Stars* expires in a few days' time," he explained equably, ignoring her truculent manner, "and as I'm not proposing to renew it, I must clear out my gear."

"In that case, I'll pack Rosamund's clothes and you can take them as well," Miss Alice said briskly, watching intently for his reaction to that.

John frowned. He had been hoping that his visit might coincide with a time when Miss Alice happened to be away, but his luck was out.

"There's not much point in me doing that," he said coldly. "Rosamund, as you surely know, has left me and is living with her father."

"Yes, I do know," Miss Alice admitted tartly. "And I never heard such nonsense in all my life! Quarrelling before you've been married five minutes—you ought to be ashamed, the pair of you!"

Without replying, John turned deliberately and walked in the direction of his own boat, but Miss Alice hadn't finished with him.

"That's right, run away!" she called waspishly after him. "That's all you young folk ever do if you don't get your own way! No backbone, that's your trouble!"

John wheeled and came back. They confronted one another, two very angry people.

"You don't know what you're talking about," he declared loudly.

"No? Then suppose you tell me?" Miss Alice snapped, quite unperturbed by this irate young man who towered so threateningly above her. "And kindly don't shout at me! My hearing is perfectly good, I'm glad to say."

"I'm sorry," John said impatiently. "I shouldn't have spoken to you like that. But this is Rosamund's business and mine. I can't discuss it with you."

"No? Even though the minx is running circles round you and you haven't a notion what to do next?" Miss Alice said quizzically.

"I—" John began, and stopped short. "Look, Miss Alice, I'm sure you mean to be kind, but really—"

"Now, as I see it, this is the situation," Miss Alice said briskly just as if he hadn't spoken. "For some reason, you and Rosamund have, to use a nice, old-fashioned phrase, fallen out with one another. No, don't worry, I'm not asking you to tell me the reason for that, though, at a guess, I'd say it's something more than just your wretched money, isn't it?"

"Yes," John admitted curtly.

Miss Alice looked at him consideringly. Rob, not unnaturally, perhaps, blamed him rather than Rosamund for the estrangement, but she wasn't so sure. Usually there were faults on both sides, and anyway, she'd always found something likeable about John, despite his inclination to scowl so blackly—as he was doing now.

"I wonder how much you know about the way a woman's mind works?" she remarked meditatively.

John shrugged his shoulders and earned a nod of approval.

"Well, at least you know your own limitations," she commented drily. "Which is more than most men do!" She paused and then went on almost casually: "But even so, of course you know that the quickest way of persuading a woman to admit that she's wrong is to apologise for the offence as if you were the culprit."

"You may be quite right," John said distastefully. "But I'm not interested in double-dealing of that sort. In any case, it doesn't apply here."

Miss Alice made no comment, but a question was so obviously in her mind that John's annoyance mounted. He'd been a fool to rise to that gibe of hers—if he'd ignored it, she'd have been left high and dry. But now—wasn't the simplest thing to tell her the truth?

"The fault for what has happened lies with me alone," he told her harshly. "Rosamund is not in the least to blame."

Still Miss Alice said nothing. John scowled. Confound this inquisitive, interfering old woman—

"She is fully aware that I admit this and also that I greatly regret—" he left the sentence unfinished and went on doggedly: "You will have to accept the fact, as I have had to, that the decision rightly rests with Rosamund. I absolutely refuse to coerce her in any way and I most sincerely hope, Miss Alice, that neither you nor anyone else attempts to do so. Is that clear?"

"Oh yes, quite clear," Miss Alice assured him placidly. "Thank you for explaining. Of course, it's a pity, but there it is, these things happen and one has to accept the fact! But one can't help feeling that, the way things have turned out, it would really have been better if your marriage hadn't been legal, wouldn't it?"

Again John turned his back on her—but not before she had had a fleeting glimpse of the desolation too deep and bitter to share with anyone.

"Oh, poor boy, poor boy!" she thought compassionately. "He'd give anything—everything—he's got to get her back! I do wonder what—but really, that matters less now than the fact that he's played himself into an impossible position! It's all very fine and noble to say that he's to blame and he won't have her coerced, but what that means is that he's robbed himself of any chance of making good in his eyes because he won't go near her. I wonder—" her eyes narrowed in the way they did when she wanted to concentrate on one particularly important detail of a painting. "Yes—I think he asked Rosamund to give him a chance to do just that—and she refused," she decided. "So now, unless Rosamund makes a move, they'll drift further and further apart—and somehow, I doubt whether she will. Not with her upbringing!"

She frowned deeply, considering this. Ruth's fangs had been drawn as regards making any future trouble, but had the damage already been done? Despite the sophisticated background which Rosamund had known, it wouldn't be surprising if she was almost completely inexperienced in the ways of men. Of course, she must have met plenty, but one didn't need to be very perceptive to conclude, particularly when one remembered past history, that Ruth would see to it that the child never had a man friend. She was far too valuable an asset to Ruth for that to be allowed to happen! Which would inevitably mean that the child had no idea that the same man could, at times, be a blundering hobbledehoy and at others, far more vulnerable and sensitive than any woman could ever be.

Nor would Rosamund ever learn that this inherent contradictoriness is an infuriating, intriguing and—altogether lovable male characteristic which makes life for a woman worth living—if she really loves her man.

"Of course, she'd say she doesn't," Miss Alice sighed impatiently. "And so long as she sees nothing of him, she'll be able to convince herself that's true! Dear me, it's very difficult to think of anything—"

The telephone bell was ringing as Rosamund and her father came into the flat. They had been to the theatre and were rather late—a fact on which Dr. Rob commented on as he picked up the receiver.

"And I hope to goodness it isn't an emergency patient,"

he commented wryly. "I'm beginning to feel my years and I need a good night's sleep. Yes, Robert Dexter speaking," he said into the instrument. "Who? Mrs. Watchett at the shop! Yes, what's the trouble, Mrs. Watchett?"

His expression changed from one of mild vexation to one of extreme concern as he listened for several moments to Mrs. Watchett's voluble flow of speech which paused now and again, but only so briefly as to give him time to say: "Yes, yes, I understand—" at intervals.

Rosamund stood rigidly beside him, unable to guess what was wrong from the one-sided conversation, but feeling more and more tense and apprehensive. It was evidently something serious—

At last Mrs. Watchett came to a breathless halt and Dr. Rob was able to speak.

"Yes, I quite understand, Mrs. Watchett," he said briskly. "And I will make the necessary arrangements without fail. I'll also ring the hospital to see if they consider them satisfactory—have you got the number?" He scribbled it down on the nearby pad. "Yes, I've got that—what's that? Yes, I'll ring you as well when it's all fitted up. Either tonight or first thing tomorrow morning. Thank you very much for letting me know! Good night!"

He replaced the instrument but stood for a moment with one hand still on it, his lips pursed. Then he slowly paced up and down the pleasant room once or twice, deep in thought.

"Father—?"

He gave a little start as if he had suddenly realised Rosamund's presence and came to a halt facing her.

"Alice has had an accident," he said abruptly. "Dropped something heavy on her foot and has broken a couple of bones in her instep. She's in hospital now, but it was some time before she was found. If I've told her once, I've told her twenty times that she ought not to be alone on that damned boat with nobody within hail—"

"Oh, poor Miss Alice!" Rosamund exclaimed with a sympathy which was yet tinged with inexplicable relief. "I *am* sorry!"

"Are you?" Dr. Rob laid his hand on her shoulder. "How sorry?"

"I—I—" Rosamund stammered, guessing what was coming.

"I've realised, of course, that you haven't wanted to go back to the canal, and that's understandable enough," Dr. Rob said deliberately. "But now I'm asking you to forget your personal feelings and to go there to look after Alice."

"But if she's in hospital—" Rosamund demurred.

"They're keeping her in until the day after tomorrow," Dr. Rob said shortly. "And that's longer than it would be if she were younger. And these days there aren't enough beds or staff to waste them on people who don't need them. No, she can't stay there, but they want her to be in the neighbourhood so that she can keep in touch with them. So she'll be going back to the *Pride of London*. But she'll be in a plaster and that means she must not be alone—and it must be a woman that's with her, of course."

Rosamund didn't reply immediately. Then she asked:

"Father, who—who was it that found Miss Alice after the accident?"

"Young Sid Watchett. Fortunately it was his day for delivering her supplies, and for once, in a way he showed some sense. He ran back to the shop and his mother phoned for the ambulance."

So it hadn't been John—she had been half suspicious, but after all, he, no more than herself, would want to go back there. Even so, it would be hard enough, but there seemed no alternative—

"All right, I'll go," she promised. "Just when will she be back?"

"I'll get through to the hospital and find out," Dr. Rob said, going back to the telephone. "You'll need to go down the day before to get everything ready."

Rosamund stood on the deck of the *Pride of London*. She had come down from Town early that morning and now, in the late afternoon, with everything spick and span for Miss Alice's reception, she had time on her hands. And that was the last thing she wanted, for in these surroundings how could she help but recall those earlier days which she had spent here?

Never in all her life had she been so happy and

confident. She had been so sure that golden days for John and herself stretched ahead in a limitless procession. But instead of that, so soon, she had found disillusionment and heartbreak. And never again, she knew, would it be possible for her to experience such enchantment. It was the sort of thing which could only happen once.

In London, it had seemed possible to accept that and shut the door firmly on the past. Even those brief meetings with John at the solicitors' hadn't disturbed her very much because it had all seemed so impersonal, as if they were both different people from the ones they had been.

But now, here, it was different. Memory stirred and would not be stilled. All the little things, all the important ones that had gone to make up those halcyon days were as clear to her mind's eye as when they had actually happened from the moment when an irate John had shaken her to consciousness when she had dropped off to sleep in his cabin to the moment of culminating bliss when he had taken her into his arms and told her that he loved her.

She beat her hand on the boatrail in a mood of hopeless frustration. Would she, no matter how she tried to forget, always be at the mercy of these bitter-sweet memories of hers? Would they, all unbidden, suddenly possess her, as they were doing now, stronger than any resolution she might make to leave them in the past?

"They shan't, they shan't," she told herself passionately. "I must forget—I *must*! There's no alternative!"

But there was. She could give John the chance he asked for—let him persuade her—

"Never!" she declared as fiercely as if someone else, not herself, had made the suggestion. "It's finished, absolutely finished!"

She would stop thinking about John, now and for all time. And instead of moping out here like this, she would get herself a meal—

She turned to go into the galley, and at that moment, John came through the gate in the hedge.

CHAPTER ELEVEN

SO it was a trap! A trap to bring John and her together again. What was more, not only John himself was responsible for it. Her father and Miss Alice, people whom she believed she could trust and rely on, were as much involved as he was.

She said as much to John, but he denied it, not indignantly, but matter-of-factly and with a suggestion of the tolerance one would show to a child encountering a problem it could hardly be expected to understand. To Rosamund, he sounded insufferably patronising and self-confident.

"Nothing like that," he assured her.

"I don't believe it," Rosamund declared stubbornly.

"You mean you think it's a put-up job?" John suggested bluntly. "That Miss Alice didn't have an accident at all? That she and your father and I put our heads together to devise a plan which would trick you into coming here?"

"Yes, I do think that," Rosamund told him defiantly.

John shook his head.

"You're wrong. Oh, I grant you it would have been a most ingenious scheme, but there's one snag. The hospital. Do you honestly think that we could have persuaded the authorities to play our game if there had been nothing wrong with Miss Alice? Of course we couldn't!"

And that, she had to acknowledge, was undoubtedly true.

"Well, if it wasn't that—" she began impetuously, and stopped short.

"If it wasn't that—then what? If, as you believe, it was a put-up job, then there's only one alternative, you know. That it wasn't an accident at all. In other words, that it was done deliberately either by me or by Miss Alice, persuaded by me. Well? Does either sound very likely to you?"

"No," Rosamund admitted grudgingly. "All the same, can you deny that you came here because you knew I'd be here?"

"Oh yes, I can deny that," John said easily. "I came down here several days ago to clear my gear out of the

Seven Stars because my tenancy was on the point of expiring. Unfortunately, I had to go to Lindacres on the day that the accident happened, and so not only was I not here to lend a hand, but I neither knew about it or that you were here until I called in at the shop a short time back."

"Well, now that you do know, the least you can do is go away as quickly as possible," she insisted doggedly. "Surely you can see that!"

But John shook his head, his jaw set obstinately.

"No, Rosamund, I can't! The way I look at it is this—you've refused to give me a chance to redeem myself in your eyes, but fate or luck, whichever you like to call it, has played right into my hands and I intend to make the most of my opportunity!"

"But you said that you only wanted me to come back to you of my own free will," she reminded him indignantly.

"I still say that, and I mean it. It's because I feel it so strongly that I'm determined *you* shall have a chance!"

"A chance for what?" Rosamund asked scornfully. "To make a fool of myself all over again?"

"If you like to put it that way," John conceded. "But as I see it, a chance to discover just what it is that your will really wants if you give it the freedom to decide. No, let me finish!" There was a new authority in his manner which checked the furious words on Rosamund's lips. "I've hurt your pride badly. I know that. I also know that you believe I've killed your love for me. Well, I don't believe that! Oh, not because I'm such a terrific chap that I'm irresistible! Far from it. No, it's on you that I'm pinning my faith. I believe that because you're incapable of feeling a shallow emotion—the sort that can easily be destroyed—you do still love me—"

"No!" Rosamund disclaimed passionately. "You're wrong—quite wrong!"

"Perhaps. But I intend to find out for certain. Is that clear?"

"Quite," Rosamund told him stonily. "But you're wasting your time."

John regarded her with an intentness that made her feel

uneasy. It was as if he was striving to penetrate her very innermost thoughts.

"It couldn't be, I suppose," he said thoughtfully, "that you're taking this line because, though in your heart of hearts you want us to make a fresh start, just as I do, you're afraid to admit it?" And then, as she didn't reply, he went on deliberately : "You can't keep on running away from life, you know, Rosamund. Or if you do, you can't hope ever to be able to live at peace with yourself."

She looked at him with wide, startled eyes. Then, with a shake of her head, she turned away and John made no attempt to stop her. But he called after her :

"Let me know if there's any way in which I can lend a hand to help Miss Alice !"

Of course she wouldn't call on John for help! Rosamund was determined about that, and really she could not see that it would be necessary to do so. Between them, she and her father had surely thought of everything. She had brought a folding wheelchair down in the car with her, and Mr. Mangell, the ironmonger, had been rung up to see if he could possibly make up a timber ramp so that the chair could be run up and down the two steps from the living quarters to the deck without difficulty. He'd turned up trumps and had brought along not only the ramp but a couple of wooden chocks to keep the chair stationary when required.

Yes, that was all right. Then food. She'd checked that over and made a few useful additions. The Calor gas supply was adequate—the water tank was full. So, if John thought he was going to ingratiate himself by being useful, he'd made a big mistake ! She would be able to manage quite well without his assistance !

She cooked her meal, ate it, though with an indifferent appetite, and cleared up. Then she settled down to read the book she had brought with her. But very soon she found to her surprise that daylight was fading. She looked at her watch. Surely the sun was setting sooner than she remembered it doing before? Oh, but of course it was ! It was that much later in the year now.

She got up to light the lamp, but first she went to the door and peered out. It was all the darker because the moon was in its first quarter. There was a mist lying like a fleecy blanket over the fields and the whisper of an evening breeze stirred the reeds. It was really rather eerie to a town-bred girl. One couldn't help thinking about tramps or poachers—she'd be glad to have Miss Alice's company to-morrow, but in the meantime she'd just have to be sensible about it. Besides, if any marauder came prowling around, she had only to shout and John would come—

She was so angry with herself for thinking of such a thing that she forgot to feel scared any more.

"I'm terribly sorry, my dear, but I just can't manage it," Miss Alice said apologetically, almost in tears. "This plaster makes me so clumsy and I'm so dreadfully afraid of falling."

Everything had gone swimmingly until now. Rosamund had been a little worried lest the ramp might be rather too steep for her to have perfect control when wheeling the chair down it. But that proved to be quite satisfactory. What even Dr. Rob had not thought of was that Miss Alice might have difficulty in getting from the chair to her bed. But here she was, completely unable to make the transfer, even with Rosamund's help.

"How did you manage in hospital?" Rosamund asked anxiously.

"Oh, two nurses," Miss Alice explained. "And of course, they have the knack—oh, I do wish your father was here! He'd know just how to hoick me over!"

"And I'm afraid I don't," Rosamund admitted regretfully. "I'm sorry—"

"But it's not your fault, dear," Miss Alice said quickly. "It's just that I'm being difficult. Shall we try again?"

But by now Rosamund felt as apprehensive as Miss Alice did. She had had little or no nursing experience and Miss Alice was a sturdily built woman. A slip might cause incalculable damage.

"I think—I'd better go and ask John if he'll lend a hand," she said in a high, unnatural voice.

"Oh, do you think he'd mind?" Miss Alice said dubiously. "As a rule, men don't like to have anything to do with illness—"

"As a matter of fact, he offered yesterday to do anything he could to help you," Rosamund told her. "I'll go right away—"

Before she regretted her suggestion to the degree where she couldn't bring herself to make the request that was obviously so necessary—

She took a torch with her and John, evidently seeing its bobbing light, came to the top of the gangplank to meet her.

"Anything wrong?"

Briefly Rosamund explained, thankful that with the light of her torch shining in John's direction, he couldn't see her face clearly.

"Right!" John said briskly. "I'll come at once. Just let me get my torch for the return journey and I'll be with you."

But Rosamund didn't wait for him. She didn't fancy even the short walk with him along the narrow footpath.

"He's coming," she told Miss Alice rather breathlessly, and a moment or so later John looked up in the doorway.

Miss Alice held out her hand to him.

"This is good of you, John! I'm sorry to be such a nuisance."

"Not at all," he replied matter-of-factly. "Obviously the most practical solution. Now, let's study the situation— yes, I think I can scoop you up out of the chair and deposit you safely in bed if Rosamund steadies your plastered foot so that you don't feel the weight of it and it doesn't hit against anything. Ready, Rosamund?"

"Yes," she said briefly.

Between them Miss Alice was settled as comfortably as possible in bed, and unconsciously, Rosamund gave a sigh of relief.

"Splendid!" Miss Alice said gratefully. "But I think I'll read for a little till I get really drowsy, if you wouldn't mind getting my book, dear. I left it on the table."

Rosamund went to get it, but John didn't follow her. He stood looking down at Miss Alice, his expression enigmatic. For a moment their eyes met. John gave a little exclamation and then, impulsively, bent down—and kissed her. A moment later he was gone, but when Rosamund returned, Miss Alice was smiling contentedly.

"I think I shall sleep quite well tonight," she said confidently.

"Yes, I quite agree, Alice, everything is going very smoothly," Dr. Rob said. "All the same, the time is coming when you'll have to leave here—and before very long at that. Autumn's on the way—there's a distinct chill in the air of a morning. If you were normally active, it wouldn't matter too much, but you're not, and the next thing will be that you start getting aches and pains that may not be so easy to get rid of. You don't want that to happen, do you?"

"Of course not," Miss Alice admitted. "But it will be at least another month before the plaster can come off, and you know what they said at the hospital about keeping an eye on me—"

"And *you* know perfectly well that it can easily be arranged for the responsibility to be transferred to a London hospital. And that's what's going to happen," Dr. Rob told her firmly. "No, it's no good you sticking out your chin in that pugnacious way at me, my dear! I know what I'm talking about and you know I do. No matter what the circumstances, I can't have you taking any more risks."

Miss Alice was silent for a moment. Then she looked at him pleadingly.

"Give me another fortnight, Rob. Then I'll do anything you say."

"You will?" he looked at her keenly. "All right, on those terms—"

"Now I've let myself in for it," she said resignedly. "And obviously you've got something up your sleeve. Out with it, Rob, let me know the worst!"

"I don't want you to go to your flat," Dr. Rob explained bluntly. "I want you to stay at mine so that I can keep an eye on you!"

"But Rob, my dear, that will never do!" she objected, a suggestion of unsteadiness in her voice. "What about your professional reputation? Even with Rosamund to chaperone us—"

For a moment Dr. Rob hesitated. Then he took her hand in his.

"There'd be no possibility of gossip, nor for that matter, any need for a chaperone," he said gently, "if you could see your way to becoming my wife, Alice."

When Rosamund heard the news she wasn't surprised. Indeed, she had often wondered why two people, so obviously fond of one another and so admirably suited, hadn't got married long ago. None the less, her feelings were mixed. For her father and Miss Alice she was unfeignedly glad, but she couldn't help wondering just how their approaching marriage would affect her. It was true that they appeared to take it for granted that she would live with them and certainly the Harley Street flat was big enough to accommodate the three of them. But there were other considerations than those. Would she really fit in with their way of life or wouldn't they be happier on their own? That Miss Alice would never do anything to make her feel unwelcome Rosamund was quite sure. She was far too nice a person for that. All the same, the constant presence of a grown-up stepdaughter could become irksome at times, particularly if, as Rosamund knew was the case where she was concerned, she wasn't a happy person or one who had any real interests of her own.

That was the trouble. Her father and Miss Alice would feel obliged to include her in their activities—do their best to "take her out of herself". And that, she was sure, must inevitably restrict their freedom and might even mar their late-found happiness.

And then, from her own point of view, it would be a strain to live with people, however dear, who were always anxious on her behalf. It meant keeping up appearances, and that Rosamund knew would be extremely difficult in her present mood.

She was restless—restless and unsure of herself. She didn't know what she wanted—a fresh start, but one that wasn't haunted by memories? But that was impossible, as impossible as she still felt it to be that there could be any future for John and herself.

John. He was the stumbling block. Her forehead puckered at the thought of him. He had spoken of the chance that luck had given him, and of his intention to make the most of it. But he had done nothing to substantiate that threat. True, he was always available if he was needed in any way, and occasionally, particularly at the weekends when Dr. Rob came down, he would have tea with them. But that was all. He never sought her out, never tried to be alone with her and rarely spoke to her except when conversation was general. They might just have been newly met acquaintances instead of what they really were.

At first it hadn't seemed to make sense. Then, gradually, she realised what John was doing. He was giving her the onus of making the first step towards reconciliation.

"But I won't do it," she told herself mutinously. "It would be almost as if I was to blame if I did. And I wasn't, I wasn't! It was his fault. And why should I risk being hurt all over again? Oh, I shall be thankful when we've left here and he can't be always—always hovering in the background like a storm that may break at any moment! Well, it won't be long now!"

But before they did leave, several things were to happen. To begin with, Dr. Rob insisted that they should get married before he and Miss Alice left for London, and although she protested that nobody ever heard of a bride going to her wedding in an invalid chair, she gave in when he told her firmly that even if she'd been a stretcher case, they'd get married just as he planned.

But he did agree that it should be a very quiet wedding. In fact, he pointed out, there was no need for anyone but John and Rosamund to be present as the necessary witnesses.

Rosamund's heart sank at the prospect. How could she leave the past behind when everything—and sometimes she felt, everybody—conspired to remind her of it? The same words, the same vows that she and John had spoken such a short time ago—she couldn't refuse, of course, but surely John could? She keyed herself up to ask what was practically a favour of him, but John shook his head.

"Sorry, Rosamund, but that's out of the question. For one thing, it's the simplest arrangement and consequently, the best for Miss Alice. But apart from that, I've no wish or intention of hurting their feelings by refusing."

"Oh well, if that's how you feel about it, there's nothing more to be said!" she said frostily.

"But there is," John told her imperatively. "It's going to be *their* day. Nothing should be allowed to spoil it. So will you bury the hatchet for the occasion? Without prejudice, of course."

Rosamund hesitated. Put that way, it was difficult to refuse, as he was perfectly aware. So, though she had the uneasy feeling that he was forcing her hand, she agreed—but with mental reservations.

Rosamund came back from what would be her last visit to the shop to see a stranger pacing impatiently up and down the little deck of the *Seven Stars*. She wondered vaguely who he was, but after all, what business was it of hers? She turned along the towpath only to be hailed by the visitor.

"Hi, there! Any idea when Lindsay will be back?"

Rosamund glanced over her shoulder.

"Not the least," she said indifferently, and went on walking.

But she didn't escape as easily as that. The man not only followed her along the path, he somehow managed to get past her so that she could go no further. She felt uneasy. He looked quite respectable, but none the less, he was obviously worked up about something. And since her father had taken Miss Alice to the hospital for a last check-up, there was no one she could summon.

"Now, listen," the man said urgently. "I don't want to make a nuisance of myself, but I've *got* to see Lindsay. I've written half a dozen times, but he simply doesn't answer. And I'm getting worried. My name's Rutherford, by the way. I'm his publisher—or his would-be publisher, I should say," he added grimly.

"Oh, I see," Rosamund said with relief. "But I'm sorry, it doesn't make any difference. I've no idea how long Mr. Lindsay will be. I didn't even know he'd gone anywhere."

"Oh, confound it" There was unmistakable chagrin in Mr. Rutherford's voice. "That's torn it. I suppose he might not even be coming back at all today."

"I don't know," Rosamund told him firmly. "And now, if you'll excuse me—"

"Wait a minute!" He pondered, frowning. "Look here, do you live on one of the other boats?"

"On the *Pride of London*," Rosamund admitted, nodding in its direction. "But—"

"Well, surely, living in such a small community, you must all be on friendly terms—it would be intolerable not to be. So you must know something of one another's affairs. Surely you can tell me, for instance, if he's writing or not?"

"No, he isn't."

"Sure?"

"My father asked him the same question a few days ago," Rosamund explained. "And that was what Mr. Lindsay said."

And again she felt the unwelcome little stab that John's admission had caused her. He had said it with no show of emotion whatever, but perhaps, just because of that, it hadn't been difficult for her to appreciate why that creative gift of his had failed him. He simply hadn't the heart to write. And she knew why—

"Oh, damn!" Mr. Rutherford sighed gustily. "And all because he was fool enough to marry a twitter-pate of a woman who hadn't the sense to recognise genius when she met it!"

"Genius!" Rosamund repeated, too startled by his use of such a superlative description to give any thought to his unflattering description of herself.

"Downright genius—and I know what I'm talking about," Mr. Rutherford insisted didactically. "Generally speaking, a publisher doesn't hope for too much because he knows he won't get it anyhow. If you could see some of the drivel I get—that doesn't get into print, of course. No, what any publisher goes for is the reasonably sound book that will earn him—and the author, of course—a decent profit. But just now and again something so good turns up that one feels the age of miracles hasn't passed. Lindsay's is the first manuscript that's come my way about which I can say that for years. But it's incomplete. And now you tell me he's stopped writing!" He brooded for a while and then said suddenly : "This girl he married—she's not one of the set he used to run around with. Dropped out of that some time ago. D'you know anything about her? Did he meet her down here?"

"I really can't discuss Mr. Lindsay's affairs," Rosamund told him frigidly. "And now—"

"I think he must have done, you know," Mr. Rutherford went on broodingly. "Probably fell for her because he thought she didn't know about his money—he's extremely well off, you know—only to find that she'd known all along and kept quiet about it until she'd got him safely hooked—"

"It wasn't like that at all," Rosamund burst out furiously. "His money had nothing to do—" she stopped short, realising that Mr. Rutherford was looking at her intently through narrowed eyes.

"You seem to know a lot about it," he commented. "I suppose, by any chance, you don't happen to be the girl in question, do you?"

"Yes," Rosamund said briefly.

"Well, well, well! Quite a coincidence! Odd, though, because you don't look the nitwit, gold-digging type."

"I told you—"

"So you did," Mr. Rutherford nodded. "And as it happens, I believe you, though Lindsay may not have done. Was that it?" He paused expectantly.

"Mr. Rutherford, you really can't expect me—"

"No, I suppose I can't," he agreed with a sigh. "Well, never mind. It's the fact that matters, not the cause. You and he have parted brass rags—"

"Who told you that?" Rosamund interrupted. "John?"

"I told you, I haven't seen him or heard from him since our first meeting. And in any case, surely you know him better than that! He's not the sort to go about snivelling that he's been hurt—and he *has* been. Why else has he stopped writing? Any chance of you making it up? No?" as Rosamund shook her head. "Pity. All that lost talent—"

Silence fell between them. Then, squaring his shoulders, Mr. Rutherford returned to the attack.

"Look, my dear," he said kindly. "It's very clear that you've been hurt as well. But don't you think it's possible that there were faults on both sides? There almost always are, you know. And one has one's pride about being the first to apologise. I know. I've been through it. Most of us have, one way and another. But you, being a woman, haven't got the same stiff-necked attitude about admitting you were in the wrong that a man has. Make the first move, my dear. I don't think you'll regret it—"

He laid his hand gently on Rosamund's shoulder, but when she made no response, he said briskly :

"In that case, I can see nothing for it but to let John speak for himself! Here—" He dropped his hand from her shoulder and unzipped the briefcase he was carrying. "This is a copy of what he's written so far! Read it—and you'll have some idea of the man you've married!" He thrust the bundle of typescript into her arms and Rosamund stood aside to let him pass.

She herself walked slowly on to the *Pride of London* mooring, but once again Mr. Rutherford hailed her and she turned.

"Ever thought how intolerable it would be to live with someone who was absolutely perfect?" he asked pensively. "Somebody who never made a mistake? See what it would mean? You'd always have to be on your best behaviour— never dare to relax because if you put a foot wrong, you'd feel so small, so inferior by comparison! Intolerable, yes, that's the right word! Much better that we should all be imperfect beings!"

He lifted his hand in salutation and strolled along the towpath. Rosamund watched him until he vanished. Then she went slowly back to the *Pride of London.*

It was not until she went to bed that night that Rosamund was able to read the manuscript of John's book without fear of interruption. She drew the curtain close over the window so that the light would not show from outside. Then she punched up the pillows to form a comfortable back rest and got into bed.

The manuscript was lying on the table beside her, and for a moment she looked at it irresolutely. Mr. Rutherford had given it to her to read, but had she really any right to? John hadn't said she might, and without his permission, wasn't it very much like eavesdropping?

Then, as if she was compelled by a force stronger than

herself, she picked it up and turned back the cover. She began to read—

An hour later, when she had come to the end of the four chapters that John had written, she smoothed the last page with a hand that shook.

It hadn't needed Mr. Rutherford's opinion to convince her that John had written something exceptional. It shone in every word.

The characters came alive from the typescript pages— they seemed as real as if she had actually met them. And one wanted to know more about them. They *mattered*.

As for the plot, though there was no more than, perhaps a third or so of the book written, one was already aware of the threads which, each arrestingly interesting in itself, were later going to be woven into an absorbing, satisfying pattern—

But while all that was so clear and though Rosamund could well understand Mr. Rutherford's anxiety for John to finish the book, it was something else which held her enthralled.

There was a perceptiveness, a sensitiveness in the way in which it was written that, more than once, made Rosamund catch her breath. This wasn't just a commercial venture. Nor was it simply a brilliant brain-child. It was something that John had written with his heart's blood.

This was John, fulfilled and whole. The man she had fallen in love with but whom she had come to believe had no existence outside her own dreams.

And yet how could a man be less in stature than the characters he created? And how could he breathe life into them so convincingly if he didn't give them something of himself? She read through several passages again and knew that she was right. It was all here—the aspirations, the hopes, the failings that are part of every human being. And something more. The warmth and tenderness that make life worth while—

It was a long time before Rosamund went to sleep, and when she did, her hand was tucked under the pillow, resting on the manuscript which lay there.

Dr. Rob and Miss Alice were married late one afternoon. They had said nothing of their intentions to anyone but the vicar, but somehow the news had leaked out and there were half a dozen or so inveterate wedding-watchers in the church when they arrived. Dr. Rob pushed Miss Alice in her chair up the aisle and Rosamund and John followed, side by side, but apart so that not even their hands touched.

One could not say that this church was really very much like that other one. It was much newer for one thing, but all churches have similar features, and when the service began Rosamund, listening, was carried back in time.

And John? She stole a cautious glance at him, but he was gazing straight ahead, his face devoid of all expression.

Then it was all over. The register was signed and they went out into the churchyard. Good-byes were said and the two men helped Miss Alice into the big, comfortable car which Dr. Rob had brought down from London. Then they were off—

"Well, that's that," John remarked briskly. "Now, you'll be wanting to get off—"

The arrangement was that Rosamund should follow the newly married couple in the smaller car. Nobody had asked John what he intended to do and he had volunteered no information.

"Yes," Rosamund agreed matter-of-factly, "I must go. Can I give you a lift anywhere?"

"Thanks, no need for that," John told her. "I'm going back to the boat—I can walk."

"Just as you like, of course," Rosamund said carelessly. "I'm going back as well—for something I've forgotten. So—?"

"I'll walk," John said shortly, and set off.

Rosamund got into the car and a moment or so later she passed John in the lane. She parked in the field and was aboard the *Pride of London* when he appeared. He came straight to her.

"I'm rather glad you've come back, Rosamund" he said in a strained voice. "No, you needn't be afraid," as she looked at him with quick, apprehensive eyes. "It's just that it's given me an opportunity of saying something I've had to admit to myself must be said—"

Her eyes dropped and she waited in silence for him to go on.

"It's just this, Rosamund—you've convinced me beyond doubt that—we're finished. It's no good pretending anything else, is it?"

"No, it's no good pretending," Rosamund agreed pensively.

"So this is good-bye, Rosamund," he told her in an oddly mechanical way as if it was a lesson which he had forced himself to learn by heart. "It may take time for you to free yourself of me, but don't worry, I'll see to all the arrangements and you needn't be afraid that I'll ever make a nuisance of myself again to you. I've had my lesson—and loving you as I do, I know that the kindest thing I can do for you, in fact the only thing that may bring you happiness in the future, is to go out of your life entirely."

"I see," Rosamund murmured.

"I suppose—no, it's too much to ask you to forgive me," he said harshly. "All the same, I'd like you to believe that I am truly sorry—"

"Yes." It was little more than a whisper.

"So that's all. Good-bye—and bless you always!" And he turned to go.

"John!"

"Yes?" He stopped but didn't turn back.

"It's going to be a lovely evening—clear and a full moon," she remarked conversationally. "It's a pity to miss it, don't you think? I really feel like putting off going back to London—"

He came back to her then and stood over her threateningly, his hands clenching and unclenching.

"You'll go *now*," he told her savagely. "Otherwise I won't answer—"

"But, John, it was *you* who told me that it was time I stopped running away from life," she reminded him. "And I've come to the conclusion that you were right."

He stared at her incredulously, a muscle flickering at the corner of his mouth.

"Don't try me too high, Rosamund," he said sternly. "I'm only a very ordinary mortal—and there are limits—"

"Yes, I think there are," she told him gravely. "Limits to my own stupidity, John."

"What!" His hands shot out and he gripped her by the shoulders—but this time she didn't resist him. "Do you know what you're saying?"

"Yes, I know," she said, her voice vibrant with certainty. "I'm telling you that I know now that there can never be any happiness for me if—I ran away from you, John!" and slipping her arms round his neck, she lifted her face to his.

With a catch of his breath, he caught her in his arms and held her close. The lips that sought hers were passionate, demanding and yet unutterably tender. There was no escape from their searching eagerness, but she had no wish to escape. To his incredulous joy he felt her respond to him as he had never thought could happen again.

When at last his arms slackened round her it was only sufficient for him to look down into her wide, glowing eyes, even now anxious to make sure that it was true. What he saw must have satisfied him, for he held her close again.

"This is—for always!" he told her huskily, and felt her breath against his lips as she repeated : "Always!"

"But *why*?" John asked at length. "What made you change your mind?"

"Oh—" Rosamund said considVeringly, twiddling her finger round a button of his jacket, "this and that! Actually—Mr. Rutherford."

"Rutherford?" John said sharply. "How does he come into it?"

"He came down here that day last week when you weren't here," Rosamund explained. "Simply bursting with rage and frustration because you'd stopped writing. He blamed me up hill and down dale for having got in the way of you finishing what he truly believes could be a masterpiece—"

"Now, listen to me, Rosamund," John said sternly, "I don't care a damn if that book would be the best-seller of all time, I won't have you sacrificing yourself—don't you understand, it's your happiness that matters to me, the book is nothing, *nothing* beside that!"

Rosamund sighed plaintively.

"Darling, don't jump to conclusions! You've got it the wrong way round. He gave me your manuscript to read because he said that if he couldn't convince me, *that* would."

"Well?"

"I think he was right, John," Rosamund said with conviction. "It is going to be a wonderful book. And I'm glad. But not exactly because it will be a success. It's because—I found you again in it—the you I thought I'd lost. But I hadn't. You were *there*, John!" Her voice lilted with gladness. "The *real* you—the you I loved. Nobody could write like that without being absolutely sincere about it. It was just as Mr. Rutherford said, it spoke for you. Now do you understand?"

"I'm beginning to," John said slowly. "And I don't know which I feel most—triumphant because you should feel like that or humble for—the same reason, I think! Do you understand?"

"I think so," Rosamund said, and gave a little bubbling chuckle which made John smile, though he looked a little puzzled.

"That was a very nice sound—and one that I haven't heard for all too long," he remarked. "But what prompted it just then?"

"Oh, something else Mr. Rutherford said," Rosamund explained. "As a parting shot, he asked me if I realised how dreadful it would be to live with someone who was absolutely perfect. It would mean, he said, that one's own faults stood out so glaringly. And I thought that seeing I can't always make up my mind about things quickly, perhaps it was a good thing that you can't either!"

"Our Mr. Rutherford seems to have talked rather a lot," John remarked tolerantly. "However, in the circumstances, I'll forgive him."

"That's nice of you!" Rosamund commented mischievously. "Personally, I've fallen for him in a big way!"

"Watch it!" John cautioned, half jocular, half serious. "Because I'm not standing for any rivals, Rosamund! You're mine! *Mine!* Understand?"

"That's how I want it to be," Rosamund said contentedly. "Yours! That's everything."

Later, they realised that they must let Dr. Rob and Miss Alice know their change of plans.

"Well, you go to the village and phone them," Rosamund suggested. "While I get us a meal——"

"Yes, I'll do that," John agreed reluctantly. "You'll still be here when I get back, won't you?"

"Yes, I'll be here," she promised seriously.

Half an hour later he was back again. *Rosebud* and the *Pride of London* were in darkness, but bright beams of light shone out from the uncurtained window of the *Seven Stars*.

John cleared the gangplank in two quick strides, confident of the welcome that awaited him.